Titles in the Cat Caliban Series

Seventh Deadly Sin

D.B. Borton

HILLIARD Harris
PUBLISHERS

Published by

HILLIARD  HARRIS
PUBLISHERS

P.O. Box 3358
Frederick, Maryland 21705-3358

Seventh Deadly Sin Copyright © 2004 by D.B. Borton

First Edition

ISBN 1-59133-052-1

Designed by **HILLIARD** **HARRIS**

Cover Illustration © S. A. Reilly
Release Date: August 1, 2004
Manufactured/Printed in the United States of America
2004

The earliest reference to the seven chief sins in any form is in the pseudo-epigraphical Testament of the Twelve Patriarchs, Testament of Reuben, which Charles dates 109-106 B.C. . . . Here seven spirits of deceit (πνεύματα τῆς πλάνης) are listed: πορνεία (fornication), γαστριμαργία (gluttony), μάχη (strife), κενοδοξία (vainglory), ὑπερηφανία (pride), ψεῦδος (lying), and αδικία (injustice).

Morton W. Bloomfield, *The Seven Deadly Sins*

Chapter One

MY DAUGHTER CONSIDERS me a bad influence. If you want to know why, you can tour my kitchen.

On the outside, my refrigerator displays the usual collection of family snapshots and kiddie crayon art, heavy on lopsided hearts over drunken letters that spell out, "I Luv You, Grammy!!" The magnets run to ads for security equipment dealers, bloody daggers, and signs that say, "This Refrigerator Is Bugged." Posted on the front is a used body target from the firing range, with bullet holes in the lower left forearm and about three inches west of the right ear. Its purpose is inspirational. Dangling from the handle is a locked pair of handcuffs that I intend to remove as soon as I find the key.

Inside, the refrigerator is well stocked with beer, Chinese take-out cartons, limes, and tonic. The limes are for medicinal purposes. They stave off the kinds of colds that can develop into bronchitis and put a sixty-one-year-old senior citizen like me in the hospital, where she is bound to catch something worse and leave in the back of a hearse. I think there may be some milk back behind the cream cheese, but if so it went sour some time around New Year's. In the freezer compartment are several bags of frozen peas marked "Do Not Eat." These serve as ice packs to treat the sprains and other minor injuries that plague people my age who lead an active life.

The cookie jar on the counter holds a set of pick-locks. But its primary purpose is to cover a small stain from a chemistry experiment that got out of hand.

The dishes in the sink are dusted with white powder. The fingerprints showing through the powder provide a record of everyone who has eaten or drunk in this kitchen in the past twelve hours—except the cats, of course. The cats have left their own traces in the small hard bits of food and kitty litter that crumble into grit underfoot.

There's an empty gin bottle in the garbage can under the sink. Fortunately, I have more.

There's a small palm tree on the kitchen table, with a hangman's noose attached to one of its fronds—a product of my studies in knot-tying. Hidden behind the palm is a small voice-activated tape recorder so sensitive that it can pick up a cat's yawn at four feet. Also on the table are a surveillance supplies catalogue and a forensic medicine textbook. When the grandkids come to visit, though, my reading matter gets stashed on top of the refrigerator.

You can see why this kitchen disturbs my daughter. It is not the kitchen of an apple-cheeked, sweater-knitting, cookie-baking, all-American grandmother. It's the kitchen of a detective-in-training.

You might think it would discourage her from bringing her son to see me. But you would be wrong. Take it from me, Cat Caliban, in these days of high-priced, heavily scheduled, demanding semi-professional teenaged child care providers, a grandma would have to be serving time to evade her responsibilities as a free and available babysitter.

That's why I spent Valentine's Day babysitting my five-year-old grandson, Ben. He brought me a trick Valentine card and left me with a bruise which blossomed like a rose tattoo across the varicose veins of my calf.

"Gee, I'm sorry, Mom," my daughter Sharon said, wincing at the vivid display of red. "Does it hurt?"

My daughter, a stockbroker, is not as stupid as she sounds. Maybe she was worried that I'd sue for workers' comp, even though I was an unpaid child care provider. Her own cheeks were flushed with the glow of a five-star dinner at the Maisonette, a bottle of French wine and whatever flammable liquid they'd poured over her dessert. Her husband Frank was not my idea of a hot date, but maybe he livened up after a bottle of wine and a pound of butter. He appeared in the doorway with a limp child slung over his shoulder.

"When I couldn't get the card open, he grabbed for it, lost his balance and ended up knocking the books off the end table," I told her. "Julia Child got me on the way down."

Julia had been my daughter-in-law Corinne's notion of a good Valentine's Day present. She probably thought I'd given up cooking because I'd run out of ideas. My son didn't have that much imagination; he'd put in his usual order at Hyde Park Florist for a mug of chrysanthemums that said *Love Means Being a Grandmother!*

"I'm sorry about the card," Sharon said. "You know how he is."

We regarded Ben as he shifted in his father's arms, turning his head and laying a sticky red cheek against his father's shoulder, eyes closed, Frank's white shirt bunched in a gummy orange fist. His Winnie-the-

Pooh sleepers looked tie-dyed, and they were sporting a new rip in one armhole. He had a rubber band wrapped around one ear. His Goofy Band-Aid, once a slash across his forehead like a pirate's scar, had been rubbed until it had shriveled up into a cowardly inchworm. His hair was shedding green glitter like fairy dust.

Yes, I knew how he was—my grandson, the peripatetic tarpit. As he moved through the world, things stuck to him and he to them. If he'd planted a single kiss on the Valentine before he'd closed the card, it was glued together for good. I told him I didn't even need to see his signature to know it was from him; he'd left a nice clear set of black partial prints all over the embossed flowers on the front.

I wasn't a detective-in-training for nothing, you know.

To tell you the truth, taste seemed to be in short supply this Valentine's Day. Even my youngest daughter Franny, a thirty-one-year-old hippie, had been led astray by a gift shop huckster and presented me with some soupy "thoughts on mothers and daughters" book, accompanied by a tin of chamomile tea and a bag of what were supposed to be aromatic herbs for bathing. After smelling both, I thought I'd try drinking the bath herbs and soaking in the chamomile.

I blamed the epidemic of bad taste on the President. Hell, I blamed everything on the President. It was the Eighties, the twenty-first century was just around the corner, and we had a nincompoop in the White House.

But not all of my Valentines came from family members. I own the small apartment building where I live, affectionately known to my tenants as the Catatonia Arms, which helps my cash flow while I prepare to launch an exciting new career as a private investigator. My housemates know me better than my kids. Maybe you find this surprising, since my kids have known me for considerably more of my sixty-one years than my housemates have. If you have kids yourself, maybe you don't.

Certain holidays are enthusiastically celebrated at the Catatonia Arms, and Valentine's Day was one of them, since nobody could think of any reason why we should be boycotting it. The music that issued from Kevin O'Neill's apartment across the hall had taken a distinct turn toward the romantic about a week before, alternating the playful, upbeat mood of Ella Fitzgerald singing Cole Porter with the slow torchiness of Aretha. Melanie Carter, my upstairs neighbor and an artist by vocation, grumbled that she thought Kevin had gone too far when he'd taped red cellophane over the hall lights, and I had to agree it gave the place all the ambiance of a cut-rate bordello. Moses Fogg, the retired cop who occupied the other upstairs apartment, complained that he couldn't see in the hall anymore and vowed we'd find his lifeless body crumpled at the bottom of the stairs come February fourteenth, guarded by his faithful beagle, Winnie. But all this grumbling went on behind the scenes. Nobody was willing to dampen Kevin's enthusiasm.

"Al thinks he's in love," Mel reported.

Alice Rosenberg, Mel's life partner and a Legal Aid attorney with considerable experience in reading people, nodded.

"I think he's met someone," she said.

"At Arnold's?" I asked. Kevin was a bartender at a historic downtown bar.

Al shrugged.

"Ain't nobody he's met," Moses put in. "Got a secret admirer, don't even know who it is. Just somebody leaving him anonymous notes."

"Mash notes?"

"Well, I don't think they call 'em that anymore, Cat," he responded. "You got to catch up with the times, girl."

"Anyway, they're probably not mash notes, exactly," Al observed. "Kevin's too romantic to get worked up over something crude."

"Oh, please!" Mel said. "Love notes on a used bar napkin?"

"Sounds creepy to me," I said.

"Sounds romantic to me," Al said.

This from the person who was giving her honey a new set of barbells for Valentine's Day.

Come February fourteenth, however, Kevin had not forgotten his landlady. When I'd wandered into the living room that morning, I'd found Sidney squashed against the front door, one paw stretched under it up to the shoulder. His tail was twitching in irritation.

"What's out there, Sid?" I asked.

Sitting in the hall was a Black Forest torte, Kevin's specialty. He always added little whipped cream flourishes for Sidney.

After work, Al and Mel stopped by with a bottle of gin and a box of Graeter's chocolates.

"Isn't that nice?" I said. "And they go so well with Kevin's present."

Me, I was giving out gift certificates to Graeter's and The Movies. But I guess I couldn't really afford to criticize anybody's taste. My own Valentine's cards came from Leon, my sometime sidekick and teenage Northside business entrepreneur, purveyor of truly tasteless cards and wrapping paper which you had to order in quantities suited more to the White House mailing list than to mine.

Mel hooted when she saw hers. "We've got two boxes of these upstairs! Kind of makes you dread Easter, doesn't it?"

"St. Patrick's Day is next," I pointed out. "Unless there's something in the box for Groundhog Day."

"Now there's a stumper," Al mused. "Wonder what you give your sweetie for Groundhog Day?"

"Something to either warm her up or cool her off, depending on Phil's prediction," Mel said, grinning.

And they went off to try out Mel's barbells.

From my kitchen window I saw Moses leave for his date with Charisse. He was moving a little stiffly, the way he always did when he was dressed up in a suit and going somewhere besides church—as if he'd ironed his underwear and didn't want to wrinkle it. He was taking his current flame to the Celestial in Mt. Adams for a romantic candlelit dinner overlooking the city. Mel had expressed the hope that Charisse would give the rest of us a Valentine's Day present and break up with Moses, taking her clunky gold jewelry, her high heels, her scent of Rive Gauche, and her attitude with her. But I didn't want to see Moses miserable, so I figured we'd just have to wait for him to come to his senses and dump her. He wasn't carrying anything, I noticed, but I happened to know that what he had for her would fit in his breast pocket. All that class going to waste on a woman who wanted to remake him into the snob she was.

I sighed, and nearly toppled over into the sink. At the moment I was standing on a stepstool, stashing my chocolates in a high cupboard before my little Valentine's date showed up.

Later, after his parents had carried my date out the door, I assembled all my tenants' presents and had my own little celebration.

When I was on my way to bed, I saw that Sidney was once again stationed at the front door, paw outstretched beneath it. A small white corner protruded, barely visible.

I opened the door. There in the hall was my final Valentine.

The card was one of Leon's. The handwriting and signature were Moses's. Stuffed inside were two pieces of paper. The first was a photocopy of a private investigator's license issued to Moses S. Fogg. The second was some kind of application form. Moses had already filled in my name at the top.

"Well, I'll be damned," I whispered to Sidney. "We're going legit."

Chapter Two

"Now, this don't mean you can go out tomorrow and take out an ad in the *Post*, Cat." Moses was looking pleased with himself. "We got a lot of work to do."

"Big duh, as my grandson would say," I said. "Does this mean you're going to teach me to shoot?"

"I reckon we'll get around to it," he said.

"So, Moses, when did you do all this?" Kevin seemed a little miffed, I thought, that something had gotten by him. When undistracted by love, Kevin, an inveterate gossip, was a walking file cabinet of information on everybody and their activities. The only reason the cops haven't found Jimmy Hoffa's body is that they haven't thought to ask Kevin. He had also been one of the earliest and most enthusiastic supporters of my new career, and the first to offer to teach me to shoot. And he'd been the source of my current firearm, an unregistered Diane that I knew just enough about to be dangerous—to myself as well as to others.

"Yeah, when did you take the test?" Al put in.

The one small barrier between me and a challenging new career as a private eye had always been the license. Even if I could have passed the test, I couldn't demonstrate to the satisfaction of the powers that be that I had the required two years of investigative experience. To the kind of men who sit on these boards, domestic detection doesn't count for anything unless it's their own socks that are missing. Then last summer we'd learned that Moses, with his long career as a police officer, could obtain a license, and I could work as his operative. Mel, Al, Kevin and I had been campaigning ever since.

"Retired is retired," he'd say. "I plan to enjoy it."

"I don't want to spend my golden years going through somebody else's dirty laundry," he'd say.

"I'm too old to be hiding under folks' beds," he'd say. "Even if I could get down there, I couldn't get back up."

Or in a different mood: "I got things to do and places to go while I'm still young enough. I got grandbabies needs playing with, a dog that needs walking."

"Cat, things are different now from what I'm used to," he'd say. "They using computers for everything, and I can't even figure out my phone answering machine."

Before Christmas, we'd worked together to find an old acquaintance of Moses's, an ex-con he'd dealt with when she'd been a juvenile offender.[*] I thought we'd made a pretty good team, if a bit gimpy, but I hadn't detected any major shifts in Moses's attitude. So his little Valentine's present had really come out of the blue. Now I learned, to my astonishment, that he'd taken the test back before Thanksgiving, and received the license last month.

"So what does Charisse think about you getting back in the ring?" Kevin asked. We all suspected that Charisse had her eye on a house in the 'burbs and a life devoted to the pursuit of culture, with the occasional NAACP gala thrown in.

Moses looked uncomfortable.

"You haven't told her!" Kevin guessed.

"Ain't like we're hanging a sign out in front of the house tomorrow," Moses responded defensively. "Like I said, we got a lot of work to do. And anyway, I plan to stay semi-retired. This business is going to be Cat's venture. I'm going to stay behind the scenes, like that guy—who's that guy I mean?"

"Nero Wolfe?" I offered.

"Naw, not him. That cat on *Charlie's Angels*—Charlie, I guess it was. The one you never saw."

"I get it," Al said. "We'll just hear your disembodied voice floating down the hall. And meanwhile, you'll just lounge around in your—say, I thought Charisse gave you a new robe!"

We all stared at the familiar brown corduroy he was wearing, balding and nearly napless, the ends of its belt chewed into a tattered fringe by a certain beagle of our acquaintance.

"She did." He sighed.

"Well, let's see it!" Kevin demanded.

"I showed you my barbells," Mel reminded him.

He went across the hall and returned a few minutes later.

---

[*] See *Six Feet Under*.

7

We stared.

"Is that velvet?" Kevin asked.

"Is that an ascot?" Al asked. "I've never seen an ascot in real life."

"Hey!" Mel said. "The colors match Cat's leg!"

The bruise left behind by my little valentine had blossomed into a wide circle of reds and purples that turned my leg into one of the gaudier Hallmarks—pink, rose, carmine, crimson, fuchsia, lavender, amethyst, aubergine. I would have made a big hit at a romance writers' convention.

"That's not a bathrobe," I observed. "It's a smoking jacket."

"So has she just, like, not noticed that you don't smoke?" Mel asked. Tact was not Mel's strong suit. "Or is she hoping you'll take it up? She hasn't asked you to change your will yet or anything, has she?"

"Maybe he'll get the pipe for Groundhog Day," I suggested.

"Well, from what I recall of that little topaz bracelet you bought her," Kevin said, "she got the better part of this bargain."

"Cheer up, Moses," I comforted him, stroking his sleeve. "I'll bet Winnie will love to sleep on this thing."

"You don't even know the worst," he said. "My daughter gave me a full-length dashiki—one of them gold and black African numbers. It's bad enough I got to remember to put 'em on when somebody's coming over. But what if they both come at the same time?"

"Just don't get sick," Mel advised him. "And don't get married. That way, you'll never have to wear a bathrobe in front of both of them at once."

Before he left for his regular Saturday morning tennis match, Kevin fingered the P.I. license again.

"I'm so pleased for both of you." He beamed at us. "And I can be your first customer! I'll hire you to find out who my secret admirer is."

Chapter Three

BUT KEVIN O'NEILL was not our first customer, as it turned out. Gussie Baer was. That's only if you stretched a point. I didn't know shit about bookkeeping, as anybody in the Fifth Third Bank could tell you, and I knew just enough about math to know that there was no such thing as a fifth third. Bookkeeping was pretty far down on the list of things I wanted to learn about detective work. So our services, for now, continued to be gratis. It occurred to me that Sam Spade, whose adventures I was re-reading in my spare time, had charged a buck; maybe he'd had trouble with addition, too.

On the phone, Gussie had the brisk, businesslike voice of someone who was about to put me through to a Rockefeller or a Trump.

"Is that Cat Caliban?"

I assured her it was, half hoping she would put me through to Ed McMahon; Rockefeller and Trump weren't giving it away, after all, at least not to profligate old ladies like me.

I'd wandered into my attached office Monday morning to celebrate the acceleration of my career with a burst of cleaning. Within five minutes I'd become engrossed in a slender book which I'd forgotten I had because it had fallen behind the computer—*Tricky Nick's Quirky Quick-Fix Tricks for Tricky Fixes.* I was leaning back in an old wooden desk chair with creaky springs, my Adidas propped up on the desk, reading about how to use chewing gum twenty ways in sticky situations.

"You know Mabel Hofstetter?"

"Oh, sure," I said. "Are you a friend of hers?"

"Who, Mabel?" she said. "No, no, I don't know Mabel. But she took this Popsicle stick sculpture class down at Alma's Arts and Crafts last spring? They made trays and purses, junk like that."

That sounded like my pal Mabel, all right.

"Anyway, this Estelle Golden was in the class, and she met Mabel. And Estelle plays bridge every Tuesday with my sister-in-law, Florence.

And Estelle told Florence that Bunny Foote, this other gal in the Popsicle stick class, had run into Mabel at the cafeteria and heard all about how you and Mabel got involved in that business down in Kentucky, and that you were a detective and I should call you."

I stuck a finger in *Tricky Nick* to mark my place, shut my eyes, and tried to concentrate.

"Bunny thought you should call me?" Who the hell was Bunny? And how had she gotten saddled with a name like "Bunny Foote"?

"No, now listen," the voice said, a little impatient. "Florence thought I should call you about my grandson. Because after all, I'm not getting any younger, and I don't want to go to my grave not knowing. And the cops are about as useful as Muppets and the kids act like somebody gave 'em a lobotomy and they forgot they had a son."

I gave up on the history.

"Not knowing what?"

"Not knowing what happened to him," she said. "Not knowing—."

Here her voice quavered, and the note of efficiency faded. "—Who killed him—or why. Not knowing if he's still out there, and if—you know—he might kill other boys."

I sorted out the pronouns. "Someone was murdered?"

"My grandson."

"Your grandson was murdered, and the police don't know who killed him?"

"I don't see how they could not know," she rejoined, "do you? In this day and age, they've got all those lasers and electron microscopes and fancy cameras. So you'd think they could tell, in spite of the water and all. But I hear sometimes they don't arrest the person if they don't think they can convict him. So maybe they're just following him around, waiting for it to happen again, I don't know. But these ones I've talked to seem like a couple of dim bulbs. I think it's a miracle they figured out how to get the police car out of Park. So what do you think?"

I thought she might be a few bricks short of a load, but menopausal women, especially sixty-one-year-old ones, are slow to judge others for being scatterbrained. At least this one is; I know scatterbrained from the inside out.

"I think maybe we should meet and talk about this face to face," I said.

That's how I ended up knocking on the door of a German-style bungalow in North College Hill. On the other side of the heavy wooden door, I could hear a series of muffled thuds, a querulous voice, and then a yowl of feline pain and indignation.

"It's the cats," said the woman when the door opened at last. "They haven't figured out the walker yet."

She was a petite woman, leaning on one of those aluminum walkers that enclosed her like a prisoner in a dock. She had wispy white hair and a dowager's hump that pushed her forward a little as if she were waiting for the starter's gun to go off. Her eyes were dark and had the intense look of some predatory bird, and she had that avian trick of turning her head abruptly as if to focus on something. She was wearing a bright floral housecoat that snapped up the front, and a pair of Air Jordans that must have added two inches to her height. She looked kind of like a baby vulture disguised as a performing parrot.

She was clutching a wriggling tiger cat. A black cat with a chewed ear regarded me from the floor near her ankles. She dropped the cat. It's not true, by the way, that they always land on their feet. Sometimes they land on other cats.

"Come on in and mind the boxes," she said, and executed a turn. She thumped down the hall in front of me. Unsteady as she looked, her progress was a marvel of precision because the path before her was narrow and uneven. All along the walls were piled boxes, newspapers, and miscellaneous junk. It reminded me of Bill's True Value Hardware, a Northside landmark where you had to wait your turn for Bill to unearth the item you needed because you'd never find it on your own—or if you did, you couldn't reach it.

The living room took my breath away. I gazed on it awestruck. Imagine the most crowded secondhand store you've ever seen, and then add about ten cats, arranged about the room in various poses of sloth, and you have Gussie Baer's living room.

"I call it Nouveau Dump," she said, and cackled. "Drives the kids crazy."

Since driving the kids crazy was a favorite pastime of mine, I grinned. I was an amateur in the presence of a master.

She toddled across the room and picked up a framed photograph off of a mantel.

"That's Peter," she said. "That's my boyfriend."

I took the photograph. Peter Baer was a good-looking kid with an engaging smile. He had brown eyes, light brown wavy hair, and clear, tawny skin with a faint rose tint at the cheekbones. His neck and broad shoulders suggested an athletic build. He seemed the picture of health.

I had remembered the case after she called. In Cincinnati, we don't get a lot of healthy, rich teenagers showing up in the river with something tied around their necks, and Peter Baer had been healthier, richer, and better-looking than most teens, until he ended up in the river. Kids die every day in the city, and the press pays no attention, but they had paid attention to Peter Baer, whose father was a bank VP and a muckety-muck in the Catholic diocese. If he'd been poor, they'd have hinted around about drugs or gang wars or child abuse. As it was, they were feeding paranoia about a psycho on the loose.

"What do you know about how he died?" I asked.

"Not much. He'd been missing for two weeks, and then they pulled his body out of the river. Well—you can imagine." She blinked a few times. "He'd been strangled with some kind of rope, like you use on boats, I guess. The coroner didn't think there was—anything else. I mean—." She swallowed. "All the other marks, he thought those came from being in the river."

The unspoken possibilities leaked out of her voice and filled the silence.

"Let's sit down." She backed herself up to a tattered recliner, and deftly scooped up the cat in possession as she heaved herself into it.

"When did this happen? I remember the case, but I don't remember when."

"Back before Christmas. After the football season ended. He played football, you know, and his team won the district title this year, but they lost at the regionals. He was just a sophomore, but he'd already made varsity and sometimes even started." She betrayed the acquired expertise of the doting grandmother. "Well, I'll never forget that phone call. It was on Friday the Thirteenth. I'd never been superstitious, but that's when I got the call. It was George who called—my son. My heart jumped right up in my throat when I heard his voice. 'Mother,' he said, 'I'm afraid I have some bad news. They've found Peter. He's dead.' Just like that. As if you could take it in right away, like any other piece of news. Like, 'Monica fell and broke her front tooth,' or 'Vanessa has poison ivy.' When they've been missing for two weeks, you expect the worse, but somehow—."

"When did they discover that Peter was missing?"

"He didn't come home that Saturday, two weeks before. November the twenty-third, that was, right after Thanksgiving. Well, he was a teenager, he had his friends, they assumed he was staying at somebody's house. They were surprised he hadn't called and left them a message— George and Vanessa had been out, and Monica was sleeping over at a friend's—but they'd been having some trouble with the answering machine, so they thought maybe he had called and tried to leave a message.

"You know these modern parents, Cat; they just don't seem to pay much attention. But George and Vanessa don't live in New York City, after all. Peter went to Seven Hills Academy, and the worst thing you could say about his friends was that they were teenage boys, and they were too damn rich for their own good—or their parents were.

"Anyway, he never came home. And when they called around, they couldn't find anyone who'd seen him or talked to him. It was just like he'd vanished into thin air."

"So who saw him last, Gussie?"

"Everybody in the family saw him Friday night at dinner. He went out with his girlfriend after dinner on a double date with a friend of his, and his parents saw him when he came home. The next morning, everybody left before he was up, or that's what they think. They know he slept in his bed."

She turned her head abruptly in that birdlike way she had. "Do you have kids, Cat?" she asked. Then she grimaced and shifted in her chair, evoking a grumpy bleat of protest from the cat who had settled on her lap.

"Any boys?" she added when I nodded.

"One."

"Then you know what they're like at that age, especially if they're athletes like Peter. Seems like all they do is eat, sleep, and play ball—football, basketball, baseball, soccer nowadays. I don't know how they get girlfriends; they don't seem to have much time for 'em. I had four boys. Nearly ate me out of house and home. My husband Ralph, he used to say, 'You going to let that boy sleep all day? Why don't you get him up?' And I'd say, ''Cause if he's asleep, Ralph, then he's not cleaning out the icebox or messing up my kitchen. Just leave him alone. He needs his beauty sleep.'"

I smiled. Even a second stringer like Jason Caliban could put away a lot of food at that age. Besides, Jason had been, in his own eyes, at least, too skinny, the ideal target for all those muscle-building programs hawked on the back covers of Superman comic books. But where sleeping was concerned, his sisters had given him stiff competition. I confess that at the time I'd considered this phenomenon part of God's plan to keep parents just on the brink of sanity. Teenagers were so hard to live with when they were awake, I'd reasoned, God had sent them long hours of unconsciousness to compensate us. Like Ralph, Fred Caliban had been of the opinion that we had a moral obligation not to let sleeping teens lie. But I agreed with Gussie. Fred never cleaned up their messes, physical or emotional, which also had a lot to do with his attitude, I'd always thought.

"So, anyway." Gussie sighed. "The police say he didn't eat anything before he died, which probably means he died earlier on Saturday instead of later. They couldn't really establish when he died, on account of—you know."

I nodded, not wanting to linger on the effects of water on inanimate human flesh.

"But why didn't he eat anything before he was killed?" I mused. "If he ate like a normal teenaged boy, it's hard to believe that he went off somewhere and was killed before he ate, unless he went out to eat."

Gussie nodded with satisfaction and tapped the crabby cat on the head to punctuate her words. "That's just what I said, Cat! And I asked Vanessa, I said, 'Honey, wasn't there anything in the house to eat?' Well, I guess she thought I was criticizing her, but I wasn't. So I said, 'Maybe you ran out of milk or cereal or bread or something?' She got kind of huffy about it, really, and said there was plenty to eat. Well, who knows about that? She probably meant brie and those skinny little imported crackers, and I meant eggs and cereal. So I thought, maybe he went out to meet a friend for breakfast. I asked Monica, and she mentioned some places he might have gone. And I was going to go to those places and ask if he'd been there, but then I broke my hip, and—well, that pretty much ended my career as a detective."

I heard a crash that seemed to come from the front hallway, but Gussie didn't bat an eyelash. Two cats hurried from the room to investigate.

"What was he wearing when he was found?"

"Just, you know, Saturday clothes—jeans and a sweatshirt."

"No jacket?" I asked. "No coat?"

"That's just what I asked!" she exclaimed and gave the cat a harder tap than before. He turned his head and clamped his jaws on her hand, but she shook him off. "Where was his jacket? It was pretty cold around Thanksgiving, I remember."

"Did his folks say a coat was missing from his closet?"

She nodded. "An old jacket of his." She leaned forward and fixed me with her dark eyes.

"I have a feeling, Cat—a premonition, like. I don't think I'm going to be around much longer. I just don't feel too good anymore. I guess it's my heart, I don't know. I have medication, but I just think maybe it's about time to check out." She looked down at her hands in her lap. "I'm ready, and I want to see my boy again. I believe I will. But I don't want to die like this, not knowing what happened." She paused. "No," she corrected herself, "it's not that. I believe I *will* know, afterward. I believe he'll tell me himself. But I don't want his murderer to go unpunished. I think about Peter, and about other people's grandsons, and I don't want that man to get off Scot free. I suppose the Lord will attend to him, in his own good time." She leaned closer and whispered fiercely. "But I haven't got that kind of time. And I want him punished!"

She straightened as much as possible and pushed back against her chair.

"Now, isn't that a hell of an attitude for an old Christian lady to have?"

On the way out the door, I tripped over an umbrella that lay with some other fallen debris in the hallway.

"I ought to warn you, Cat," Gussie said, as I caught myself on a nearby box, "my kids think I'm nuts."

"Gussie," I said, "I know just what you mean."

Chapter Four

THE CINCINNATI POLICE Department ran on God's timetable, it seemed, not Gussie's. Lucky for me, the case was being handled by an old friend of Moses's and mine, "Rap" Arpad, but like God, he had a lot to do, and it was Thursday before he could find the time to pay us an informal visit. Moses insisted that I talk to the cops before I talked to anybody else, even Peter's immediate family.

"It ain't just about stepping on toes, Cat," he pointed out. "You don't want to mess up their case if they have one. Besides, it ain't like the immediate family invited you in, and parents can get mighty strange when their kids have been killed, if they weren't strange before. You need to know what you walking into. Grandma may be the family wacko."

Arpad had never met Gussie, which meant she'd been questioned by someone else, and if she'd called up to complain about the pace of the investigation, she'd probably been passed off to someone in community relations. He was a handsome, distinguished-looking black man in his fifties, and I was conscious of his dark suit, beautifully tailored, as he sat down on Sophie's favorite sleeping spot. He brushed a few cat hairs off one knee before crossing his legs.

"It bothered me, too, Cat, that the kid hadn't eaten anything, but the parents didn't seem concerned about it. Hell, he was a football player, a sixteen-year-old football player! He wasn't a linebacker, but even so, boys that age don't go twenty minutes without eating. I should know; I've got an eighteen-year-old hockey player at home."

"Hockey?" Moses echoed.

"Hey, all the brothers don't play hoops these days, Foggy," Arpad said. "We diversifying. Kid's studied French for two years so he can curse like a Canadien."

"Is there a league in Cincinnati?"

"Nah, they just go down to the rink. Kid's got ankles as big as my thighs. Doria says we should just be grateful he doesn't play goalie, after all the money we've spent at the orthodontist."

"So do you think Peter Baer was going out for breakfast?" I asked.

Arpad shrugged. "Maybe. But where? Let's overlook for a minute the unlikelihood that a normal, healthy sixteen-year-old boy would leave the house without stopping off at the fridge for something to sustain him on his way to breakfast. Where would he go? Kid lives in one of those big mansions in East Walnut Hills."

Arpad emphasized the "east," and we didn't have to ask why. It was the code which distinguished a wealthy, predominantly white neighborhood from the less affluent black neighborhood next door, the intact mansions from the ones that had been divided into apartments and allowed to deteriorate.

"Okay, he can't drive legally, but he has his learner's permit, and his folks say he was a reasonably good driver for a teenager. But he didn't take one of the family cars. So he's on foot. Where's he going? To have breakfast with his killer?"

"He could take a bus," I offered.

"Kids from that neighborhood don't take buses, Cat. Cabs, either. That's for the hired help."

"Bike?"

Arpad shook his head. "Not at his age. With kids that old, it's real wheels or nothing."

"So he was picked up in a car," Moses speculated. "He could have gone anywhere."

"And nobody talked to him that morning?" I asked. "Friends? Teammates? Girlfriend?"

"Nobody," Arpad said. "We know some calls came to the house, answering machine apparently picked up all of them. The only outgoing calls are ones we've matched to the parents."

"So if he's going to meet somebody, he's set that up ahead of time," Moses said. "You ever hear of a boy making a breakfast date with somebody?"

"Only with a college recruiter," Arpad said. "And he wasn't that far along."

"Could have been a lunch date," I pointed out. "He wakes up late, realizes he's not going to make it in time, doesn't even stop for something to eat on his way out the door."

"You ever know a male teenager to care about being late to anything except a game?" Arpad asked. "To care more about being late than eating?"

"Was he a runner?" I asked. "Most athletes do some running; it's part of their training. He go out for a run that morning?"

Arpad nodded at me. "That's the best explanation we've been able to come up with. The clothes might have fit, though most runners don't run in jeans. He was wearing athletic shoes, but not his running shoes. We're talking about a family that can afford trainers to suit every occasion. And then there was the jacket."

I saw where he was going. "Runners don't wear jackets," I said. "Or maybe they do in the dead of winter. If they're cold in November, they add another t-shirt or another layer of sweats."

"What's the girlfriend say?" Moses asked, frowning.

"The last she saw of him was Friday night. They double dated with another football player, who drove, and she got dropped off around eleven-thirty. Then the driver, a kid named Mark Drew, dropped off Peter. That's the last anybody saw of him."

"Except his father, who checked on Peter when he got home," I said.

"Right," Arpad said, after a slight hesitation.

"You don't believe him."

Arpad sighed. "It's a fundamental principle of criminal investigation, Cat, that everybody is lying about something, right? You just have to figure out which lies are relevant. What I think is that if my sixteen-year-old son had just been found murdered, I wouldn't like to admit that I hadn't even bothered to check on him the night before to make sure he'd made it home okay."

"So you think he didn't go home that night?"

"What I think, since you ask my opinion, is that he was dropped off by Mark Drew. I'm keeping an open mind on what happened after that."

I unfolded a city map and spread it out on the coffee table.

"Okay, so all we know is that wherever he went, and however he got there, his body ended up at the Four Seasons Marina at nine in the morning on December eighth." Gussie had told me that much. She'd also described the rope as something used on boats.

"One of the maintenance men spotted a floater," Arpad said. "It took a few days to check out the missing kids and match the fingerprints. The parents ID'ed him."

"Time of death?" Moses asked.

"Can't say for sure, but probably not long after he went missing," Arpad said. "I don't think you want me to explain about body gases, and how long it takes a body to float, but that all depends on water temperature. You can't get an exact answer, but given the relatively mild weather we were having, the coroner thinks two weeks is about right. Fingernails were just starting to loosen up."

I swallowed, and turned my attention to the map. "Any theories on how far the body traveled?"

"Too many variables," Arpad replied. "It's not just the current, because the body could have gotten hung up on something, and then worked loose. I think we can rule out Pittsburgh, though."

"Well, that's a relief."

"No, seriously, Cat, the farthest point upriver he could have been dumped might be Portsmouth, but I doubt he was that far from Cincinnati," Arpad said.

"Could he have been dumped at the marina?" I asked. "That's kind of a ritzy place, isn't it? Wasn't it some kind of boat rope he was strangled with?"

"Sure, he could have. There's always a chance he'd been banging around the dock for a week, and nobody noticed."

I thought of the smiling boy in Gussie's photograph and winced.

"You checked out all the rope at the marina?" Moses asked.

"Yeah, but you know, Foggy, that's a needle-in-a-haystack type of thing." Arpad made a face. "A lot of folks are going to have the same type of marine rope, so the best you can hope for is some kind of match on the cut, but that's only if you get lucky and the perp used a dull, rusty knife or something. We're talking about plastic here, not fiber. Most of the time, you cut this rope with a sharp knife, it's all going to look the same. And yeah, the Baers own a boat, got the same kind of rope in their own garage and on their boat in drydock. Only difference is that theirs is yellow, and the rope used to strangle Peter was orange, so it doesn't match.

"And before you ask, the Baers don't have any ties to the marina. They belong to another club, a couple of miles downstream. And they couldn't think of any associations Peter might have with the place—no summer jobs, or friends with sailboats there, nothing like that."

I traced the wide blue loop that separated Ohio from Kentucky with my finger.

"Where else might he—might he have been put in the water?" I couldn't bring myself to say "dumped," as if he were a load of laundry or a bin of garbage.

Rap gestured toward the map. "Could have been anywhere, Cat. Even if you didn't take a boat out."

"This bridge?" I put my finger on the thin red line and squinted. Damn, they make that print small. As if people who were lost all had twenty-twenty vision, and only got lost on bright, sunny days. "It's the 275 bridge south of the marina."

"The Combs-Heil," Arpad said. "Yeah, could've been there. Or almost anywhere along the Ohio or Kentucky riverbanks. Hell, he could've been dumped in the Little Miami." He pointed to a narrower blue line that connected up with the Ohio just below the marina. "Except my experts don't think he would've cleared that bend in the river without getting caught up on something."

Now all of a sudden, Peter sounded like a competitive kayaker.

"Not what you'd call a promising line of inquiry," Moses said. "So what'd you get from the family and friends? Any resident nutcases?"

"Just the grandmother," Arpad said, glancing at me. "We took a hard look at the father. Had both the parents in for questioning several times, but couldn't crack them. They're both acting weird, but parents usually do."

"Weird how?" I wanted to know.

"Cold. Reserved. Bragging about the kid one minute, angry at him the next. More angry than anything, far's I can tell. But that's how it hits some people."

"Yeah," Moses agreed. "The old 'I told him to be careful, and look what he went and did' line. Don't mean the grief ain't real, Cat."

"Kid's got no other male relatives in the area," Arpad continued. "No male neighbors or teachers or coaches or even older brothers of friends with sexual assault records. Nothing obvious."

"So you think it was sexual?" I asked.

Arpad shrugged.

"In sex crimes, Cat, the weapon of choice is a ligature or a knife," Moses volunteered.

"Coroner can't confirm anything, but that doesn't mean he wasn't molested, just that we didn't find anything." He crossed a leg and studied the pattern of cat hairs on his knee. I decided to pursue this particular line of questioning with Moses later.

"And you think it was somebody he knew, because he probably went with them voluntarily?"

"We don't get a lot of abductions by Jehovah's Witnesses, March of Dimes mothers, and kids selling candy bars, Cat," Rap pointed out. "So he either went to meet somebody he knew, or somebody he knew saw him out walking and offered him a ride."

"He was an athlete," I observed. "It wouldn't have been easy to talk him into anything he didn't want to do unless you were holding a gun on him."

"Right."

"What do his friends say?" Moses asked.

"Friends say he was a great kid. Honor roll, student council president, football player, track star, homecoming king—an all-around great guy. Mister popularity. Did a little of everything—not just Student Council, but National Honor Society, choir, Computer Club, Key Club. Even had a small part in the fall play—nothing he couldn't rehearse between football practices, just a walk-on. Had a good relationship with his girlfriend, as teenage romances go."

"Too good to be true?"

"You might think so, Foggy, but damned if I can get anything on him. Of course, the parents probably shook down the room before we got to it, it was too neat, but Huesinger can usually find the stashes that the parents miss. This time, the worst thing she found was a *Playboy*. Just one. Otherwise, he was clean—no drugs, not even cigarettes or an empty beer can, nothing."

"Just one?" Moses echoed in surprise.

"Yeah." Arpad grinned. "In mint condition, too. Like somebody just gave it to him for his birthday."

"Did he have anything in his pockets when you found him?" I asked.

"Clean as a whistle. No house key, nothing."

"And he was wearing a sweatshirt and jeans?"

"A UC sweatshirt, yeah, jeans, underwear, socks, sneakers. Looked like every other male teenager in the city. In fact, the first clue we had to his identity, apart from his age, height, and weight, was one of these woven bracelets that the kids wear, and we wouldn't have had that if he'd been in the water much longer. His sister told us he had this black and white one on his right wrist. His folks didn't remember it. Don't ask me what they're for or why they're popular, but kids tie them on and then don't take them off. They come in all different colors. We had two other kids on the books with black and white ones, but one was a girl, and the other was much smaller than the body we had."

"So," Moses said, "you got no suspects, just suspicions. The case gone cold, and you ain't got time to work it if it hadn't. Do I take it that you don't mind if Cat pokes her nose in your business?"

"Be my guest, Cat," Arpad said.

"And you'd start where, if you had the time?" I asked.

He picked some cat hairs off his coat sleeve. "I'd start with the parents, maybe the sister. I don't think they're telling the whole truth, and I wish I knew what they were holding back. Maybe you can get something out of them."

"You know Cat," Moses said. "She's the soul of tact, restraint, and discretion."

I don't know why they thought that was so funny. I can be discreet if I want to. I didn't breathe a word to Arpad about the ring of cat fur he was wearing on the seat of his pants as he headed out the door, laughing.

Chapter Five

OKAY, LET'S GET one thing clear: to say I am not a morning person is like saying Elvis had a following. Moreover, since my long-delayed but momentous arrival at menopause, I've been short on patience, cheerfulness, humor, memory, and good will toward men. Shorter than usual. Especially toward men. My hot flashes light up my nights, keeping me awake half the night. Trips to the bathroom account for the other half.

So at ten-thirty on Sunday morning, I was in my usual antemeridian stupor. I had my elbows propped on the kitchen table, a cup of coffee between them, and my thumb and forefinger were holding my eyelids open. I had missed the target on my first pass with the kitty crunchies, and Sophie was fastidiously picking them up off the floor. Sidney, however, was after bigger game. He was posed in front of the calendar, which hung on the wall facing me but too far away for me to read in my present state. I suspected it was a holiday, probably some president's birthday, probably not Reagan's. He casually stretched two paws up, dug in his claws, and raked them down the calendar page.

"Give it up, Sid," I said. "Turkey is for Thanksgiving, and ham is for Christmas and Easter, but whoever heard of celebrating Washington's birthday with tuna fish?"

That's when the pounding started, and I swear that at first, I thought it was in my head. Damn, I thought, maybe I should give in and go see my gynecologist after all, like everybody had been campaigning for me to do. Last I heard, brain tumors were not symptoms of menopause. Forgetfulness, yes, but not the sound of Big Foot breakdancing on your skull. But maybe I'd forgotten this symptom.

When I realized that it was somebody pounding on the door, I pulled myself to my feet and gave myself a little push-off to propel me in that direction. Sadie was sitting by the door, ears back, staring at it in annoyance.

I opened the door to a man in a suit and tie.

"Catherine Caliban?"

"More or less."

"I've got one thing to say to you," he said, his voice coiled with tension like an overwound clock. "Stay away from my mother, stay away from my house, and keep your damn nose out of my business!"

"Do I know you?" I was still too stunned to be angry. Besides, there was a good chance I was in bed having a dream, which tells you something about what my dreams are like when I do get to sleep.

"I'm George Baer," he said. "And no, Mrs. Caliban, you don't know me, and we're going to keep it that way."

"You're dressed for church," I observed, passing the time while I worked up to my Sam Spade imitation. "I can tell by the cross on your tie tack."

George Baer was a rather short man with a forgettable face, but he behaved like a man accustomed to power. What I noticed most about him was the Masonic ring he was shaking in my face.

"I'm not just playing around here, Mrs. Caliban. You stay away from my family, or I'll get a court order to keep you away! Is that clear?"

"Let's get something straight here, George," I said. "Your mother contacted me, I didn't contact her. She asked me for help, and I agreed to help her. She doesn't need you to sign a goddamn permission slip for her, she's a grown-up."

"She's an old lady with half her marbles gone, and you know it!"

I stared him down on that one. He actually started looking the teensiest bit uncomfortable. Good Catholic boys are trained to be polite to women, out of deference, I suppose, to Mary. What they always forget is that Mary didn't die right after they painted all those pictures of her with the Baby Jesus. She lived to be an old lady, like me.

"That might be, George, but with the marbles she's got left, she wants to know who killed her grandson. Now that sounds like a pretty goddamned reasonable request, if you want my opinion. Or even if you don't want my opinion, my opinion, like my services to your mother, are free of charge."

"This is a police matter!" he shouted. "I won't have you bumbling around and screwing up their investigation. And as for charges, your services goddamn well better be free, because if you extort a nickel out of that old lady, I'll sue you so fast it'll make you head spin!"

He sounded like a guy who had a law firm in his hip pocket.

Kevin chose this moment to put in an appearance. His door jerked open across the hall.

"Yo! Mr. Potatohead! Some of us are trying to sleep here!"

Baer swung around to confront the apparition of Kevin, red hair in cowlicks that made him look like a space alien, dressed in a lavender nightshirt that had electric pink cartoon bunnies romping all over it. He was carrying his teddy bear, a venerable creature named Simon. The nightshirt had been a present from his mother, but all Baer saw was a Catholic boy gone bad.

"You need some help, Mrs. C?" Kevin asked, scratching his antennae.

"Don't even think about it," I cautioned Baer. "Underneath those bunnies is a body that can bench press two hundred."

To be honest, I didn't know whether Kevin could do that or not. But one night at Arnold's, I'd seen him throw a two-hundred-pound drunk across Eighth Street, which was close enough and more to the point.

"I don't think so, Kevin," I said to him. "Thanks, anyway. I think George has said his piece."

"Well, if he's got any more of it to say, I hope he'll turn it down a few notches," Kevin said grumpily, and shut the door.

Baer turned back to me.

"I've said what I came here to say, Mrs. Caliban. Don't fuck with me! The chief of police is a friend of mine."

"I don't care if you're swapping underwear with him. I haven't done anything illegal, no matter how many goddamn lawyers you want to shell out for. Don't fuck with me, either! And don't slam the door on your way out!"

"You haven't heard the end of this!" was his parting shot.

We'd both descended into childish clichés.

I stood at the door and watched him.

"Now, what bent his bow, I wonder?" I asked Sadie.

Chapter Six

"MONICA. WE'LL HAVE to get Monica involved."

That was what Gussie said when I called to tell her about my little heart-to-heart with her son.

That's why I was sitting in Gussie's kitchen the following Wednesday afternoon, eyeing with trepidation a plant in a large clay pot that was perched on a pile of boxes and magazines over my right shoulder. It looked like a Christmas cactus that had last bloomed in December of 1967. I swear, every time I set foot in Gussie's house, I felt like I should be wearing a helmet and a full set of pads.

Monica was Peter's sister. She was a chubby girl with messy brown hair and intelligent brown eyes. She wore a rumpled navy school uniform. The collar of her white blouse was pulled askew over the jumper. Her white knee socks were wrinkled and loose from overstretching, and they were in constant motion: they would creep down her calves to her ankles, where she would seize them with ink-stained fingers and yank them back up again, leaving pale blue streaks on them. She wore scuffed Oxfords. She also wore black wire rims, an assertion of personal style that I gave her a lot of credit for. As she methodically worked her way through a package of Fig Newtons, I thought of her as a Franny in the making. Her deference to the rules was nominal; every wrinkle and stain was a token of rebellion. I bet she, like Franny, drove her parents nuts.

"We don't talk about it much at home," she said. "Mother thinks it's healthier that way."

I couldn't resist.

"What do *you* think?"

"I think they're weird."

So we had consensus on that point.

"Were you close to your brother?"

She threw me a look of exasperation and slipped her tongue inside a Fig Newton. Gussie intervened.

"Remember, honey, Cat isn't a reporter, she's an investigator. She doesn't know anything about Peter or your family, and she needs to find out."

"You know that show, *The Addams Family?*" Monica asked me. "That's us. Except nobody likes anybody, except me and Peter. And Grandma Gussie, but she doesn't count, because she doesn't live there."

"So your parents didn't love your brother, is that what you're saying?" I asked.

"No, I think they loved him—more than they love me, anyway."

She said this with thought, not bitterness, as if she were trying to clarify the complexities of the familial relationships. I took it with a grain of salt, knowing that all teenagers go through periods when they feel unloved and secretly hope to discover that they're the adopted offspring of a wealthy rock star who's having second thoughts.

"They were proud of him," she said. "He did everything right. I just don't think they really wanted kids all that much." She scored one side of the Fig Newton with a dirty thumbnail, tore it along the line, and unwrapped it. "They never really knew what to do with us. And now that he's dead they don't really know how to handle it. So they're mad at him, which is totally creepy and bizarre, if you ask me. But it was practically the first thing he did wrong in his life—getting killed like that."

A tear slipped down her cheek, and she ignored it.

"Did you ever see anybody creepy hanging around Peter—apart from your parents, that is? You know, a man or an older kid?"

She grinned. I'd demonstrated my willingness to play her favorite game: Trash the Parents. She licked her unwrapped Fig Newton, and then popped it in her mouth. One hand reached down to a sock and pulled it up.

"No, there wasn't anybody like that. And even if there had been, Peter would have beat him up. Peter was real strong. He worked out a lot."

"So what do you think happened?" I could tell she'd given it a lot of thought.

She frowned. "The cops think Peter went someplace, like maybe he met this guy or the guy picked him up. Well, the guy must have had a gun, right? Otherwise, Peter would never have gone anyplace with him. And the kind of weirdos who hang out on playgrounds don't usually have guns, just candy bars and drugs."

Her sophistication unsettled me. This was not a subject on which any of my three kids could have ventured an analysis when they were Monica's age.

D.B. Borton

"So maybe this guy was trying to rob Peter, you know? Maybe he thought Peter was carrying a lot of money. Or maybe Peter never even went out—that's what I think. Maybe some guys came to rob the house. Sometimes they call first, to see if anybody's home, but if they called that morning, Peter would have been asleep and wouldn't have picked up the phone. Or he could have been in the shower. So maybe they came expecting the house to be empty and Peter surprised them, and maybe recognized them or at least saw them, so he could identify them, and they had to kill him to shut him up. But they didn't want to use a gun, because that would be loud and messy. And if they hit him with something, that would be messy, too. And maybe by now, they were so scared, all they wanted was to get out, and make it look like they'd never been there. So they strangled him because that's the quietest way to do it, unless you hold a pillow over somebody's face, but can you see anybody trying to do that to Peter and getting away with it? And then they, like, took his jacket so nobody would know what they'd done. You know, they panicked. That's why they didn't steal anything."

I stared at her, awestruck. Damned if I didn't like her theory better than Arpad's. I assumed that Arpad had investigated the possibility of an intruder, and dusted the house for prints to match against prints in their databases, but I would have to ask.

"Actually," she added, "I think at first they were just going to tie him up. That's what the rope was for. But maybe Peter threatened them, or, like, tried to run, and they panicked, like I said."

"Do you read mysteries?" I asked at last.

She nodded. "I've read all of Nancy Drew and most of the Hardy boys."

"Have you thought about what you want to be when you grow up?"

"A psychologist. That's kind of like being a detective, you know, except you're trying to figure out people's minds. I like to do that."

"I have a daughter you should meet," I said, though in fact psychology was only one of Franny's many erstwhile majors. "So, listen, the night before Peter disappeared, you were at a friend's?"

"Abby Hargreaves's. She's my best friend. She's a writer."

"And you got home when?"

"Not till around five-thirty. We went Christmas shopping." The tears were flowing faster, and her nose had turned pink and runny. She licked her upper lip.

"And you didn't notice anything out of place?"

She shook her head. "Mother and Daddy were out, and I figured Peter was out with his friends. The house looked empty, and—normal."

28

My focus shifted to take in the kitchen, crowded with junk and knicknacks and cats. I could smell a ham in the oven, and at least six cats were in sight, some keeping a more casual eye on the oven than others. Gussie had just pulled herself up and done her six-footed shuffle over to the refrigerator, which was disguised as a message board crossed with a filing cabinet. Monica's tears dripped from her chin onto a petite tabby that occupied her lap. Grandma Gussie's must have appealed to a little girl who lived in an empty house.

"What can you tell me about Peter's friends?"

"He had a ton of friends. Which ones do you want to hear about?"

I groaned inwardly. How many people would I have to interview to get nowhere?

"How about his girlfriend?"

She shrugged. "Kristin's okay."

"Did they have a good relationship?" I prodded.

"I guess. We didn't talk about it much."

"Who was his best friend?"

"That would be Mark. Mark Drew. They were out together the night before Peter disappeared."

"Do you like Mark?" I had the feeling I was running in deep sand here.

"Yeah, he's funny. He teases me a lot, but I don't really mind. He doesn't treat me like I'm stupid."

"Look, Monica, I'm really sorry you lost your brother. He sounds like a great guy. I assume you'd like to know what happened to him."

"I guess so," she said, uncertainty drawing out the words.

She guessed so. I'd fed her a conventional line, and she'd refused to follow the script. Everybody assumes that when somebody is murdered, their loved ones want to know what happened, like Gussie. But Monica already had her own version of what had happened. And the advantage of her version over the one Arpad was developing was that it had no sexual content, and little violence. The death she had in mind was no doubt quick and painless, with little time for Peter to become scared. I didn't have to tell her that the alternatives were scarier.

"I do, honey," Gussie told her. "I want to know. Will you help us?"

She swallowed her tears and thought. "I guess," she said.

"Monica, did your folks clean up Peter's room before the police saw it?" I asked.

She nodded.

"Did they find anything? Take anything out of the room?"

"I don't know. They did it after I went to bed. I heard them in there, talking and moving around. The next day, it looked different—neater. Not that Peter was messy or anything, but he was pretty busy."

"When was this?"

"Saturday night. They called a bunch of his friends to try and find him. They asked me where I thought he was. Then they decided to wait till the next day to call the police. They went into his room to see if they could find anything that would tell them where he was."

"Why was that?"

"I told you, they're weird. I don't think they wanted the neighbors to see a cop car come to the house, especially if it had its lights on. And they kept rationalizing it, saying maybe he was with a friend, or maybe another girl, and he didn't want Kristin to know. He knew people all over the city."

"Had he stayed out overnight before and not told them?"

"Not exactly like this, but sometimes he stayed out when he told them he was going someplace, and he knew they'd go to bed before he got home, anyway."

"Who'd he stay out with? His girlfriend?"

"Uh-uh. I think with some of his football buddies. Mark would know."

"Well, here's what would help me a lot, and you're the only one that can do it. I can't search his room, so you'll have to do it for me. Maybe we should start with an inventory of everything in his room, and anything you can find put away that used to be in his room. Do you think you can do that for me?"

"I guess so," she said in a small voice.

"If he has a date book or a phone list or a diary or anything like that, I would love to see them. I can photocopy them if you want me to. Any postcards on his bulletin board or notes stuck in his mirror, letters in drawers, especially anything recent."

"Okay."

"I know it's going to be hard for you," I said. "I know you miss him. But it's important to make sure that nobody else loses their brother the way you did. Does that make sense to you?"

She nodded.

I stood up, thanked Monica and Gussie, and had started for the front door when I remembered the question I had forgotten to ask.

"Say, Monica, was the house unlocked when you got home that Saturday?"

"No," she said. "But if it was burglars, they could have taken Peter's keys, and locked the door when they left."

She began to sob.

"I should have been there," she whispered. "It was so stupid. We were just shopping! I should have been home with Peter."

She had thought of everything, including a way to make herself responsible for her brother's death.

Chapter Seven

ON SATURDAY, I picked up Gussie and we met Monica and her friends at Northgate Mall, where somebody's mother had dropped them off. We took them to lunch, Gussie and I in slow motion while they circled us like comets whose path took them close to every store window featuring girls' fashions and then looped back around to rejoin ours. One of them had pronounced Gussie's Air Jordans "radical." Our lunch covered the four basic food groups: meat, potatoes, soda pop, and fat.

"I can think of worse places to die than Northgate Mall," Gussie announced. "Like hospitals."

They were a gaggle of gigglers, Monica, Abby, and Mary Pat, but Monica had taken her assignment seriously enough.

"I didn't find too many letters, and he wouldn't have kept a diary or anything like that. That's girl stuff," she told us.

"Oh, bummer!" exclaimed Abby, and she exchanged a look with Mary Pat.

"What?" Monica said. "What?"

"Nothing," Abby said, glanced at Mary Pat again, and burst out laughing.

"She wants to know if him and Kristin were fooling around," Mary Pat explained. "Abby has a dirty mind."

"I do not! I'm just—interested, that's all. Inquiring minds want to know."

"Kristin wasn't 'that kind of girl,'" Monica said.

"That's what she said," Mary Pat pointed out. She grinned, showing a mouthful of braces.

"She was saving herself for marriage," Abby gasped. She was wearing tight jeans and a cropped knit top that rose to expose her midriff and a decorative little belly button when she laughed. It made me cold just to look at her.

Now even Monica cracked a smile. "Well, some of herself, anyway," she said.

I found this whole conversation fascinating. Had my girls talked like this when they were ten years old? Somehow, I doubted it. At ten, I'd swear they knew so little about the mechanics of sex that it wouldn't occur to them that there were parts of yourself you could give away or hold in reserve. I'd always heard that Catholic schools were the places to go for the best sex education, however informal, but I didn't think that was it. I suspected that these girls had seen more on television than I saw on my wedding night.

"Here," Monica said, handing me a small notebook. "This was everything I could find."

I flipped it open to a meticulous and detailed inventory, practically down to the last sock and handkerchief.

"Wow!" I said. "I'm impressed!"

She flushed with pleasure. "And his letter jacket is gone; I checked. And here's the piece de resistance."

She pronounced it like any American kid would who'd built up her vocabulary by reading Nancy Drew. She reached into a shopping bag and brought up one of those old familiar blue binders, softened and soiled by use, with writing all over the cover.

"It's his notebook. I stuck his phone list in there for you, and any other little pieces of paper I could find that looked interesting. He didn't have a phone book, just that list he made on notebook paper. There's also a Seven Hills phone book in the back."

"Woo—oo!" Abby rolled her eyes. "Aren't they special!"

"It probably accounts for the last zillion dollars on the tuition bill," Mary Pat commented.

"Thanks," I told Monica. I opened the notebook and found the list tucked inside the front pocket. "Do you know all these kids?"

She shook her head. "Some of them I do, because they came over, or I saw them at games and meets. But since we didn't go to the same school, there's a lot of people I don't know. Like this guy, Scott, I think he was the treasurer of the Student Council, but I never met him."

"Scott Demarkian? I know him." Abby was studying the list over my shoulder. "He's a real dweeb. He'll be a pencil pusher when he grows up and make megabucks on the stock market. And this girl? Myra Smith? She plays killer guitar! She's in that all-girl rock group, Femagination. They're awesome!"

"Yeah!" Mary Pat enthused.

"So what did you girls think of Peter?"

"Peter was a hunk!" Abby said.

"Get your mind out of the gutter, Ab!" Mary Pat scolded her. "Everybody liked Peter, Cat. We all did. We were so bummed out when he died!"

"Yeah." Abby frowned. "And I hope they catch the guy that did it and fry his nuts!"

"Ab-bee!" Mary Pat wailed, glancing at Gussie and me.

But Gussie said, "Here, here!"

"See, that's why it would make more sense if it was burglars or something," Monica interjected, "somebody who didn't know him at all. Or, like, accidental. Because everybody who knew him liked him."

I didn't want to tell them that a significant number of killers are crazy people who see the world differently from everybody else. Instead of rose-colored glasses, they wear a pair of funhouse mirrors that distort everything and turn it ugly. There was a chance that someone had looked at Peter and had seen him that way, not the way he was, but transformed into some kind of monster—the popular all-American kid they could never be, a reflection of their own inadequacies. If Monica did become a psychologist, she'd find out soon enough.

"Hey, Monica, look!" Mary Pat stage-whispered, elbowing her.

"Speak of the devil!" Abby said.

"Don't everybody turn around!" Mary Pat whispered, now mortified that five heads had swung around to see what she was looking at.

I strained a neck muscle responding to her urgency; I now looked casual and in pain. But Gussie continued to stare.

"It's Kristin," Monica told us.

"Yeah, and she's with a *guy*!" Abby announced.

"Who is it? Can you see?" Mary Pat craned her neck.

"No. Ooh, come on, boy! Look over here!" Abby said this under her breath.

"Well, that was quick!" Mary Pat said. "I thought Peter was the love of her life."

"You guys!" Monica protested. "This guy could just be a friend of hers."

"That's it, honey, turn your head a little more this way," Abby coached him.

"It's Mark Drew!" Mary Pat was scandalized.

"Well, why wouldn't she be with Mark?" Monica asked. "They were friends, and they both loved Peter."

"No, I'm telling you, girl, they've got packages! They've been shopping together!" Abby pointed out.

Monica gave her a look, and shook her head. "Well, so what? Are we in a shopping mall, or what? Why shouldn't she go shopping with him? You guys act like they're sleeping together or something."

"I don't know, Mon," Mary Pat said. "They look pretty intense."

"They're not holding hands." That was Gussie, putting in her two cents. "You kids still do that, right?"

"Excuse the interruption," I said, miffed at being the only person at the table who hadn't even glimpsed the topic of conversation, "but could you introduce me, Monica, and ask if they'd be willing to talk to me about Peter?"

"Sure," Monica said, with a defiant glance at her friends. "Come on."

So she marched me over and introduced me to the notorious Kristin Brannigan, as well as to Mark Drew, who actually stood up to shake my hand.

They seemed like nice kids to me. Kristin had the long, silver-blond hair that someone named "Kristin" should have, delicate features set close in a doll-like face, and honey-brown eyes. Mark had a more southern European look: black curly hair with one of those heartbreaking curls bisecting his forehead as if arranged there by a portrait photographer, and sleepy green eyes. He had a smattering of acne along his jaw line which seemed calculated to emphasize rather than detract from his good looks.

They did not seem embarrassed by our intrusion. In fact, it was clear they both liked Monica, and would be happy to help her.

"Sure, Mrs. Caliban," Mark said. "Anything we can do."

"We don't think we know anything, though," Kristin warned me. "We've talked and talked about it. Nothing we can come up with makes any sense."

I didn't have a business card to give them yet; Moses and I were still bickering about whether to print any, and what they should say. But I took down their numbers and promised to call them soon. I wanted to look over what Monica had given me before I talked to anyone else.

On our way out of the mall, we stopped in at the lingerie department at Penney's because Gussie wanted to look at pajamas.

"I've always worn nightgowns," she said, "but now they just wrap around my legs and get in my way. I'm afraid of tripping in the middle of the night, and falling and breaking the other hip. My kids would pull the plug faster than you could say 'medical power of attorney.'"

Looming over a display of women's underwear on sale, I spotted two friends of Kevin's, whom I knew only as Allen and Wags. Allen was holding up a pair of vivid red women's underpants, studying them critically, when he noticed me.

"Before you say anything, Mrs. C," he said, using Kevin's favorite nickname for me, "I want you to understand that we're shopping for my mother."

Wags laughed. "Yeah, right, Allen. Cat really believes that your mother wears size nine undies."

Allen turned as red as the Valentine's leftovers he was holding.

"Well, where do you find the damn sizes on these things, anyway?" he grumbled.

Allen and Wags were a couple in their mid-fifties. They'd been together as long as anybody could remember, according to Kevin. Allen was of Korean descent, and worked as a highly paid systems analyst, while Wags, a Paris-trained chef who practiced his art at the Netherland Hotel downtown, was from Martinique. In a crowd, you would never have put them together, and yet I'd met few couples who seemed more happily matched.

"How is your mother?" I asked Allen. She'd had a stroke two years ago, at the age of eighty-eight.

"Feisty as ever," he said. "She's in a nursing home now, in Kenwood. She likes to shock the staff." He gestured with the red underpants. "I'd buy her a red French bra, but that's even harder to size."

"And speaking of red," Wags said, "how's our favorite redhead? We haven't heard from him in ages."

"He's never home," Allen complained, "and I refuse to talk to his answering machine. What's up with him?"

I sighed. "I think he's got a new friend."

"That's nice," Wags said. "Anybody we know?"

"I don't think so. I'm not even sure Kevin knows him."

I told them about Kevin's Secret Admirer.

"Somehow, I don't think it's a secret anymore, though," I said. "I haven't seen much of him, either, and based on past experience, that usually means he's got a new flame."

"Maybe they got together on Valentine's Day," Wags speculated. "Wouldn't that be romantic?"

"I don't know," Allen said. "After they break up, Valentine's Day will be ruined for him."

"That's true," Wags agreed. "He'll probably always wonder why he feels so depressed on February fourteenth."

"But maybe they won't break up," Allen said. "After all, look at us."

Wags looked at him in surprise. "But we broke up, Allen, lots of times. Don't you remember?"

"Oh, yes, we used to break up all the time," Allen conceded. "But then we gave it up for Lent one year, and got out of the habit."

As I promised to remember them to Kevin and moved away, I realized why I'd found the encounter unsettling. What if Kevin did meet someone, and form a long-term attachment? I mean, I wanted the best for him and all, but I doubted he'd stay in his cozy little apartment with a live-in partner. If the truth be known, that was one of the things I was holding against old Charisse, Moses's current squeeze: she was a threat to the Catatonia community. Like an old tabby, I liked things the way they were. Change—at least change of the interpersonal kind—unnerved me.

Well, I thought, there'll be time enough later to drop hints about Kevin's Grand Ole Opry collection and his Barry Manilow imitations, if things get too serious.

I didn't have an opportunity to scrutinize Monica's inventory that night, because I was once again babysitting Attila the Munchkin. Under the mistaken impression that I could get Ben to sit still for longer than five minutes, my daughter Sharon brought along a video movie for us to watch: *Bedtime for Bonzo*. I opened my mouth to protest, but she was already gone. Shit! It wasn't enough that I had to watch Ronald Reagan on the nightly news, now he was invading my primetime entertainment. What's more, you'd think my daughter would know enough by now not to trust a five-year-old with a plot.

But I have to admit it was kind of cute, and not without its ironies. Al, who was on her own while Mel attended a martial arts seminar, wandered in about the time the young Ronald decides to teach the chimp Bonzo to be ethical.

"See, Bonzo was about to be shipped off to a research lab, and then Ronnie comes along. He's a psychology professor, Professor Boyd, and his father is an ex-con, so he's got a vested interest in proving that environment is more important than heredity in how somebody turns out. So he's adopting Bonzo to raise like a kid, so he can teach Bonzo to be good, but he needs a nanny—that's where the Diana Lynn character comes in."

"If Ronnie thinks environment is so fucking important," Al grumbled, "why's he cutting all the social services?"

"But why's the monkey wearing diapers, Grammy?" Ben wanted to know. "Can't he use the potty?"

At five, Ben was less interested in ethics than in excrement.

Ben drifted off to sleep, curled up on the floor with a crayon still clutched in one fist, right after Papa Ronnie called the fire department to get Bonzo out of a tree. And really, the movie focused more on the ethical drama and on romance than on chimp action after that. But Al and I were hooked, raising glasses of wine when Papa confesses to Mama, "I guess I have a lot to learn about being a father."

"Here, here!" Al cheered. "Let him be Welfare Queen for a Day, and we'll see how he likes it!"

"So tell me, Cat," she said as the credits rolled, "did you ever look like Diana Lynn when you were a mama? You know—get up in the morning, put on a dress and makeup and fix your hair, and then make your family breakfast?"

"I think I did," I said. "It lasted about a week. Then I took them on a tour of the kitchen, pointed out the refrigerator, pantry, and sink, and told them to wake me up when it was over."

Moses came home a short time later after being eliminated from his bowling tournament. He wasn't depressed, though; bowling was too hard on his back for him to view elimination as a tragedy.

"I need me a new sport," he grumbled. "Something you can do while lying flat on your back, or from a recliner."

"I think it's called channel surfing," Al offered.

Sharon came and collected Ben, and I showed Moses Monica's notebook.

"I gotta hand it to her, she wrote down everything—every album he owned, every piece of sports equipment, every photograph he had stuck to his bulletin board. I kind of like the burglar theory, though," I said wistfully.

Moses shook his head. "Homeowners usually get shot, not strangled, and burglars don't usually take the body with 'em. It's a possibility, I guess, but it's statistically unlikely."

"Well, what about Monica's explanation that they had to be quiet, and they didn't want the cops on their trail right away?"

"I'm just telling you, Cat, it don't usually happen that way. Now, there's a first time for everything, I ain't saying there's not. But it's not where I'd start. Most murders are committed by somebody the victim knows."

"So where would you start?"

"Well, you've alienated the parents, so I'd start with his teachers and friends. Minister, if he had one—I guess it would be a priest. Coaches. Neighbors. But especially his friends."

I sighed. "That's what I thought you'd say."

"What's the problem? Kid's got friends, right?"
"Oh, yeah. They'd fill the bleachers at Riverfront."

Chapter Eight

ON SUNDAY I went through Monica's inventory and Peter's notebook with a fine-toothed comb. Don't ask me what I expected to find. A collage of words cut out from magazines, arranged in the message, "You're next!" or "I'm coming to get you"? I reminded myself that I wasn't seeing anything that Arpad and his men hadn't already seen.

There were a few things even Monica couldn't identify—a group photograph taken at a picnic table, a school photograph of a guy she didn't know, a couple of pictures of Peter with kids she didn't recognize. Also posted on the bulletin board were: a caricature of Kristin, a dried rosebud, several ticket stubs from rock concerts, a year-old graduation invitation, photographs of Peter himself with Mark or Kristin, several cartoons reflecting negatively on the intelligence of football players, and a student council election flyer promising conscientious representation from Peter Baer. Monica had even spelled "conscientious" correctly, doing the nuns proud. I also found a program from a production of *Our Town*, a flattened cardboard crown, an invitation to the high school formal, several photographs of Monica, and a fortune from a Chinese fortune cookie. The last said, "Your sunny personality warms everyone around you."

To tell you the truth, it all looked like normal kid stuff to me. Not that I could translate the chemistry, computer science or math notes, or the Spanish homework, but I didn't think any of it was some kind of sinister code.

The pockets and the cover interested me more. Peter's own phone list was long enough, but there were a few others as well: Student Council officers, football team members, National Honor Society members. I clipped these lists together. Then there were miscellaneous numbers: Bill, Sweetsers, Jody (TC), Jen D., T.F., PW, Shoe, UC lib, PL, and Hoagey, and a few that were unlabeled. Some of these appeared on small slips of paper, and some were written on his notebook, scattered among the graffiti. Not all of it was written in his hand, which I could now recognize—a relatively neat, round script, with everything slanted backwards like a thunderstorm out of the west. I made a separate list of these miscellaneous numbers.

None of the graffiti was threatening. In fact, Kristin had drawn a red ballpoint heart with an arrow, and added, "Love Ya, Bear! Kristin." Another hand had scrawled in black magic marker, "For a good time, call 551-1212." I wasted a good five minutes checking the number against my lists, then stopped to remember what teenage boys were like; sure enough, it was Peter's number. Someone else had put a blue ballpoint line through the number, and added a second below it. That number belonged to the football coach.

At the front of the notebook, Peter had a daily planner that went back to August. Many of the notations concerned schoolwork—exams, papers, homework, things he had to bring from home for class projects. The names of other area schools also appeared, followed by notations of either "home" or "away." Without overloading my mental circuits, I deduced that these were his football games. There were SC meetings and NHS meetings—student council and National Honor Society?—as well as a "CC to UC," which I decided meant the computer club had taken a field trip to the university. But I was well aware that my translations could have been wrong. I'd have to ask my sources.

I'd already pegged Peter as a music lover from the number of tapes and albums on Monica's meticulous inventory, so I wasn't surprised to see two notations for rock concerts, one for jazz at the Hyatt, one for the CSO, and one for "TF—blues at Cory's." I was impressed by the kid's range; not too many teens frequented the Hyatt and Cory's in Clifton, and it wasn't because they couldn't get fake IDs. The ones who did probably didn't frequent Cincinnati Symphony Orchestra concerts.

Other notations fell in the category of appointments with a particular person or group: "Pick up Monica at MP's" and "K—7:30," that kind of thing. These were worth scrutinizing.

Then it occurred to me that something was missing from the inventory. Peter had been in a computer club; surely he owned a computer. I knew just enough about computers to be dangerous myself, but I was willing to bet you didn't send your kid to Seven Hills nowadays without one. I went through the inventory again, but no, no computer. I made a note to ask Monica about it.

After two hours of this kind of work, my back was sore and my eyes were crossed, so I took a break and rewarded myself with a lunch of macaroni and cheese—the really sticky, school-bus-yellow, disgusting kind out of a box that I hid behind the stone-ground wheat flour in case my youngest daughter came snooping around in my kitchen. When she gets in the mood, she turns into a dietary storm trooper, and pitches anything in my kitchen that has more than three grams of fat or the slightest trace of a chemical preservative.

But I'm here to tell you that stuff must contain powerful stimulants, because as soon as I sat down again to look at Peter's calendar, I began to notice a pattern. The notation "P" often appeared on Saturdays, and only Saturdays—every other Saturday, in fact. That meant that on the Saturday Peter disappeared, probably the Saturday on which he was killed, there should have been a similar notation. There wasn't.

So who or what was "P"? And what, if anything, did it have to do with Peter's death?

Okay, it could be anything, I realized that. Since there was no time attached, it could even be a reminder to do something, like pick up P's mail, or go to special practice sessions. Maybe his parents were out of the house every other Saturday; I would need to ask Monica about that. He had two friends with first names starting with "P"; did he meet either of them regularly on Saturdays to do something? If it had been a teenage girl, and the notation appeared every four weeks, I would have known what that meant, but I couldn't think of anything comparable that teenage boys kept track of.

I made a note to ask Gussie and Monica about "P."

I waded through a lot of other stuff, mostly cute little love notes from Kristin, who seemed to like using hearts instead of dots over the "i"s in her name. The majority were uninteresting—ripped scraps of notebook paper that said things like, "Did you see me walk by third period, or were you too busy cooking chemicals?" and "Love that smile! —K" and "What's wrong? You look like you lost your best friend! Call me later!!!"

Then, accordion-folded and crammed into the bottom of the notebook pocket, I found a note that said, "Can't do this any more. Maybe I'll see you some time. P." The handwriting was cramped, less legible than Peter's, and slanted in the other direction. So "P" wasn't Peter. Was she or he the "Pat Martin" whose name appeared on the student council list? Phil Young from the football team? The "PW" whose phone number was scrawled on a corner of Peter's notebook? And what did the note mean? What couldn't "P" do? Meet Peter on Saturdays? Figure out her math homework? I made another note about "P."

A phone call to Gussie did not reveal the identity of either "P," but she promised to phone Monica and give it more thought herself. The prospect of working a whole case in which I couldn't pick up the phone and call the victim's sister made me tired.

I lay down on the carpet in the living room, my back flat on the floor with Peter's remains all around me, and studied the inventory of his books for some insight into his mind. Many were obviously textbooks. Others may have been. My kids had never read Plato's *Symposium* in high school, but they hadn't attended an academically high-powered private academy, either. Some of his books were paperback copies of the kind of novels they usually taught in school. Some were hardback biographies of figures meant to inspire adolescent boys, with an emphasis on military and sports figures. There were other sports-related books as well, and several computer books. Like any good Catholic boy, he had a Bible. And he boasted a small collection of paperbacks with lots of exes and zees in the titles, books I took to be fantasy or science fiction—enough to register interest, but not enough to suggest the obsessiveness of a true junkie.

But what did any of this have to do with Peter's murder? After all, without seeing the books, I couldn't even tell if he'd read them. Did they represent his taste, or the taste of the people who gave him presents? Was his Bible well-thumbed, or relatively pristine? And even if I knew his tastes in reading material, I doubted I'd be any closer to figuring out why anyone would want to kill him, unless he'd spotted a plagiarism.

His tastes in music were eclectic, but otherwise unrevealing. A collection strong on heavy metal music might have aroused my suspicions about the crowd he was running with, but that seemed to be one of the few musical genres he didn't have covered. In addition to the extensive collection of rock albums and tapes, he owned some classical music, some folk music, some bluegrass music, some jazz, some R&B and soul, and single-artist recordings by everybody from Patsy Cline to Aaron Neville, from Judy Garland to Barbra Streisand to Paul Simon. If there was a clue here, I didn't see it. I hoped I wouldn't have to smuggle the whole damn collection out of the house and play it backwards.

When Al called, I was sound asleep, hands folded across my chest like a corpse, fingers numb because the blood was having a harder and harder time running uphill these days. I rolled myself to a standing position and went into the kitchen to answer.

Al wanted to know if I'd help Mel and her position a picture they were hanging.

On the landing outside Al and Mel's apartment, I ran into Moses. He'd been asked to hold the picture.

We were standing in the middle of Al and Mel's empty living room when a crowd of people jumped out and yelled, "Surprise!"

Don't ask me where they jumped out from; the apartment isn't that big. Some of them must have been hiding under the sofa. Now the closet, kitchen, and bedrooms emptied out like a clown car at the circus. They were singing, at the top of their lungs, "For they are jolly good fellows!" If this was a party, some of them had already sampled the punch.

I gazed at them in a sleepy stupor, irritated at their rowdy cheerfulness. This was going to take me some time to warm up to. And I hadn't even figured out the occasion yet.

But Moses was already grinning, glad-handing folks and slapping them on the back. When I turned around, I noticed a banner, draped between a curtain rod and a poster from Judy Chicago's "Dinner Party"; it read, "Congratulations to Fogg and Caliban, Inc.!!!"

"Congratulations, Cat!" my friend Louella shouted, squeezing my arm. "Welcome to the ranks of the fully employed!"

"Congratulations, Mom!" My daughter Franny hugged me and I caught that faint musty odor that had lingered about her since her earliest days as a hippie. "We knew you could do it!"

"Congratulations, M-m-miz Cat!" Leon shook my hand. "M-m-my brother s-say, this be a g-good time to ax you for a raise, b-but I don't need no more m-money," he reassured me. "I b-been thinking about your b-b-business cards, though."

"Gimme five, baby!" This was Moses's friend, Chuck, who caught me up in a hug before I had time to react to the prospect that Leon might produce our business cards. "I give you credit for getting the old man off his ass. Jus' remember, though, he ain't as young as he used to be. Don't wear him out, now."

Junior, the enormous brown hound dog Louella had acquired during one of my cases, planted a paw on each shoulder and dragged a tongue like a wet washcloth across my face. Junior was convinced, despite all evidence to the contrary, that we were great chums. I was now fully awake.

Everybody was there, if we don't count my two most disapproving children and Charisse. I doubted they'd been invited.

"Let's hear it for Fogg and Caliban!" somebody shouted.

I stole a glance at Moses's happy face. From the way he looked now, you would never have believed that he'd been dragged kicking and screaming out of retirement and into semi-retirement, as if an investigator's license were the first step along the path to a new career with the CIA.

The main entertainment for the occasion was the unwrapping of gifts by Moses and me.

As I surveyed the pile of presents, Louella said, "Now y'all are partners for real—got joint property and everything."

"That's right, Foggy," one of Moses's police cronies chimed in. "Y'all better not split up, be worse than a divorce."

Moses unwrapped a present from his grandkids first—a month's supply of vitamins and a First Aid kit, complete with Ben-Gay.

"Aww, thanks, kids," he said, and took the littlest one on his knee and gave her a hug. "Me and Cat will get a lot of use out of this."

"Are you and Cat getting married, Grampa?" she asked.

"No, sweetie, I already been married," he said. I could tell from the way Al and Mel traded looks that they took this as a hopeful sign that he intended to remain single. "We business partners, like your daddy and Uncle Branson. I ain't gonna marry Cat, I'm gonna train her."

"Well, somebody's gonna train somebody," I heard someone mutter in the back.

All in all, we received: a professional make-up artist's make-up kit; a set of pick-locks (from one of the active cops, while the others made a great pretense of not noticing); a pair of trick pens full of pepper spray; a pair of binoculars; matching t-shirts that announced, "Don't Look Now! I'm Following You"; a hand-crocheted wall hanging from Mabel that said, "In God We Trust, All Others Pay Cash" (with the last "a" looking like an "o"); a boxed video set of the Pink Panther movies (from Allen and Wags); an honest-to-god sword cane (where did people find this stuff?); a reverse telephone directory; a pair of soup cans painted and decorated as pencil holders; a set of paper body targets for use at the firing range; a Sherlock Holmes deerstalker hat for Winnie with ear slits and a rubber squeak meerschaum; a jar of invisible ink; a bottle of bourbon to put in our desk drawer; a forbidding sign that read, "WARNING! THESE PREMISES ARE PROTECTED BY AN ATTACK DOG!"; and books on covert surveillance, arson investigation, handwriting analysis, skip tracing, con games, and conflict resolution in a business environment.

Rap Arpad gave us a jumbo box of disposable plastic gloves and one of assorted plastic evidence bags, with the admonition that if I ever found any evidence relevant to one of his cases and didn't use the gloves and bag, he'd have me arrested on as many charges as he could think up.

But the hit of the evening was Leon's present. He had shopped the yard sales and come up with a secondhand Polaroid that worked. His brothers had thrown in a supply of film and some coupons for free film processing.

"It d-don't have n-no case, but I c-c-cleaned it up, and it t-take real good pictures," Leon assured us.

"It's a great present, Leon," I said. To tell you the truth, I was kind of choked up. It was sort of like I'd cast my bread upon the waters by buying all of those hideous greeting cards, and it had been returned to me a hundredfold.

Leon was saying, "Thanks for the v-v-valentine, M-miz Cat. I thought m-m-maybe you was going to s-send me the b-b-broom one, on account of h-how I sweep the h-h-hardware store for Mr. B-bill sometime."

"No," I said. "I knew you liked fruit, so that's why I sent you the talking bananas. The broom one is a little too sentimental for my tastes."

"W-w-what that m-mean? That 's-s-sent-mental'?" he asked, frowning.

"Mushy."

"Oh," he said. His face brightened. "Maybe you c-could ax Kevin if he w-w-want to t-trade some cards with you. He like them m-m-mushy k-kind."

Ever the business entrepreneur, striving to keep his clientele satisfied—that was Leon.

One of Leon's brothers was already showing Moses how to load it, with Kevin kibitzing over his shoulder. This was, in fact, the longest amount of time I'd spent with Kevin in a while, but he left early.

By the time the party broke up, everybody had been photographed at least once and everybody had looked up their phone numbers in the reverse directory to see if the directory had it right. The cats were playing lino hockey in the kitchen with Winnie's meerschaum. Winnie was happily chewing on the conflict resolution book. She'd already thrown up a piece of chocolate cake she'd managed to swipe off the coffee table, which spoke volumes for Moses's skill as a trainer.

Al was studying the place on the carpet where Leon had spilled the invisible ink.

"My guess is we're okay as long as we don't turn the heat up too high," Mel speculated. "It's not like we're going to run a candle flame under it."

By now I was three sheets to the wind. My partner asked me how the case was going.

"I don't know, Moses," I said. "I've got a shitload of information, but I can't tell what it adds up to, if anything. It might all turn out to be worthless."

"Might," Moses agreed drowsily. "Can't ever tell. You got to just keep looking at it, Cat, like of them Escher prints, and maybe some day something will jump out at you."

"I start on the Seven Hills crowd tomorrow."

"The who?" Al asked. "Is that a teen gang?"

"That's where Peter went to school," I said. "Seven Hills Academy."

"A poor little rich boy, huh?" Al commented.

"What are the seven hills, anyway?" Mel asked. She was a recent transplant to Cincinnati, having moved here only ten years ago.

"Like the seven hills of Rome," Al explained. "That's why they named the city after that Roman guy, what's-his-face—"

Al had clearly consumed her share of the alcohol.

"Cincinnatus," I said.

"Right. Him."

"I know that," Mel said. "I mean, what are the seven hills? You know, like, which ones are they?"

"Let's see." Moses frowned. "Bond Hill, College Hill, Price Hill—"

"Mount Adams, Mount Auburn, Mount Lookout," Al added.

"What about Mount Washington and Mount Storm?" I asked.

"That's more than seven," Mel said. "And what about Mt. Airy? Does that count?"

"How about Indian Hills?" Al asked. "And Walnut Hills?"

"Those are 'hills', plural," I said. "I'll bet they don't count."

"Did somebody say Mount Healthy?" Al asked.

"That's a whole mess of hills," Moses pointed out. "Way more than seven."

"Where's Kevin when we need him?" Al complained. "He always knows stuff like this."

"We could call the public library, if they were open," I said.

"We could call the mayor's office, if they were open," Mel said.

"Well, all I can say is I hope this kid doesn't have a friend I need to talk to on every goddamned hill in Cincinnati," I said, "but I ain't optimistic."

Chapter Nine

THE THING ABOUT pessimism is, it never disappoints you. Have you noticed that? If you expect your cats to throw up on your new carpet or your grandson to break the most valuable thing you own, you won't be so unhappy when it happens. You'll be unhappy, but this small, submerged part of you will feel the satisfaction of having been right all along. I'd always leaned toward the optimistic side myself. But menopause was teaching me a lot about pessimism.

Take March. Groundhog or no groundhog, every year I expect March to show signs that spring is just around the corner. Mel and Moses start seeds in the basement, and the smell of damp earth seeps up through the heat vents. When I trip over the snow shovel on the front porch, I think about putting it away. If the thermometer rises above freezing, I start lobbying Moses to bring the screen doors up from the basement and take the storm doors down. I put my boots away. I take my coat to the cleaners.

Not this year. This year, the way things were going, I fully expected a major blizzard that would cover the snowdrops, kill off any other vegetation struggling to emerge, and blow all of my neighbors' dead branches into my yard. I expected the snow plough either to break down before it hit my street, or to leave a minor Himalayan chain across the entrance to our parking lot. I expected an ice storm to follow.

So when the storm moved in that night, I was psychologically prepared. By the time I cracked my eyes open next morning, there were two inches of snow on the ground, and the snow was still falling. My back ached from falling asleep on the floor the day before. I couldn't get warm—an irony not appreciated by someone who'd awakened in the middle of the night, sweating like a steam room attendant. If hot flashes were power surges, someone should invent a fabric that absorbed the heat and released it later when you really needed it.

What I needed to do most was make phone calls. But everyone I tried to call was at work or at school. Most of the answering machines I spoke to featured cheery greetings from a grown-up or messages recorded by the kids which ranged from cutesy to flip to unintelligible. I collected last names to go with most of the phone numbers I had. I told them all that I was looking into Peter Baer's murder, and would like to talk to anyone who knew him.

There was no answer at "Jen D."'s number, or at "T.F."'s.

I brought out my new reverse telephone directory, and looked up these numbers. The first belonged to an "R. P. Deemer" and the second to a "Wm. Frank." At least I would have something to say in my thank-you note, I thought. Then I looked up the unlabeled numbers on Peter's list. The first was for a La Rosa's Pizza. The second number was for a "Thos. Goff," who didn't answer his phone. The third was for Monica's school. But the fourth piqued my interest: "Youthline."

"Youthline," a youngish male voice said. "How can I help?"

"May I ask what kind of service this is?"

"You dialed the number, ma'am," the patient voice said. "What kind of service did you think you were calling?"

I could tango with the guy for ten minutes, but if he was a pro, I wouldn't get anywhere, so I decided to come clean. I told him that I was investigating the murder of a sixteen-year-old boy named Peter Baer, and that this telephone number had appeared on his school notebook.

"I see," he said.

"We don't have any leads in this case," I continued, when it was obvious he didn't intend to fill the silence. "So I'm wondering if anyone there knows him or spoke to him at any time last fall before he was killed."

"And your name is—? Your first name, I mean."

"Catherine."

"Hi, Catherine; my name is Michael," he said, that quiver of sincerity in his voice that told me he really was some kind of counselor or else he'd known a few in his day. "And I work for a youth hotline, a place kids can call and talk about their problems. Now, as far as your second question goes—whether or not Peter spoke to anyone here—I couldn't tell you that, even if I had the information. All of our conversations are strictly confidential. I know you can appreciate why. But I'll tell you what I can do. I can ask around and find out whether anyone here was a friend of Peter's. Sometimes our friends do need to get in touch with us when we're on duty."

"I'd appreciate that," I said. "But suppose the police were to ask you if Peter had ever contacted the hotline. Wouldn't you have to tell them whether he had or not, even if the content of the call were confidential?"

"I doubt it," he said. "I'm sure our directors would fight it. You see, most kids have to feel confident that their calls are kept secret, otherwise parents could try to coerce them into revealing what they talked about. And I don't think the police want to put us out of business, because we perform a valuable service. Besides, we don't ask for last names, or record them in our log book, so unless you know what Peter called about, it's unlikely that anyone here could tell you for sure whether they talked to him or not."

"Give me some help here, Michael," I said. "What kinds of things do kids call about, hypothetically speaking?"

"Oh, everything from school problems to love problems to things like physical and sexual abuse. It's a very wide range, so I don't want you to leap to any conclusions about Peter, even if he did call. We take every problem seriously, because if a young person is upset enough to call, their problem is serious to them, even if it's a B instead of an A on their math homework. Kids can be really vulnerable, you know."

"I know," I said. "The one I'm dealing with is dead."

He gave that a moment of silence.

"It's a terrible tragedy," he said, "when they're taken so young. It tests our faith, doesn't it?"

My ears quivered at the word "faith." Was this a Catholic outfit? I was pretty sure Michael wasn't an archangel, but was he a priest? "He wasn't 'taken'," I said. "He was strangled."

"It must be so hard on his family and friends," he said. "Tell me about him."

He was good. On the other hand, the more I talked, the more opportunity I had to win his support and gauge his reactions. So I told him about Peter.

"Yes, I remember reading about it in the paper now," he said. "I thought at the time, 'What a terrible waste!' We can only trust that God has a hand in all things, and that Peter is at peace with our Saviour. And what about you? This must be very painful for you."

"Look, I wasn't a friend of Peter's," I said. "I didn't know him. I'm just a detective doing my job."

"I see," he said slowly. "Well, I'll be glad to ask around, as I say, in case anybody knew him. But if not, I wouldn't attach too much significance to our phone number, if I were you, Catherine. We publicize it a great deal, you know. We encourage kids to write it down in case they ever need it—or even in case their friends do. 'Maybe you'll never have a problem that serious,' we say, 'but maybe a friend of yours will, and you'll be glad to have our number handy.' That usually gets them to write it down. Then sometimes it even gets them to call, as I'm sure you can imagine. They say, 'I have a friend with this problem,' and we accept what they say and talk things out with them."

"When you say you publicize the number, how do you mean?" I asked.

"Oh, lots of ways," he said. "The Yellow Pages, of course, ads on buses, in sports and concert programs, participation in social service fairs, youth events of various kinds, flyers and cards in the schools, rec centers, parks—every place we can think of where kids hang out."

"Sounds like a big operation," I observed.

"Pretty big, I guess," he admitted. "We have lots of volunteers."

Yeah, I thought, but are they paying the printing and advertising bills?

"So are you a nonprofit organization?"

"Yes, church-affiliated."

"Catholic?"

"Protestant."

"Which one?"

"The church is called New Life Ministries. New Life sponsors Youthline and many other programs for young people—as well as programs for adults, of course."

"Could I find out if Peter Baer attended any of those other programs?"

"I really don't know, to be honest," he said. "I suppose you can find out whether he was a member of the church."

"That's a good idea," I said. "I'll do that. Thanks for talking to me, Michael."

"Not at all. I'm sorry I couldn't be more helpful," he said.

I hung up and gazed at the faded black number against the grainy denim background of Peter's notebook. Had Peter experienced a crisis that nobody so far either knew or was willing to talk about? If so, had it been a crisis of faith? And if so, had he secretly left the Catholic fold and become a religious renegade?

And what difference did it make if he had? Last I heard, the bishop wasn't sending out hit squads to bump off lapsed Catholics.

I called New Life Ministries anyway. The woman who answered sounded like she had, not a frog, but a full-grown prince in her throat.

"New Life Ministries," she croaked. "How can I help you?"

I doubted she could help anybody. But I explained what I was looking for, and why. I told her the truth, which is usually simpler to start out with, unless you have reason to fabricate. I asked her if she could tell me whether or not Peter Baer was a member of their church.

"I don't know," she wheezed. "Nobody's ever asked me that before. I really should check with Mrs. Van Heusen to make sure it's okay. She's in a meeting right now, though."

She sounded ready to keel over, so I leaned a little.

"This is a murder investigation," I said. "Anyway, it would be highly unusual for church membership rolls to be secret."

I lied with the assurance of a veteran prevaricator. Every mother understands what I mean and I'm not just talking Santa Claus and the tooth fairy. What I knew about church membership rolls could be balanced on the head of a pin.

"Well," she said hesitantly, "we do share our mailing list with other organizations. . ." Her voice trailed off as if she didn't have the energy to continue.

"There you are," I said. "I don't even want the mailing list, after all, or even the address. I just want to know if his name appears on your roll."

"Okay," she said, giving up. "You'd better spell his name. I'll see if I can pull up the list on the computer."

She breathed like a bellows into the phone. I could hear the tapping of keys.

"Doggone this thing!" she said. "I don't—." She sighed. "That's not it," she said. "Maybe if I—." More tapping. "Oh, drat! Now it's going to go back to—. That's not what I want." She breathed into the phone.

"You sound awful," I observed while we waited.

"You should hear me from this side," she said. "I know I should be in bed, but I just hate to take sick days. There's always so much work to do around here. I know the Lord sends sickness to try us, but He doesn't send temps to fill in for us when we're down."

At last, she said, "I'm sorry. This is all new to me. We're just now in the process of putting this list on the computer, and I—. Wait. No, that's not it. I'm sorry. You'd better call back when you can speak to Mrs. Van Heusen. She understands this machine better than I do."

"Okay, thanks," I said. "I really appreciate your help. Take care of yourself."

"You, too," she said. "Don't get what I got."

So I'd have to wait to find out whether Peter Baer had left the Catholic fold and joined the New Life church or not. Maybe he'd called the Youthline once; he could have discussed anything from an embarrassing fumble in the homecoming game to family alcoholism. Or maybe he'd written the number down to pass on to any one of his five hundred intimate friends. I'd probably never know.

But talking to a sick person had made me even colder. I did laundry to warm myself up.

I called New Life an hour later, and my sick friend told me that Mrs. Van Heusen had been called out of the office. She would take down my number and ask Mrs. Van Heusen to call me.

This was the kind of day when my mother would have relined all her kitchen cabinets, but I wasn't my mother. I got out my new pick-locks and tried to break into everybody's apartments.

The locksmith wasn't answering his phone, either. When he called back, I could hear the wind howling in the background as he speculated that he might be able to come by on Wednesday. When he asked me what was wrong with the lock, I hung up on him. Maybe I'd just let Moses handle it. After all, it was his door.

I started to read about skip tracing. At least I fell asleep on the couch this time.

My daughter-in-law Corinne called and woke me up to ask me how to get ketchup stains out of a white sweater. Corinne calls me "Mom" and appears to have me confused with Heloise. I half suspected that these little appeals for advice were really attempts at mother-daughter-in-law bonding. I advised her to call Sharon, since my grandson Ben collects more stains than a demo carpet.

I heard Mel moving around upstairs, and wondered if she'd noticed the new scratches on her lock.

Kevin came stumping in the front door as I passed through the entrance hall with an armful of laundry.

"Yes, Kevin, the case is going fine, thanks for asking," I said. "I've alienated the parents, which leaves me with a ten-year-old and a gimpy old lady in my corner. The kid knew half of Cincinnati, and all I have to do is figure out whether his killer is in that half of the population or the other half. There are no noticeable clues."

"I'm sorry, Mrs. C," Kevin said, looking contrite. "You know I take an interest. It's just that I've been busy lately with this guy I've met. You know how it is." He appealed to me sheepishly.

I couldn't remember that far back, to tell you the truth. I assumed that there must have been a time when I found Fred Caliban distracting in a romantic kind of way—there were some soupy wedding pictures to prove it—but I found it hard to imagine now.

"I will take you shooting some time, I promise," he said. "I've just been spending a lot of time with Ron."

"Okay, so when do we get to meet this guy?" I asked. "I haven't seen him around. Is he tiptoeing in and out with his shoes in his hand?"

Kevin actually blushed.

"Well, I don't know, Mrs. C."

I heard Mel's door slam, and the clatter of her boots on the stairs.

"He's kind of shy, and private. We don't go out much. He's—."

"Closeted," Mel said, brushing between us. She looked back from the open door. "And married."

I stared at Kevin.

"He's married?"

"Well, right now he is."

"Right now is when you're having an affair with him, isn't it? Or have I missed something?"

"Yeah, well, I know, but he's trying to work through some things, that's all. It's not like his wife doesn't know. She's got her own friends. But they're trying to stay together until the kids are out of high school."

I dropped a pile of underwear in frustration and spread my arms.

"Kevin, are you listening to yourself? Can't you hear what you're saying? What did you tell Francie Fiedelhors when she was dating that married guy? You remember that guy—the one who was staying married for the sake of the kids, but had an understanding with his wife? Are you or are you not the one who told her to dump him and get on with her life? Your exact words, as I recall, were, 'There's absolutely no future in dating married men, and nobody but a masochist would put up with it.'"

"I meant straight married men," he said. "A lot of gay men are married, but they don't sleep with their wives. It's harder for them than for straight men, because they don't want to embarrass the kids, and so they come to some kind of arrangement—."

"And you're satisfied to be a part of that arrangement?"

He leaned back against the wall, looking deflated.

"No," he said with a sigh, "but it's the best I can get right now."

"Kevin," I said, "it's not good enough."

"You're right. I know you're right."

"Kevin, it's not *me* that's right. I'm repeating things I've heard you say a million times. I just happen to agree with the old you. And anyway, you're not the kind of guy who collects boyfriends. You're looking for a long-term relationship with somebody. Are you going to wait for the kids to leave home? How old is the youngest?"

"Fourth grade."

"So we're talking years before you can even live with the guy, right? And he's closeted? Whatever happened to 'closets are for clothes' and 'remember Stonewall'? Are you reading your own refrigerator these days?"

Cat Caliban, spokesperson for gay liberation. My late husband would be turning over in his grave.

"I don't know," Kevin said. "I really think I'm in love with him, Mrs. C. He's so—oh, romantic and sweet. Everything you're saying is true, but—my heart just won't listen."

I knew he was sincere, and that this was one of the most serious conversations we'd had in a long time. But as usual, I led with my mouth.

"Oh, gag me with a spoon," I said. "You got that line out of some old movie with a soundtrack heavy on violins. You hardly know this guy."

Sadie, a connoisseur of tragedy, had joined us in the hall, which looked like the site of a major underwear explosion. She was sniffing at a pair of drawers to see if it was what she thought it was.

Kevin just looked at me.

"Well," I said, "just think about it, will you? I don't want to see you hurt."

"Yeah, I know," he said. "I will."

I forgot all about the seven hills. I was picking up far-flung bras and underpants when I heard him fumbling at his lock.

"Boy, this lock sure is stiff! Maybe I'd better ask Moses to oil it for me."

But Moses wasn't much in a lock-oiling mood when he appeared at my office door later in the afternoon. Between thumb and index finger he was holding a small bent metal rod.

"This belong to you?"

"Hey, I've been looking all over for that! Where'd you find it?"

But he was already shaking his head at me.

"Cat, if you going to practice breaking and entering—"

"I didn't enter!"

"The whole damn apartment smells like Downy. Anyway, you broke. So if you going to practice breaking, why don't you break your own lock?"

"Where's the challenge? I can get in my own door any time I want."

"You can get in my door any time you want, too—you the landlady."

"Oh, yeah, I forgot. Well, don't worry, Moses, I've moved on." I held up the book I was reading—the one on handwriting analysis. "So would you—?"

"No."

"Please?"

"No."

"Just a short note, that's all!"

"No, Cat, I ain't going to have you comparing my handwriting with some sample in a book and telling me I'm psycho!"

"It doesn't have to be neat, if that's what you're worried about."

"It ain't about neat. Charles Manson probably got handwriting just as messy as mine."

"But, Moses, how am I going to learn stuff if my partner won't cooperate?"

"I cooperated. I got a busted lock to prove it. Why don't you analyze your own handwriting?"

"It didn't work on mine. Tell you the truth, I got my doubts about this book."

"Yeah? What'd it say about you?"

"Never mind."

"Cat—."

"It says I'm bossy and manipulative. Also I've got mental problems. Of course, I've got mental problems! I'm a menopausal sixty-one-year-old woman working on a murder case, for crissake! Damn! What time is it?"

"Four-thirty. Why? Where you going?"

He followed me out to the living room, where I began the long process of dressing to go out in the cold.

"Skoomf," I said into my muffler.

"Where?"

"School. I got to go to school."

As I was closing the door, I heard him muttering, "Well, if you get sent to the principal's office, and they give you one phone call, don't call me! And don't boss everybody around!"

Chapter Ten

SEVEN HILLS ACADEMY was situated in a wooded area north of the city. It was protected on all sides by green space—woods and lawns and playing fields invaded here and there by the concrete of parking lots and tennis courts, all of it covered with snow for the present. Wealthy parents from all over the city sent their kids here, decked out in Izod shirts, Eddie Bauer skirts, Guess jeans and jackets from Land's End, to spend four years boning up for the SAT's and accumulating Advanced Placement credits. Here, too, they began sculpting the resumés that they would one day present to law schools and medical schools. Rumor had it that they played sports here my kids had never heard of, like field hockey and lacrosse. It didn't seem to be a suitable place for a fashion trend running to simple woven bracelets, but you never knew with kids.

I crossed the lot to a brick monolith that looked like high school gyms everywhere, however well-endowed and well-equipped. I snagged a tall towheaded kid that looked like he could dust the rafters on his slam dunk.

"I'm looking for Mark Drew," I said.

"Out there."

The kid, who was wearing earphones, was wired for sound, and if I hadn't seen the cord I would have known by the muted noise of rock music that reached my ears six feet away. I thought maybe he hadn't heard me right.

"It's Mark Drew I'm looking for."

"Out there," the kid repeated, nodding in the direction of the door at the end of the hall—a door clearly marked with an exit sign.

I pushed it open and stepped out onto a sidewalk, gritting my teeth against the cold blast of air that slapped me in the face. Across a crowded parking lot, in the middle of a snow-covered open space, was a track. I could see that the track had been cleared because there were kids running on it. As I got closer, I could see that the inside lanes were wet with trampled snow that had melted. I stood and waited, numb fingers inside thermal mittens tucked under my armpits. Only a teenager would be out running around in this kind of weather.

Mark waved at me as he went past, as if I were a college scout who'd dropped by to watch instead of a frozen woman in the age bracket highly susceptible to pneumonia. If he was a killer, he'd found an easy way to do me in.

"One more!" he shouted on the next pass.

I stood, shoulders hunched, and tried not to wonder what frostbite felt like. Maybe he would speed up as he headed toward the finish line.

"Hey! How's it goin'?" he gasped when he reached me again. He bent over, blowing clouds of smoke like a steam engine. When he straightened up, he said, "You know, you really ought to move around to keep warm, Mrs. Caliban."

"Keep warm" implied that I had been warm, and at the moment I couldn't recollect having been warm since I'd taken the clothes out of the dryer. That's the thing about menopause; the memory lapses make you forget the hot flashes. Besides, I was wearing so much clothing I felt like a Sumo mummy. It was a goddamn miracle I could move at all, now that I had no feeling in my feet, except for the shooting pains in my toes. I said a prayer to the patron goddess of old ladies that all young men could be cursed with our circulation for just twenty-four hours, to improve intergenerational understanding and communication.

"Is there someplace we can talk?" I asked, then amended, "Someplace warm?"

He nodded. "Let's go in the gym."

So we sat on those hard wooden bleachers, and his eyes followed the basketball players up and down the court as we talked. He couldn't think of anything relevant to tell me about Peter's death. As far as he knew, Peter didn't have any enemies, though he might have been the target of envy or jealousy. He couldn't think of anything that singled Peter out as a murder victim. He had his hands stuck in the front pockets of his hooded sweatshirt, and he shrugged a lot.

Nothing strange had happened the night before Peter had disappeared. They'd double dated, but he'd dropped the girls off first because Peter lived closer to him. In a private school that enrolled kids from all over the city, distances between close friends could be greater than usual. The conversation had been unremarkable; Peter hadn't mentioned any plans for the next day.

Mark filled in some of the gaps on the phone list, but he didn't know anybody named Deemer or Frank. And he couldn't explain why Peter would have written "P" on alternate Saturdays in his date book.

I asked if he'd ever heard of Youthline, ever heard Peter talk about it, knew whether Peter had ever called. He looked surprised.

"I've heard of it," he said, "but it doesn't seem like the kind of thing Peter would do—call a hotline, I mean. I could see him as a volunteer maybe, answering phones. He might be interested in something like that."

I hadn't considered this angle. The young man I'd talked to at Youthline had been older—in his twenties, I'd say—so it hadn't occurred to me that teenagers might also be answering the phones there. But why not? With the right training, they'd probably make better teen counselors than older people. I would have to check into it.

"Did Peter own a computer?" I asked.

"Sure," he said. "He was good with computers. His folks put in a dedicated line, you know."

I didn't know. I didn't even know what a "dedicated line" was.

"He had friends all over the city—well, all over the state, really. People he met at student government conventions and football games and computer contests and stuff. So he used to write some of them letters over the Internet."

"The Internet?"

"Yeah, its, like, this communications system developed for the government, only now ordinary people can use it. It's pretty cool."

I would have to ask my cousin Delbert, the computer geek, to explain the Internet to me. I would also have to ask Monica what had happened to Peter's computer. Surely the cops had looked at it.

"Y'know," he said at the end, "it really gets to me when I think about how ordinary that last conversation was. I mean, I was talking about graduating in June, and going on to college, and how he was going to be a football star and we'd meet on the field some day, playing for different schools. I didn't tell him I'd miss him, because guys don't say stuff like that, you know?"

He was watching a guard break out of the pack with a steal and run it down the court, but his eyes were wet and his voice husky. He sniffed ostentatiously as if the cold had made his nose run.

"I never figured on something like this happening. It's like I wasn't exactly ready to say goodbye, you know? And now I really miss him."

"Maybe he knows that," I said. "Maybe he misses you, too."

I got out while the getting was good, before I embarrassed myself by revealing the depths of sentimentality to which I can sink when the right stimulus comes along. I could always send him one of Leon's sympathy cards.

When I arrived at Kristin's house, she met me at the door. She was wearing a short down jacket, tights, leg warmers, boots, and some kind of fake fur earmuffs.

"I was just going for a walk," she said. "Want to come?"

"A walk?" I echoed, horror-struck. I'd come within a yew bush of cracking my head open on the ground when I'd slipped on a patch of ice in her driveway.

Taking that as a 'yes,' she headed out the door. From where I was standing on the threshold, I could see past the front hall to a cozy conversational grouping in front of a fireplace in the living room beyond, and I could smell brownies baking.

"I just get so restless when I'm cooped up in school all day," she confided. "Plus, I just love to walk in the snow, don't you?"

I spat out a yew needle and waddled after her.

It soon became obvious that I could either talk or breathe, but I couldn't do both at once, and they were equally painful. Talking froze my teeth, and breathing made me feel like I had swallowed the whole damn yew bush.

But Kristin was a self-starter. She knew that the family was always suspect in murder cases—she'd watched enough cop shows on television to know that—but she didn't think Peter's parents made very likely murderers.

"His dad's kind of a cold fish, not real emotional, like you expect murderers to be," she said.

Thinking back on my brief encounter with Peter's father, I speculated that Kristin had never had occasion to see him roused.

She seemed to read my mind.

"I mean, he can get angry, I guess. I've seen him angry. But it's like this cold fury, know what I mean? I could see him, like, cutting Peter out of his will or something, but I can't see him strangling him. And his mom is sweet and vague and kind of ditzy, but, like, totally under Mr. Baer's influence. No way she would strangle anybody. Which leaves Monica, who's got her own problems, but she adored Peter in that wistful kid-sister way."

"You say Monica has her own problems, but what were Peter's problems?" I asked.

"Oh, I don't know. He didn't get along well with his father, I know that. I think a lot of the stuff he did he did to impress his father, but I don't think his dad really knew how to show approval. It's weird, really. Lots of fathers would love to have a son like Peter, who had that much talent and brains and all. And I think his dad probably really was proud of him."

"Monica seems to think so," I gasped.

"See? So he just wasn't good at expressing it, I guess. Anyway, his mom's big thing was to keep everything running smoothly. It's not like she didn't care, I just think she didn't want to know if anything was wrong or anybody was unhappy."

"So what are Monica's problems?"

"Oh, Monica, well she's probably too smart for her own good. She's really bright, you know, and they ought to send her to Seven Hills for high school, but they'll probably keep sending her to Catholic school 'cause she's a girl. So she's bored in school, and probably feels unappreciated at home, and some day she'll probably really rebel, and get into drugs or something and dye her hair purple. I hope not. But with Peter gone, there's nobody to really keep an eye on her."

She dispensed all this wisdom while striding at a pretty fast clip along a sidewalk that alternated between salted cement and snow packed into ice. She took the first corner like a sailboat rounding the final marker in the America's Cup.

Me, I slid into it like a base runner, and landed on my well-padded hip.

"Kristin," I said as she stopped to pick me up, "you're going to have to slow down."

"Gee, I'm sorry," she said, trying to get some leverage on my bulk so she could roll me to my feet. "I guess I walk pretty fast normally, and I get hyped up every time I think about Peter. I mean, who would want to kill him? Everybody liked Peter."

I mentioned jealousy or envy as a possible motive, even though I didn't really believe that strangulation with a ligature was the method of choice for the pathologically envious. Manual strangulation, maybe, in a fit of rage.

She shrugged. "I guess that's possible, but the thing is, Peter was so friendly to everybody, it was hard for anybody to resent him. I guess if somebody really schizzed out, they might do it, or a dopehead or somebody like that. But I really don't think it's going to turn out to be anybody who knew him. Everybody who knew him just loved him."

Since we appeared to be on the home stretch, I concentrated on survival, hoping she didn't have a kick as she neared the finish line. In any case, I couldn't have extracted a piece of paper from my pocket if I'd wanted to; I wasn't sure my fingers were still there, and I doubted they'd respond to any instructions from me if they were. I was hoping for a brownie to wrap them around.

"Want to go around again?" she asked over her shoulder, as we reached her front walk. She must have taken my open-mouthed gasps for a verbal response. "I guess not, huh?"

I got my brownie. My fingers felt like sausages, but I managed to extract the list of phone numbers from my pocket. Kristin studied it through her bangs. She reached "PW," followed by my notation, "Whitney."

"I don't know who this is," she said. "Let me get the directory."

The school directory listed no Whitneys whose phone numbers matched the one I had. Nor, for that matter, did any of these particular Franks or Deemers appear to be students at Seven Hills.

"They could be from anywhere, really," she said. "Peter represented the school a lot, not just in football and track, but at, like, conferences for kids in student government, youth leadership conferences, stuff like that."

She didn't know of any activity involving a "P" in which Peter engaged on alternate Saturdays.

"Geez, I guess it could be anything, huh? Except I can't think of anything that starts with a 'P'."

"Do you know if he ever called or volunteered for a crisis hotline called Youthline?"

"Youthline?" She seemed a little startled. "I've heard of them. He wasn't a volunteer, I can tell you that, but he might have thought about it sometime. I can't imagine him calling them, though, to talk about a problem he was having. I mean, he was a pretty private person. He didn't like to talk about his problems. He'd never talk to a total stranger like that."

She stared into space as if conjuring up Peter's image.

"How can I say this? He didn't like to ever admit that there was anything wrong in his life, you know? It's partly the guy thing, but his whole family was like that, too. You were just always supposed to be strong."

"What did he have to be strong about, for example?" I asked.

"Oh, well, just—you know—anything. If he had a bad game or if the coach didn't play him one week, or if his father got on his case about something, or if somebody complained that the student council wasn't doing something it should be, or if his biology experiment got screwed up, or if he lost a file on the computer. Anything. I mean, things go wrong for everybody sometimes, right? In my house we scream bloody murder, or we cry, or we call up everybody we know for sympathy, and then we go out and buy ourselves a hot fudge sundae. But in Peter's family, you pretend that nothing's wrong, everything's fine. And you just—go on."

I put the next question carefully.

"If Peter was that adept at hiding his problems, is it possible that he could have been in some kind of serious trouble without your knowing it? Whether or not you knew what it was, that is, would you have known he was in trouble?"

I expected her to reassure me, but she considered. "I think I would have known," she said, "but maybe that's because I hope I would have known. But he could be really protective—not tell me things he thought would upset me. The worst fight we ever had was about that."

She traced an invisible pattern on one knee with her finger and studied it.

"Seems like a dumb thing to fight over now," she said softly, "when you think about what most couples fight about."

"Yeah," I said, feeling discouraged and miserable. Now that my toes had thawed, they were throbbing and I could feel something cold and wet in the bottom of my right boot.

At home, the light on my answering machine blinked at me in urgency. Twelve people had returned my phone calls. They didn't think they had anything to tell me, but they were all eager to talk to me about Peter. "Everybody who knew him just loved him," Kristin had said, and for the first time, I found myself wondering whether that statement could apply to his killer.

After dinner had restored me to a moderate funk, I let my fingers do the walking. I was trying to ascertain over the telephone which of Peter's friends and acquaintances should be interviewed in person. But nobody had any significant information to add to what I already knew. Nobody could think of anybody who hated or resented Peter.

But I found that what interested me most was what people didn't know. Nobody knew what was special about Peter's Saturday afternoons. Nobody knew of any association Peter might have had with Youthline. Most intriguing of all, nobody knew anyone named "Deemer" or "Frank." These were probably kids from other schools, as several of my informants pointed out, but still.

Once again, I talked to numerous answering machines—humorous ones, abrupt ones, seductive ones, inept ones with truncated messages, musical ones, communal ones with choral greetings. Whatever happened to staying home to study on school nights, under the watchful eye of wise and supportive parents? I talked to some parents, who seemed vague about the precise whereabouts of their offspring, as well as sisters, brothers, and grandparents.

And then I got lucky. I dialed the phone number for "T.F." for the seventeenth time, and actually reached "T.F." himself, who turned out to be a kid named Tony Frank. An adult man, presumably Tony's father, had answered the phone, and after listening politely to my explanation, said that the name "Peter Baer" didn't mean anything to him, but maybe the boy was a friend of his son's. He'd put the kid on.

Tony's was the first voice I had heard that sounded the least bit tentative or wary, and I developed an immediate interest in him for that reason. Tony told me that he'd met Peter Baer during some kind of youth leadership conference the previous summer; it had been a weekend program held at a camp in Northern Kentucky.

"We were both interested in computers," Tony reported. "We talked about getting together. I was going to show him this design program that I developed for my dad. Anyway, like I said, we talked about getting together, but it never happened. I called him a couple times, and he called me a couple times, and that was about it. We were both pretty busy."

"When did you talk to him last?" I asked.

"Ages ago," he said. "Probably September. So I didn't really know him very well at all. I read about his death and all, and I—I really felt bad." His voice shook a little, and he stopped.

"I'd like to talk to you," I told him. No one else I'd talked to on the phone so far had seemed quite this shaken up three months after his death.

There was a pause.

"I don't really see the point," Tony said. "I mean, like I said, I barely knew him. He was a real popular guy, though, from what I could see and from the stories in the newspapers. There must be a million people who knew him better than me."

"Even so," I said, and let it hang there.

"I just think it would be a waste of your time, ma'am," he insisted. "I didn't live in his neighborhood or go to his school or anything. I couldn't tell you anything."

"That's okay," I said. "I'd just like to hear more about what you talked about when you met him. I'm trying to get to know him, and it could be really valuable to get the impressions of a relative outsider."

If I was trying to make him feel important, I wasn't succeeding.

"But why me?"

"Your phone number was written on the cover of his notebook, but beside it were only your initials, not your name."

"So?"

"Don't you think that's odd?" I asked. "I think so, especially since he'd only met you once, and had so many other friends, as you've pointed out. If it were me, I'd be afraid of forgetting what 'T.F.' stood for."

Okay, so sixteen-year-old boys aren't as forgetful as sixty-one-year-old women. This objection did not seem to occur to Tony.

The silence stretched on.

"So, how 'bout it, Tony? When can I come see you?"

He sighed. "Okay, look, I have to stay home with my sister on Thursday afternoon. Maybe you should come then."

He'd chosen a time far enough away to give him a chance to think up excuses. I wrote down his address in Mt. Adams, an artsy little hilltop enclave above Eden Park.

I was eager to talk to him. His nervousness represented the first palpable wrinkle in the smooth fabric of Peter Baer's life. And Mt. Adams, while distant in consciousness and ambiance from East Walnut Hills, where Peter lived, was not very distant in miles.

Around eight-forty-five, I made one last attempt to reach the few people on my list who didn't have answering machines. "Jen D."'s number was answered by a woman's sandpaper voice. I asked if Jen was home.

"No," the woman said, "she's not."

I explained that I was interested in talking with her. I was about to give more information, but I was cut off.

"That makes two of us," the woman said. "You find her first, tell her her mother says to get her butt home."

There was something in her voice besides anger. I asked if Jen had come home from school that day.

"Are you the truant officer?"

I didn't even know they had truant officers anymore, but I assured her I wasn't one.

"Look, lady, it's none of your business, but Jen hasn't been home from school in three weeks. You want to find her, it's okay with me."

"You mean, she's missing?" I felt a cold finger touch the base of my spine.

"Like I said, three weeks."

In the background, I heard young voices raised in argument, and then a wail.

"Will you kids be quiet?" The woman's shout was muffled. "I can't hear myself think!"

"Mrs. Deemer?" I said tentatively, using the name I'd gotten out of the reverse directory.

"Yes," the woman said into the phone.

"Mrs. Deemer, have the police been notified?"

"Oh, sure, they've been notified." She sounded bitter, but then a note of suspicious defiance crept into her voice. The wailing in the background continued unabated. "A sixteen-year-old kid goes missing, you don't think her own mother would report it?"

"No, no, I'm just—I'm trying to take in what you're telling me, is all," I assured her. "What do the police say?"

"Oh, the police wanted to know where my ex was. And even though I told them the kid hated his guts, they had to go look under his bed, I guess. So when they didn't find her there, they started in on giving me advice about how to get her picture on grocery bags. Grocery bags! Can you believe it? When's the last time you saw a teenager on a grocery bag? Or noticed? The country's full of runaway kids. The cops don't know how to look for 'em, don't have the money and time, or don't give a shit."

The wailing increased in volume, and she raised her voice to talk over it, picking up steam.

"This is just like her, too! Just like her! Of all the months out of the whole fucking year, little brat picks February to run away! February! Do you know all the things that can happen to a teenager on the streets in fucking February?"

I flashed on images of Peter's body floating in the river. Yes, I knew what could happen to a teenager on the streets. And I dreaded having to tell her what I knew.

Chapter Eleven

I TURNED UP Winton Road with Spring Grove on my left, dark and silent behind a stone wall. It was the city's largest cemetery—not an auspicious sign. On my right was the Lazarus discount store, where they sent their mismatched socks and scratch-and-dents. I passed the Winton Place VFW's antiaircraft gun, which guarded the cemetery from aerial attack, and drove up the long hill to a cluster of blocky brick apartment buildings which squatted in a large open space below the reservoir.

Mrs. Deemer met me at the door. She was preceded by a bulging laundry basket. Attached to one leg like a lamprey was a mop-headed kid of indeterminate sex, diapers bulging under its overalls. The diapers needed changing.

"Do you mind?" she said, thrusting the basket at me so unexpectedly that I almost let it fall. "Bebe needs a clean gym shirt, and I got to go now or I'll never get a dryer. Come on, kids!" To my consternation, she directed this last over her shoulder. "I don't have all night."

Still, we were delayed by a skirmish over coats. Nobody could find one for the lamprey, so Mrs. D. went back in to find it, dragging the leg with the kid attached. Two little girls of about six pitched a fit when it was suggested that they also needed coats.

"But why?!" they chorused. "We're not cold."

"Because I said so," their mother replied.

I set the basket down in the hall. I had been here before. These kinds of disputes could take longer to resolve than the Korean conflict.

Mrs. Deemer was back, the dead weight on her leg made bulkier by a coat. A muffled wail of sibling solidarity issued from just under Mrs. Deemer's left kneecap.

"Where's Jordy?" she asked. With an air of distraction, she hung two kids' coats on the ends of my arms as if I were a coat rack, and turned back. The two girls regarded the coats with loathing.

"I hate that coat!" one said.

"My pocket's ripped," the other said.

Mrs. Deemer reappeared, dragging a toddler. He was trying to gain a foothold on the carpet with his sneakers, pulling back against her arm with all his strength. His face was bright red and he was screaming.

Philip Marlowe, I thought, had to put up with a lot, but he never had to put up with kids. Why was that? I seemed to meet them wherever I went. It occurred to me to wonder if he would have turned in his license if just once he'd been met at the door not by a well-bred butler or a conspiratorial blond or even a gangster's thug, but by a pack of kids in full cry.

The laundry room had the garish yellow light of a Hopper painting. It bathed the yellowed linoleum of the floor and counters. The air was humid, and smelled of strong chemical perfumes that overpowered the odor of cigarette smoke. The roar of washing machines was punctuated by the rhythmic thumps of spin cycles and dryers. Mrs. Deemer gave the latter an appraising look before taking the basket from me, dumping its contents on the counter, sorting them and feeding them into two adjacent machines.

We sat down in orange plastic chairs molded to fit the bodies of space aliens. Mrs. Deemer nodded at two women seated nearby. A third woman was folding clothes, and a fourth was feeding coins into one of the dryers. Coming in the door, I'd nearly tripped over a baby who'd been crawling around on the floor. Sitting on the floor with her back propped against a washer was a little girl with a large book spread across her lap. She was reading to a younger boy leaning on her shoulder.

The Deemer brood staked out their turf in the middle of the floor and produced coloring books, crayons, and a small portable tape player playing loud children's marches. The red-faced toddler, inspired, began a one-man parade around the island of washing machines. The lamprey slithered to the floor and noisily sucked its thumb.

Mrs. Deemer was a woman of medium height and bulk and generous hips. Her permed black hair showed lighter color at the roots. She wore a full complement of rings on each hand like brass knuckles.

"So, like I told you, she just took off," Mrs. Deemer said, as if we'd been engaged in a conversation that had just been interrupted.

"And you're sure," I ventured, "that she's run away? I mean, that she left of her own free will?"

Mrs. Deemer shrugged. "She threatened often enough. And she took some of her stuff with her—some clothes, and some of her tapes. She wouldn't leave those behind. Oh, no! Can you picture it? Kid's wandering the streets, maybe starving, but at least her life has a goddamn sound track until the batteries run out."

"Does she have any relatives she could have gone to visit? Apart from your ex-husband, I mean."

She expelled a puff of air through her nostrils.

"I'm the only one that would put up with her. And don't think she didn't know it. My mother told me a long time ago that that girl would give me trouble, and she was right."

"Does the name 'Peter Baer' ring a bell?" I asked. "Did she have a friend by that name?"

Mrs. Deemer shook her head. "Don't ask me who her friends were! I'm just her mother, after all. But if Peter Baer was a weirdo, he was probably a friend of hers. That's the kind of friends she had."

"But it doesn't sound familiar?"

"Not to me, it doesn't."

But Peter Baer had not been a "weirdo," as far as I could tell. Whatever that term meant to Jen's mother, I was pretty sure she wouldn't have described Peter that way, if only because nobody else had. On the other hand, the kind of person who would strangle a kid like Peter might well be described that way.

"When you say Jen's friends were 'weird,' what do you mean?"

"Oh, you know," she said. "Weird."

"Rebellious?" I prompted.

"Well, when they don't give a damn how they look, and wear jeans that are ripped and stained and their fathers' t-shirts and flannel shirts and these combat boots and camouflage jackets from the army-navy surplus stores, and then cut all their hair off short, or wear it long in ponytails if they're boys and get their ears pierced—well, I call that rebellious, don't you?"

I would, but I wouldn't say they had no interest in fashion. It sounded to me like they were cultivating a look as carefully as a New York designer.

"Had any of them been in trouble with the law?" I asked.

"Not that I know of, but how would I know? I sure wouldn't find out from Jen."

"Was your daughter religious at all?"

She snorted. "Jen? Not Jen."

"So she never had anything to do with a place called 'New Life Ministries'?"

"Not unless it was a place where weirdos hang out. Hey, c'mon!"

She bounced up and grabbed my arm. A dryer had just been vacated. We stood in front of it, and she gave the room a quick survey.

"Stand right there," she commanded, positioning me to suit her.

She pulled something out of the bottom of her laundry basket, and turned her back on me. I glanced around, wondering if she were feeding slugs to the coin box or engaging in some other criminal activity to which I was becoming an accessory. Nobody was paying us the least attention. When I looked back at her, she was moving away. There was a new sign taped to the dryer window. "OUT OF ORDER," it read.

"It's not like my daughter gave me a whole hell of a lot of information," she continued, steering me back to our chairs. "But she didn't go out a lot, I can tell you that. Not like I did when I was her age. 'If you'd fix yourself up nice, and wear some of the decent clothes you've got in your closet, maybe you could get a date,' I told her. Hell, when I was a girl, I couldn't wait to wear makeup! That's what I spent my allowance on—lipstick and nail polish and eyeliner. She couldn't have been less interested. She wasn't a bad-looking kid, either. You'd think she'd want to go out with boys, and go to parties and all. But when she went out at all, they all went in this one big group. I just don't understand kids today."

To tell you the truth, Jen Deemer sounded to me like a kid with a pretty healthy attitude. But she didn't sound like a killer, or even a killer's moll. So the connection between her and Peter Baer was looking tenuous, and the more we talked about her interests, the more tenuous it sounded. She was not involved with student government or intermural athletics. She did not hold any leadership positions, did not belong to any clubs that her mother knew about. She didn't have any regular Saturday appointments, only occasional babysitting jobs on Saturday nights. She could have met Peter anywhere, anytime—at the mall, at the movies, at a rock concert. None of the other names on my phone list meant anything to Mrs. Deemer.

I had a murder to solve, I told myself. I didn't have time to find a runaway teenager. Kids ran away from home all the time, so it shouldn't be surprising that one kid among Peter's wide circle of acquaintances had done it, even if the timing was a little suspicious. Nevertheless, I asked the questions I would have asked if I were going to look for a runaway.

Eventually, it occurred to Mrs. Deemer to ask why I wanted to talk to Jen, and I was forced to tell her about Peter. Even in the yellow light, I could see her turn a few shades paler. She agreed to dig up a photograph of Jen and let me see Jen's room as soon as the clothes were safely deposited in the dryer—an operation that went off without a hitch, I'm relieved to report.

The room, which Jen shared with the twins, had a split personality. One half was all pink flounces, however faded and threadbare. The other was a study in simplicity—a madras bedspread and a small braided rug thrown over the pale blue carpet. Two vacant-eyed dolls dressed in Scarlet O'Hara crinolines graced the top of the girls' beds, crowded though they were by the detritus of the school day, from discarded slips to gym uniforms and schoolbooks. Jen's bed was clean. The walls on the girls' side were decorated with cheap silhouettes of them, paint-by-numbers puppies with bows around their necks, and mass-produced prints of rose bouquets. On Jen's side was a bulletin board.

Mrs. Deemer gave me a tour of the latter, or at least the parts of it that weren't self-explanatory. I was holding in my hand a school photograph of a bored sixteen-year-old, her hair blond with reddish tones and worn straight and short but in need of a haircut, or even a combing. It curved around her pierced ears and fell over her eyebrows, close to her sage-green eyes. The same girl appeared in some of the photographs tacked to the bulletin board. Sometimes she was in the company of other kids in the photographs, but none of the other kids was Peter.

Leaning forward to study the pictures, I said, "Do you know if she knew a kid named Tony Frank?"

"He a weirdo?" she asked.

"I don't know," I admitted. "I haven't met him yet."

"Never heard of him," she said. "But like I said, that doesn't mean much. He could've been her boyfriend, and you couldn't prove it by me."

"Who's her best friend?" I asked.

Mrs. Deemer put her finger on a picture of Jen with another girl.

"Natalie," she said. "Natalie Bassey. But she's not around any more. They moved to Michigan."

"When was that?" I asked.

"Last summer," she said. "Jen was crushed. Well, I remember what that was like, don't you? I had a friend named Sally Middleton who moved away right before high school, and I thought the world was going to end. I wrote her every day for the first two weeks, and then once a month for three months, and then on her birthday. And then I stopped writing. I saw her once, when they came back to visit a year later, but we didn't have much to say to each other."

"Yeah," I said, "I remember what it was like. Best friends. I don't suppose there's any chance she's trying to hitchhike to Michigan to see Natalie?"

"The Basseys haven't seen her, and Natalie swears she doesn't know where Jen is. I don't know whether to believe her or not, but the police talked to her, too. That would have scared it out of me, if I knew, but with today's kids, who knows?"

Otherwise, the bulletin board featured the same items you'd see on the average bulletin board kept by the average teenager: postcards (none from Peter), a few cartoons, some pictures cut out of magazines, a bumper sticker that proclaimed "SHIT HAPPENS!", a few smaller pictures and childish notes in crayon, a sappy poem, and a Chinese fortune that read, "You are a person of unique possibilities." Maybe all these kids had met at a Chinese banquet.

I studied the photographs again, trying to memorize the face. Then my eyes grazed something else—no more than a shadow.

"Her hands," I said. "I need to see a recent photograph that shows her hands."

Mrs. Deemer left the room, and returned. She handed me several snapshots. The first, in which Jen was trying to cover her face to avoid the camera, was out of focus, but the shadow was still there. The next, taken a moment later, showed it clearly: a woven black and white bracelet worn on her right wrist.

Chapter Twelve

"I DON'T KNOW where she got that," Mrs. Deemer had told me, "but you can see how ratty it looked by the end of the summer. I said, 'Why don't you trade that one in, and get a new one?' But she said it was bad luck to take it off. I guess it got washed some when she went swimming, but still. Then one day, I noticed she wasn't wearing it anymore."

"Did you ask why?"

"God, no! Are you kidding? If I'd said anything, she would have run right out and got herself another one. I just figured the fad was over. Next thing I knew, she had this silver tube thing wrapped around her ear. You know what I'm talking about?"

"I think they're called ear cuffs."

"Yeah, that's right, ear cuffs." She sighed. "So what I want to know is, when are little pearl studs and gold lockets coming back into style?"

She was asking the wrong person. If anybody was waiting on me to set the trend, they had a long wait. And my own consultants on teen culture, Leon of the tasteless cards and my cousin Delbert, the computer geek, were both sartorial iconoclasts who seemed oblivious to fashion trends.

"When did she take the bracelet off?" I asked.

"Oh, I don't remember. After the summer some time. September, maybe, or October? When you've got as many kids as I do, you're lucky if you remember their birthdays."

"If Jen were upset about something—if she were really missing Natalie, say—do you think she would call a crisis hotline?" I asked. I was shooting at anything that moved, hoping I'd hit something.

"Oh, who knows what she'd do," Mrs. Deemer said. "She spent a lot of time on the phone with Natalie, until I had to make rules about how often she could call and how long she could talk. 'You know how to write,' I said. 'Write her a letter.' 'It's not the same,' she said, and I knew she was right, but I've got five kids to raise on a bookkeeper's salary. I felt sorry for her and all, but I've got to buy diapers, right?"

"So Jen didn't use a computer to correspond with Natalie?" I asked. I could see there was no computer in the room, and I hadn't expected one. "At school, I mean. Did she take any computer classes?"

"She took a class," Mrs. Deemer said. "I don't know what she got out of it. She passed it, I think, which is all I care about. But I don't know anything about writing letters on the computer. If she did, she didn't tell me."

"So she wasn't in a school computer club or anything like that?"

Mrs. Deemer snorted. "She wasn't exactly a joiner, if you know what I mean. Not Jen."

I couldn't think of anything else to ask.

"It's not like she's got a hard life," Mrs. Deemer complained as she walked me to the door. "Though you'd never know it if you listened to her. I've got my hands full as a single parent, but I don't want you to think my kids are starving. Even without the child support that her bastard of a father never remembers to send me, I do okay, if I'm careful. I'm head bookkeeper for Shur-Good—you know, the Shur-Good Biscuit Company?"

That rang a bell, and I nodded.

"And then I sell Avon on the side, though you'd never guess from looking at my daughter." She gave me an appraising look. "Hey, you ought to let me give you a beauty makeover some time. I got some eye shadow that would make your eyes just light up your whole face, and some concealer that would make you look ten years younger."

I told her that I was allergic to makeup, which was more polite than telling her that I had other ways of getting lit, and that I'd earned every goddamned wrinkle I had.

"Thanks, anyway," I said.

"Look," she said, "Jen's a pain in the ass, but she's *my* pain in the ass, if you know what I mean. I wasn't so worried at first, but I thought she'd be home by now. What I mean is, I'd be really grateful if you could find her."

I said I'd keep my eyes and ears open. That was as much as I could promise. She said she'd better go see if the girls had put their brother in the dryer yet, and headed off down the hall in the opposite direction.

I called Gussie Baer and asked her to have Monica call me. A few minutes later, the phone rang. It was Monica.

"I can barely hear you," I said. "You sound like you're in a tunnel."

"I'm in the closet with the portable phone," she whispered. She was getting into her role as Deep Throat.

"Did you know a friend of Peter's named Jen Deemer?" I asked.

"Never heard of her," Monica said. "And if you tell me Peter was secretly having an affair with her behind Kristin's back, I'll wet my pants."

"I think she was just an acquaintance," I said. "I'm trying to figure out where he met her. What about Tony Frank or somebody named Whitney?"

There was static on the line.

"What did you say? I didn't hear you," I said.

"Hold on," she said. "The antenna's caught. There. Can you hear me now? I said I didn't know either of those guys."

"Okay," I said. "Can you tell me about Peter's bracelet? What was its significance?"

"You mean the black and white thing? I don't know what that was about."

"Why do kids usually wear them?"

"Uh, hmmm, well, I think originally it was this political thing—something to do with Central America."

If that was the case, I could talk to my daughter Franny, fashion consultant to the politically correct.

"But then I think kids just started wearing them because they were cool, you know?"

"What about Peter? Was he the type to make a political statement like that?"

"Not really. I mean, he was interested in politics, but he never, like, put bumper stickers on his locker or anything like that. I thought maybe Kristin gave him the bracelet. He just called it a good luck charm."

That made two teenagers wearing good luck charms who'd had really rotten luck. I didn't like the sound of it. I was almost afraid to find out if Tony Frank wore one of these bracelets.

Of course, Mrs. Deemer and Monica had both been right about teen trends. Maybe every teen at Jen's and Peter's respective high schools had worn a black and white bracelet at some point. Arpad had said they came in all colors, but maybe some colors were trendier than others. And maybe that particular color trend had come later to Seven Hills Academy than to Aiken High, where Jen went to school.

"Okay, tell me this. Peter had a computer, right? But there was no computer on the inventory. What happened to it? Do you have it?"

"No." She sounded disgusted. "I wanted it. But my folks said that it was a really expensive computer, so Dad took it to his office. 'When you're in high school,' they said, 'if your grades are good, we'll see about a computer.' God! You'd think I'd asked for a Porsche or something! It's not as if they couldn't afford a new computer for Dad's office. They really piss me off sometimes!"

"Yeah," I said. "Geez!" I wanted to strengthen my bond with Monica. I didn't want her to start thinking of me as a parent myself. In fact, I didn't want to think of myself as a parent anymore. I'm sure my kids had said the same things about me when they were Monica's age, and in just that tone of outrage.

"Fucking unfair," she muttered, but there was a tentativeness in her voice, as if she were testing me to see how far she could push.

"Yeah," I said. "Fucking A." To tell you the truth, I wasn't even sure what the "A" stood for, but this was an expression I'd heard young people use on television. I had my suspicions about the "A," but it hadn't occurred to me to ask around on the possibility that I'd be adding this expression to my repertoire, which, as my kids would point out, was pretty extensive already.

"So, Cat," Monica said conspiratorially, "anything else I can do for you?"

Cat Caliban, friend to the downtrodden teen.

I called Rap Arpad at home, and shouted to be heard over the din. The heavy bass beat made my eardrum vibrate. Was this a hip-hop hockey player I was listening to? I heard Rap's voice, shouting, before he spoke into the phone. The music dropped to a grumble.

I told him I'd just talked to Monica Baer, and I described the inventory she'd given me.

"So, I'm assuming you guys looked at the computer, right? I mean, apparently he wrote letters on it to some of his friends. You read all that, right?"

There was now an ominous pause on the other end of the line.

"He had a computer?" Rap said at last.

"Supposedly," I said. "He was in this computer club, went to computer contests—whatever they are."

"Yeah, but Cat, they got this fancy computer lab at school," Rap said. "He spent a lot of time there."

"Right," I said. "But he had a computer at home, too. His parents put in a dedicated line." I said this as if I knew what the hell I was talking about. "You never saw it?"

"Shit."

I let the silence lie there, not wanting to alienate him by saying the wrong thing.

"A dedicated line? You shittin' me?"

"That's what his sister said."

"Shit. How'd we miss that?"

I couldn't answer, since I didn't know what a "dedicated line" was, much less how big or how visible it was.

"You ask her where the computer went?" he asked.

"She said her father took it to work."

He chewed on that. There was no point in asking me when Baer had confiscated the computer; he'd done it before allowing the cops to search Peter's room.

"Looks like I got a few more questions to ask Mr. Baer, huh?" He didn't sound happy.

"Yeah, well, sleep tight," I told him. "And if you get anything out of Mr. Baer—."

"You'll be the first to know."

I couldn't tell whether or not he was being ironic.

Much as I wanted to find out if anybody in the Whitney household wore a black and white bracelet, it was too late to call and introduce myself to strangers. So I took a bath with Raymond Chandler, gin on the side. Sidney perched on the edge of the tub and tried to read over my shoulder, but I angled the book away from him.

"I don't want you getting any ideas," I said. "You're tough enough already."

The next day I went to school. If I couldn't call a meeting of Peter Baer's friends down at Riverfront, which was beginning to look like a damn good idea, I would do the next best thing.

I parked in a spacious, well-plowed lot, squeezing my little Rabbit between a BMW and a Porsche, and wondered whether these cars belonged to the students or the teachers. Either way, it was an unnerving thought. I followed my nose to the cafeteria. I had timed my visit for lunch.

Most mothers learn early that nosiness is a survival skill, so kids expect that from them. Nobody seemed to think it strange that I was looking for kids who had known Peter Baer. On the other hand, kids for their part learn to be guarded in their responses to maternal inquisitiveness, just in case there might be unforeseen repercussions lurking behind the most innocent of inquiries. Nevertheless, in a short time I found myself at the center of a large group of kids who claimed a greater or lesser friendship with Peter.

Four were athletes, judging by their build and the numbers of cheeseburgers piled in front of them. Three kids on the fringes looked to be arty types, their wardrobes color-coordinated in black and their hairstyles running to punk—or as punk as it got in suburban Cincinnati. If the rest bore signs of any particular clique, I couldn't identify them, although two of the young women were perky enough to be cheerleaders, and pretty enough in a Miss America way. The word had spread that I wanted to talk about Peter, and the circle was growing larger. Everybody wanted to tell me what a great kid Peter was. A few of them had already told me so on the phone.

I asked whether anybody knew of a school activity that took place on alternate Saturdays. Nobody did, although I got some interesting suggestions, mostly from the boys.

"That's how often Carruthers changes his socks."

"That's when Mandy goes out with Bobby. The other Saturdays, she goes with Jim."

"Aw, you're so bogus, Eddie! She doesn't want to listen to your jive!"

I tried out the names on my list: Jen Deemer, Tony Frank, P. Whitney. Nobody knew any of them. Again, I collected a few suggestions.

"Hey, wait! I recognize that first one! Isn't that the name from the last stall in the men's john on the first floor?"

"Yeah, right next to your sister, Boka!"

"You mean, right next to where you wrote those other two names!" Boka retaliated.

"That was ba-a-ad!" The speaker traded high fives with Boka.

"Anybody in the computer club?" I asked.

"Are you kiddin'?" someone said. "Geeks don't eat in the cafeteria, they're plugged in."

"Shows what you know, asshole," somebody else said. "Josh here's in the CC."

A tall, skinny kid in jeans, t-shirt, and glasses askew on a thin nose, looked a little embarrassed.

"You recognize any of these names, Josh?" I asked, and repeated them. "They could be kids you've met at a computer competition."

"Whitney, maybe," he said. "He go to Mt. Healthy? There's this kid named Paul on their team. He's good."

"You know him?" I asked.

He shook his head.

"Peter know him?"

He shrugged.

I asked about the bracelets some of them were wearing.

"Lots of kids wear these now," a girl said. "We think they're cool."

She fingered a blue and orange one.

"Do they have any special significance?"

"What do you mean?"

"She means, like, do they mean we're going steady or something, Whiz Kid," a boy said. "Nah, it's just a fad."

An intense young woman with long hair and wire rims said, "It is for you. For some people, it represents solidarity with the Nicaraguans in their struggle to maintain self-determination against the CIA-backed Contras." I noticed that her bracelet was blue and white.

Someone gave the faddist a playful shove. "Yeah, doofus. Not everybody's a slave to fashion like you."

"Mine's supposed to represent a victim of domestic violence," said another young woman, holding out her wrist to me. Her bracelet was purple and green. "You know, like a woman who died."

I looked around, but didn't see any black and white bracelets.

"So are the colors significant?"

"The blue and white are the colors of the Nicaraguan flag," said the first young woman.

I looked at the second. "Yours?"

She shrugged. "I don't think so. You just pick colors you like."

"How about the rest of you?" I asked, looking around.

"It's like she said," said a slight young man with his brown hair pulled back in a ponytail. "You just pick colors you like."

"So these bracelets," I continued. "They're not for good luck or anything?"

"If they were for good luck," he said, "I'd be wearing ten of 'em. Radford's givin' this bitchin' exam in Civ today."

"Are any colors more popular than others?" I asked. "Peter wore a black and white one."

"This one matches my eyes," a boy said.

"Let me see, Sanders," another said from the back of the group. "Is it red?"

"John's got a black and white one," a girl pointed out.

The kid with the bracelet, one of the arty kids in black jeans, t-shirt, and boots, shrugged, and looked a little abashed to be singled out. "It goes with my wardrobe," he said.

I couldn't argue with that. I watched his face out of the corner of my eye as I asked if any of them had ever heard of Youthline. He blinked, and I thought he looked uncomfortable, but I couldn't be sure.

"Yeah, I heard of them," an athletic type said through his cheeseburger. "Crisis hotline, run by NLM."

"NLM! I know that one!" one of the boys said. "That's that band Dorsey used to play in!"

"Don't listen to him, lady! He don't know jackshit."

"It's a church." This voice was quieter, and female. The last speaker turned on her.

"Get out of here! A church! You think they name churches like plumbers—A-1 or Triple-A or something?"

"Yeah! The Acme Temple!" someone else put in. "Can you dig it?"

"No, Tammy's right," another girl said. "It's that minister that came to the anti-drug assembly in the fall. 'NLM'—that was his church."

"Yeah, Jay, so back off!"

"Tell me about this assembly," I said.

"Hey, don't ask me!" one boy said. "I was catching some z's in the back of the room when it was going down."

"Some z's?" Another boy hooted. "Give me a break! You mean you were too hung over to keep your eyes open."

"Aw, it was just the usual bullshit," the kid named Boka said. "You know, do drugs and you'll screw up your life."

"Yeah, one puff of weed and your brain is fried for life," said another.

"You oughtta know," someone said.

"Look who's talkin', Airbrain!"

"So what do you know about 'NLM'?" I asked.

"New Life Ministries," a girl said. "They have a lot of programs for young people."

"Are any of you involved with them?"

"I've gone a few times," one girl offered. "You meet kids from all over, and they show films and have speakers—you know."

"Angela Rodriguez goes all the time," someone else said. "And so does what's-his-name—that sophomore who played drums in Zach Wang's band."

"Do they meet on Saturdays?"

"No, Sunday afternoons is when I've gone."

"Aw, shoot!" one of the boys said. "That's when I've got choir practice!"

"Does anybody know if Peter attended the New Life Ministries programs?"

"Peter was Catholic," somebody said.

"That don't mean he couldn'a attended some programs at another church, moron!"

"I never saw him there," the girl said, "and he never mentioned it to me. But it's possible he went to a program there. Like I said, I only went a couple of times."

The expert on Peter's Catholicism spoke up. "See, Peter wasn't just Catholic, like somebody might be Presbyterian or Episcopalian or something, he was *Catholic*. He had an uncle who was a priest, and his whole family practically built the church they belong to. His dad's a Catholic big shot. I mean, he doesn't come from the kind of family that goes church-hopping in their spare time."

"I see what you mean," I said. Cincinnati had a solid contingent of old Catholic families, mostly of German extraction.

I looked for the arty kid with the black-and-white bracelet. I wanted to ask him if he'd heard of NLM, and if he'd ever been there. But he was gone.

"Is there something I can help you with?"

The new voice belonged to a grown-up, someone who, by the look of her in her tailored suit and silk blouse, carried authority.

I straightened up in my chair. "I don't know," I said. "I'm investigating the murder of Peter Baer, and I wanted to talk to his friends."

"I'm afraid we can't allow people to just wander the halls and interrogate our students," she said, steel beneath her smile.

She struck me as the kind of person who might drive an expensive car. I think that's why my better judgment lost the battle.

"Do I look like I'm wandering the halls?" I asked. "This is a cafeteria, so I figured the kids were on their own time. I don't think I interrupted any important academic activities, unless they were conducting a biochemistry experiment on the cafeteria food."

This drew a laugh from the gallery.

That's how I found myself back on the sidewalk leading to the parking lot, muttering, "I been thrown out of better places than this!"

I half hoped I'd trip on the ice and break my ankle, so I could sue them.

Chapter Thirteen

WHEN I RETURNED to the Catatonia Arms, I met a tall blond man wearing cologne in the hall. With the light from the front door behind him, I couldn't see him clearly, but as I approached from behind I had the impression of an overcoat that was well-tailored and expensive. He turned, as if in surprise.

"Can I help you?" I asked.

He smiled. He was a handsome man with the kind of rugged good looks that made his age hard to guess.

"No, thanks," he said. "I was just leaving."

He didn't look like a burglar, but a career in motherhood had made me suspicious.

I persisted. "Were you looking for someone?"

"I found him," he said. "Mr. O'Neill."

He smiled again and turned to make his escape.

"You wouldn't be Ron by any chance?" I asked.

He was reaching for the door but that stopped him. He looked back at me, his face registering surprise. "Well, yes, I would."

The encounter with authority had put me in a bad moon. "The Ron with the wedding ring and wife and all," I said. "That Ron."

I saw something flare in his eyes but I couldn't tell if it was alarm or temper.

"I have a wife, yes," he said with caution, as if he couldn't imagine why his marital status should concern a stranger.

"I'm Cat Caliban," I said. I held out my hand.

"Oh," he said, showing recognition. "Mr. O'Neill's landlady." He shook my hand with a firm grip.

"Kevin's friend," I said, and squeezed back.

He didn't hold my gaze for long. "Well. Nice to meet you."

And he left. I glanced at my watch. His lunch appointment must have canceled.

Late in the afternoon, I called the Whitney residence. A woman answered.

"Hello, I'm looking for someone named 'P. Whitney,' a teenager, probably, who might have been a friend of a boy named Peter Baer," I said.

"Who is this?" the woman said sharply.

It seemed rather an odd response.

"I'm a private investigator looking into Peter Baer's death at the request of his grandmother," I said. It was best to be as open and clear as possible, in case she was a friend of Peter's parents.

"Look, I already talked to the police about that. I'm not going to go into it again. If you have news about my son, fine. Otherwise, I don't have anything to say to you."

"News about your son?" I echoed.

"He's missing," she snapped. "He's been missing for months. If you don't know that, then you must not be doing your job. The police certainly don't seem to be doing theirs."

"Did he wear a black-and-white woven bracelet, by any chance?" I asked.

That caught her off guard.

"How do you know that?" she asked. Then she gasped. "He isn't—. They haven't found him, have they?"

"No, no," I reassured her. "Nothing like that. But Peter wore one. And so did another girl who's missing, a girl named Jen Deemer. Do you recognize the name?"

"Jen Deemer," she repeated. "No, I don't think so."

"Your son's phone number was written in Peter's notebook."

"Yes, the police told me that. I can't explain it."

"Did they find Peter's phone number anywhere in Paul's room?"

"No, they didn't."

"Do you know why your son wore this bracelet?"

"No, I don't," she said. "Apparently, it was something the kids at school were into."

"Was Paul into computers?" I asked.

"Well," she said, "he was in the computer club at school. He didn't talk about it much."

"But he doesn't own one?"

"No."

"Do you?"

"No," she said. "I don't know the first thing about them. My husband says we'll have to learn eventually, because of the business."

"What business are you in?"

"We own the Good News Bookstore, in North College Hill."

I began to feel that prickle of recognition on the back of my neck. "Is that a religious bookstore?"

"Yes."

"What church do you belong to?" I asked.

"North Side Baptist," she said. "The Whitneys and the Tannens have been Baptists for generations."

"Do you know anything about an organization called New Life Ministries?"

"Yes, I've seen them on television. They're a very big organization."

"Do you know if Paul ever had anything to do with them, or with their teen crisis hotline, Youthline?"

"Paul's a Baptist, like the rest of the family," she said. "So I can't think why he would've had anything to do with New Life. Unless it was through school. They do school assemblies, I think. I think he went to one last year some time."

"But as far as you know, he never volunteered for Youthline?"

"Paul was very involved with the youth ministry at church," she said. "And he was a serious organist. He wouldn't have had time for anything else."

"And as far as you know, he never called them to talk over his problems?"

"This is a very close family, Mrs. Caliban," she said. "We talk over our problems with each other and with God."

"Can you tell me if Paul had any standing appointments on Saturday afternoons?"

"Yes, he practiced organ on Saturday afternoons, at CCM," she said. "You know what that is?"

"The College-Conservatory of Music at the University of Cincinnati?"

"Yes. He made arrangements to play one of the organs there every Saturday. He took the bus. As I say, he was very serious about his music."

"Can you tell me about his disappearance? When was it? What happened?"

"It was in the fall, on a Wednesday. September eighteenth is when it was. Paul just didn't come home from school. It got later and later, and I—I was irritated with him because we had Bible study that night, and we had to eat early, you know. When Keith—that's my husband—when Keith got home at five-thirty, I called one of Paul's friends. He said Paul hadn't been in school that day. Well, I didn't know what to think when I heard that! It wasn't like Paul to skip school, he was a good student. I called everybody I could think of, but nobody had seen him all day. So Keith and Bobby—Bobby's my oldest—they got in the car and drove to CCM, and everyplace else they could think of where Paul might've gone, but nobody had seen him. It was just like he'd walked out of the house and vanished into thin air!"

She paused to gain control of her voice. Occasional sniffs told me she was crying, and her voice was thick with tears. She began again in a soft voice. "You never think it's going to happen to you, Mrs. Caliban. You never do. You read about other mothers losing their children. You see it on television all the time. You feel so sorry for them. But you never think it's going to happen to you."

"Mrs. Whitney, I really appreciate your help," I said. "Can you tell me one more thing? Do you have any theories about Paul's disappearance? Any ideas you gave the police? Did anything change right before he disappeared? Did he act differently at all? Anything?"

She hesitated. "I don't have any theories. Not really. I think somebody must have kidnapped him, but I don't know why." Her voice wavered, and I didn't interrupt while she struggled to control it. "I feel that he's alive. I know mothers always say that, but it's true. I feel that he's alive, and as a Christian, I believe that he is in God's hands." Then she gave a little gasp. "You know, now that you ask me about that bracelet, I remember something. He'd stopped wearing it before he disappeared."

"How long before he disappeared?"

"I don't know. I just remember I looked down one day and it was gone. I didn't ask about it. I just remember thinking, 'I hope the next thing the kids are into isn't any worse.' You know what I mean? It's funny that I hadn't thought of that—about him not wearing that bracelet. You don't think it's important, do you?"

"I don't know, Mrs. Whitney," I confessed. "Right now, I just don't know."

So now I had one dead teenager and two missing ones. I propped my Adidas up on my office desk, leaned back in my chair, and thought. The creak of the chair aroused Sophie, who was curled up in the trash box, but she just stretched her toes, resettled herself, and went to sleep again.

The boys had both known something about computers, and there was a missing computer in the case. But if Peter's father had deliberately kept the computer out of the hands of the police, that implied that he was guilty of something. But what? Of strangling his own son?

I thought about the *Playboy* under the mattress. Maybe it had been so pristine because Peter had access to other kinds of pornography. I remembered my cousin Delbert swapping soft-core porn with other teenaged hackers—busty babes wearing skintight body stockings disguised as space suits, action-posed with legs apart and hair flying. According to Delbert, such pictures constituted the currency of hackdom; if someone did you a favor, you thanked them by sending them your favorite space babe. Maybe Papa Baer wasn't as tolerant of such practices as Cousin Cat. Maybe he'd removed the computer to prevent the kind of exposure that might get him funny looks the next time the diocese met. Assuming that dioceses met.

Mrs. Deemer hadn't known whether Jen had any particular interest in computers, and hadn't thought she'd belonged to a computer club. But Jen had had access to a computer at school. And maybe Jen hadn't wanted to tell her mother that she'd joined a club. She might have been embarrassed to admit that she'd taken an interest in something; some kids don't want their parents to know things like that. Suppose that Peter, Jen, and Paul had met at some citywide computer contest. Maybe the bracelets were a way for teen computer geeks to identify each other, like Masonic rings. Of course, Peter was an odd candidate for geekdom, but he'd been serious enough about computers to join the computer club.

Or maybe the kids hadn't met in person, or not at first, anyway. Thinking about Delbert reminded me that he had friends he'd never met—like the boys he swapped space babes with. I was vague about exactly how he'd first become acquainted with them, but it had to do with writing letters on the computer. Maybe there was a lonely hearts club for teen computer geeks.

Then there was the New Life Ministries connection. Both Peter and Paul had attended school assemblies put on by New Life. Was that even constitutional? Did the schools give equal time to anti-drug programs from the Muslims, Jews, Buddhists, Hindus, theosophists, and atheists? Or even the Catholics and Episcopalians, if it came to that. But if the bracelets were somehow tied to New Life, I figured the other kids would have known. Unless—? Unless you had to attend services to get one. But the Seven Hills girl, Tammy, who had attended didn't seem to recognize the bracelet from my description, and hadn't been wearing one herself.

There was a rustling sound at my elbow and Sidney emerged from the open bottom desk drawer, a dust bunny impaled on one ear.

I leaned down to scratch his forehead. "Sid," I said, "I think it's time to get me a new life."

Chapter Fourteen

I DON'T HAVE the kind of wardrobe that runs to flower-print dresses. And my last pair of pantyhose had been donated to last summer's garden to tie up the tomato plants and keep the borers out of the squash and cuke vines. But I did have a polyester pantsuit in pastel pink that my daughter-in-law had given me two Christmases ago. No doubt she thought that pink polyester was missing from my wardrobe by oversight. Or maybe she thought it matched my gin-flushed complexion.

I found some old make-up in the back of a drawer, but the foundation had dried to dust and the lipstick was a garish color I'd used to paint blood on somebody's fangs one Halloween. I examined my short white hair in the mirror. Needless to say, I didn't own a curling iron. I found a flowered chiffon scarf that had last seen duty when I painted the kitchen ceiling. I folded it to hide the paint splotches, and tied it around my neck. I did have some old clip earrings—the big, heavy kind with pink daisies on them. I clipped them on.

"Yow!" I said to Sadie, who was sitting in front of me, contemplating my ensemble.

I didn't look like anybody's grandmother, which I was, of course. Even in the pink polyester pantsuit, I looked like a shorter, heavier Andy Warhol in drag.

Sadie approached me warily and sniffed at my pant cuffs.

"Good point, Sades," I said. Under the bathroom sink, way in the back, was a bottle of cologne that my grandson Ben had picked out for me. It's the little things that create the air of authenticity, I thought, and doused myself with it. Maybe it was just as well I had to cover my handiwork with a coat.

On my way to the car, I spotted Leon clomping down an unshoveled sidewalk—mine, in fact—with his book bag slung over one shoulder. He stopped and stared at me. He may be retarded but he doesn't miss much. I saw him cock his head in bewilderment and tried to imagine what he'd seen that had puzzled him. The pink polyester peeping out from below my quilted winter coat? The daisies winking provocatively out from underneath my ear muffs? He approached me, his nostrils quivering like the nose of a cat who has caught an interesting scent.

"You got a n-new outfit, M-m-miz Cat?" he said.

I shook my head. "I'm undercover today, Leon."

"Oh," he said. He nodded in comprehension. "I knew y-you was d-d-different. S-say, M-miz Cat. I g-got vacation coming up, you b-be needing an o-operative?"

Leon had helped me on a few cases before, and he had some extremely useful talents.

"I don't think so, Leon, but I'll keep you in mind if something comes up," I said. I opened the car door.

"You c-could hire me to v-vestigate Kevin's new b-b-boyfriend," he offered.

I paused, and rested my elbow on the doorframe. "What do you know about Kevin's new boyfriend?"

"He a realator," Leon reported. "G-g-got a b-big fancy c-car he park up the s-s-street, got a s-sign on it, s-say, S-s-seven Hills Realaty. Don't want n-nobody seeing h-him when he visit Kevin. He always be looking around, l-like he afraid he g-going to run into s-somebody he know. But he don't know me."

I grinned at him. Leon was observant, and within his own small territory, he knew as much about what was going on as Kevin did.

"Thanks, Leon," I said. "That's good to know. Maybe you'd better keep an eye on him. He sounds like a shady character to me."

"O-okay," he said. "I g-got to go to s-school now. Good luck w-with your w-work. You d-don't look like yourself, M-miz Cat. N-not the tiniest b-bit."

"Thanks," I said. "If I solve this case, you can send me a congratulations card—the one with the donkeys on it."

The "world headquarters" for New Life Ministries, unlike the world headquarters for Fogg and Caliban, was in Mt. Auburn, just the other side of the University of Cincinnati campus and, I noted, an easy walk from the College-Conservatory of Music where Paul Whitney was supposed to have practiced the organ on Saturday afternoons. It was across the street from Christ Hospital on Auburn Avenue, at the top of Mt. Auburn. The building was part old, part new, and very big, in keeping with the world headquarters theme. Cantilevered out from the hillside in the back was a circular structure, maybe an auditorium or studio, which appeared to be built out of dark glass. Behind that, higher than the cross on the front of the building, was something that looked like a television tower. A short distance from the parking lot, off to one side, was a pre-fab two-story house tricked out to look like a fairy-tale cottage. I couldn't even begin to guess what that was.

I parked my rabbit between a "Happiness Is Being Born Again!" bumper sticker and one that read, "God Already Made My Day!" I congratulated myself on having had the foresight not to decorate my bumper with the sticker Franny had given me, which proclaimed, "God Is Coming and Is She Pissed!"

I pushed open a heavy wooden door in the older part of the building and followed a female voice into a large office to the right of an elegant staircase. The office was nicely but not newly furnished. The woman who was talking had the phone wedged between her ear and shoulder, one hand in what looked like a date book, and the other suspended over a large calculator. She smiled at me vaguely and raised the finger generally used to indicate "one minute."

I took off my coat and ear muffs to give her an unimpeded view of my granny outfit, and sat down on a comfortable couch to wait. I almost put my purse on the floor, then decided that it was not a grandmotherly thing to do. I held it on my knees. Details.

"Uh-huh," she said. "Uh-huh. Uh-huh. No, that's right. The third. Uh-huh. No, I'm looking at it right now." She craned her neck slightly to look at the book. "Uh-huh. No, hold on, Emery. Let me put on my glasses." The glasses were resting on an ample bosom, and were attached to her neck by a chain. She held them out in front of her and looked through them. "No, it's not an eight, it's a three. Uh-huh. A three. Uh-huh, plain as day. No, that's okay. It's just, with Margie out sick—. Uh-huh. Well, I do, too. I appreciate that. Oops—gotta go! My other line's ringing."

With an apologetic smile at me, she punched a button on the phone. "New Life—. Yes, Edna, I told you it was. Uh-huh, that's just what I told you. Did you find it? Well, look again. Sometimes things fall back behind the whozit. Uh-huh, that's right. Bye!"

She hung up with one hand, the other reaching up to fluff her curly light brown hair. I caught a flash of peach nail polish that matched the peach lipstick and the peach blouse she wore.

"My goodness, the Lord is trying me today!"

I tried to give her a sympathetic smile.

"Days like this, I think I should've been named 'Job' instead of 'Joy.'"

I laughed. I suspected this was a well-worn joke.

"What's your name, honey?" She had the kind of Southern accent you hear a lot in Cincinnati. It usually signaled a native Kentuckian.

"Catherine," I said. "Catherine Caliban."

She stared at me for a moment, and then she began scrabbling through a pile of paper scraps on her desk. "Was I supposed to call you yesterday? Do I have a note here about it?"

I had forgotten. Since yesterday, I'd decided to change my tactics. Forgetfulness was a liability for a detective, and no doubt a reason why more menopausal women don't take up private investigation. What most of them don't realize is that skill at lying can cover a lot of mistakes. But Margie was out sick and the note, when Joy found it, said nothing about Peter Baer.

"I am so sorry that I didn't get back to you. I would have, though! Well, Catherine, what can I do for you?"

"Well," I began, trying to seem nervous. To tell you the truth, I didn't have to try too hard. "It's about my grandson. He lives with me, you see. And he's getting to be quite a handful."

"How old is he?" she asked, as if she really wanted to know.

"Sixteen," I said. I leaned in and lowered my voice. "I didn't approve of the divorce, and I tried to tell my daughter that she and Frank should think of the boy. But you can't tell young people anything these days. They get married and unmarried so fast! It doesn't mean anything to them."

She clucked and shook her head. "Don't I know it!" she said. "Now me and my husband, we're going on twenty-two years."

"See there?" I said. "That's just what I mean. You stuck it out. You had some hard times, I'll bet, but you stuck it out."

"Well, we get on pretty good now, but we had us some fights in the early days. I mean, real name-calling, throwing-things-at-each-other kinds of fights."

I nodded. "Everybody has those. But you get past them."

She nodded. "We were so young! Still, I don't believe—." The phone rang. She gave it a tired look, then glanced up at me with a mischievous smile. "I think I'll just let the machine answer that. No, like I was saying, I don't believe we would have made it without our faith, you know. So many young people have never invited Christ into their lives, don't you think that's true? We get so many young couples in here now in need of spiritual guidance. Later, they tell me, 'Joy, it was God led us to Reverend Armbruster, and his spiritual guidance has made all the difference.'" She beamed at me. "I feel so blessed to be part of all that healing, I can tell you."

"Well, that's what I wanted to talk to someone about," I said. "You see, someone told me that you have wonderful programs for teenagers here. And I thought maybe if I could get Ben involved—."

"We do," she said. "Reverend Ted just does wonders with the kids. We have a very active group of nice, Christian young people."

"Reverend Ted? Is that Ted Armbruster, then?"

"No, no, honey. Reverend Armbruster is the head of New Life," she explained. "He built this ministry. But like a lot of churches, it got so big, he couldn't look after everything himself."

Kind of like God, I thought, but I didn't know if she'd appreciate the comparison.

She continued, "Reverend Ted Settles is the person in charge of our teen ministries program."

"Maybe he's the one I should talk to, then," I said. "You see, I don't know that Ben will take to the idea of coming here, to a church. In fact, I know he won't. He won't take to anything that isn't his idea. So everything I suggest just falls on deaf ears."

"Honey, I know just what you mean," she said. "What church do y'all attend now?"

I was prepared for this one. I'd already figured out that it would be a bad move to claim an affiliation with Shintoism or some other religion that didn't have regular services. When the kids had been young, we'd sometimes attended a Presbyterian church, and I'd come away with an impression of Presbyterians as pretty laid back. I'd looked through the *Yellow Pages* for a church to belong to—one that was far enough away but not too far. I didn't want her meeting their secretary for lunch.

"Sixth Presbyterian," I said. "It's in Madeira."

"All the way out there?" she said. "Well, I hate to disappoint you, but Reverend Ted's not here right now. He's—."

The door swung open and a dolly laden with boxes pushed through, followed by a bearded young man in blue jeans, a flannel work shirt, and a denim jacket.

"Where you want these, Joy?" he asked. Then he saw me, and smiled. "Sorry for the interruption."

"Oh, my," Joy said, and hopped up. She came out from behind the desk and stood contemplating the boxes, one hand to her cheek. "That's a lot, isn't it? I thought it would be less this time."

He had a pleasant laugh. "You know him, Joy. Always a few hundred extra. Can't hurt anything, he'd say." Then he leaned toward her in a show of confidentiality. "But you ask me, there's some kind of loaves-and-fishes thing going on between the time they pack the boxes in the back of the truck and the time they arrive here."

She sighed. "Well, I guess you'd better put them in the conference room. There's nobody in there today. Though how I'm going to get rid of 'em all before the breakfast meeting tomorrow, I don't know."

She opened another door for him.

"Will Margie be back tomorrow, you think?" he asked.

"I don't think so, not with the weekend coming up, and sick as she is," Joy said. "I told her to go home and rest and not to even think about coming back before Monday."

I felt a slight tug under my hands. By the time I reacted, my purse was sliding off my lap. I grabbed for it, but a pair of small brown hands took a firmer grip on it and yanked it from my grasp. I gave a little squeak of surprise as it disappeared around the corner of Joy's desk.

Joy emerged from the conference room as I was getting to my feet. She noticed me leaning over to look around the side of her desk. I caught a glimpse of pink cloth.

"What's the matter?" Joy asked. Then, as she drew nearer, she said, "Oh."

"Do you have a purse snatcher on your staff?" I asked.

She went around the other side of her desk. "It's just Evie," she said. "She has a thing about purses."

As I watched, fascinated, she bent down and began to scold someone I still couldn't see.

"Evie, now you know that's not nice! Give it back." She reached down, and began to tug. "Evie, you're being very naughty. That's not your purse, you know it's not."

Some odd sounds I couldn't place began issuing from under the desk.

"You know you can't take things without asking. It's not polite."

I glanced at the young man. He was leaning on the dolly, looking on, amused. The battle for the purse was intensifying, but he made no move to interfere.

Joy reached down with her other hand, then disappeared under the desk. The sounds were becoming more familiar, but what were they?

"Evie, if you don't give me that purse, I'll tell Papa on you," Joy warned. "You know how disappointed he'll be."

A small explosion occurred behind the desk. I saw my purse fly up, its contents shooting through the air in all directions. Someone grunted. A brown and pink streak appeared from behind the desk, leapt onto the dolly, and climbed to the young man's shoulder. He reached out to catch it and threw an arm around its waist.

It was a chimpanzee, just like Bonzo. Except that this chimp was wearing a frilly pink dress, and, if I wasn't mistaken, ruffled underpants. And she was laughing, baring her teeth with glee at the spectacle of a bedraggled Joy surfacing from under the desk.

The young man was laughing, too. I felt my own face crack into a grin.

"Don't encourage her, David!" Joy scolded him. "You know you'll only make her worse. You could have helped, you know."

"Sorry," he said. He tried to swallow his laughter and look contrite. But behind rimless glasses, his green eyes were liquid.

Joy looked at me. "I am so sorry, Mrs. Caliban," she said. "Evie gets loose sometimes, and she can be a little terror when the mood hits. But don't worry. We'll find everything."

The young man took a few steps and bent to pick up my purse. Her joke over, Evie made no attempt to snatch it from him when he held it out to me.

"Evie's sorry she was so inhospitable," he said, "aren't you, Sis? And to show you how sorry she is, she'll help pick up your things."

Joy was already crawling around on her hands and knees. He put the chimp down, but didn't, I noticed, let go of her hand. She did her little bow-legged chimp waddle over to the desk, leading him, and bent down to pick up my Swiss Army knife.

Damn! I thought. My disguise was too superficial. I should have removed the knife and crammed my purse with make-up and lace handkerchiefs.

"Give it back to the nice lady," David instructed.

She held it out to me. Our eyes met. And I could swear she was looking right through my disguise. If David and Joy wanted to think of me as a nice lady, that was their business, her eyes said, but she knew a hellraiser when she saw one. She gave me a knowing grin. I was fascinated, but more than a little unsettled.

"Is she yours?" I asked David.

He shook his head, and squatted down to retie the bow at the back of her dress. "Evie's an Armbruster," he said. "I'm just her caretaker. I guess you've never caught one of the reverend's sermons on evolution." He gave her a swat on a rump that sounded like it was padded with disposable diapers. Here's where I had a leg up on Spade and Marlowe, who, as far as I could tell, hadn't been near a diaper since they'd worn diapers themselves, much less had the opportunity to sample the distinctive sounds of cloth diapers and disposables.

"No," I admitted.

"Evie's the star of the show," he said. "You wouldn't know to look at her that she had a calling, but she does."

I wasn't quite sure if he was putting me on or not. "How old is she?" I asked. It was the kind of thing you asked about small critters wearing diapers.

"Just two," he said. "Lucky for us, she's not at full strength yet."

Joy was still on her hands and knees, reaching under the desk for something. She brought out a set of pick-locks and frowned at them. I might as well have brought the goddamned gun.

"Joy," I announced to distract her, "you've got something on the bottoms of your shoes."

She rose up on her knees and screwed her head around to look at her heels.

"Oh, those are my 'stomp the devil' stickers," she said. "I guess I must be stompin' him pretty hard, 'cause they're nearly worn through so you can't read 'em anymore."

She pulled herself up awkwardly and held out two handfuls of junk from my purse, with the pick-locks crowning the pile. I opened my purse wide and she dumped it all in.

I felt David's eyes on me. I fished out the pick-locks and held them up. "I found these in my grandson's room," I said, and looked at him. "Are they what I think they are? I've been meaning to ask somebody, but I'm not sure I want to know."

"If you think they're pick-locks, that's just what they are," he said.

"Mrs. Caliban wants to talk to Reverend Ted about her grandson," Joy explained.

"Sounds like a good idea," he said. Then he looked down at Evie, who had picked up a stapler off the desk and was trying to staple her dress to the coffee table. "Come on, kiddo. Let's find out how you got out this time."

He hoisted her to his hip and left with his dolly.

"He seems like a nice young man," I observed.

"David is wonderful," she said. She raised her hands for emphasis. "I don't know what we ever did without him."

"Is he new here?"

"Well, not too new," she said. "I think he started in the fall. It's hard to remember sometimes, because now it seems like he's always been here. He fits in so well, you know."

I nodded. "Is he a minister?"

"Oh, no," she said. "His main job is to take care of Evie—at least, it was at first. But now he helps Reverend Ted with the youth ministries, too. And he's handy, so he fixes things. I guess he does just about everything, when you think about it." She gazed at the door, a speculative look on her face. "There's something about him, though. Margie and I think—well, we think maybe he has a tragic past." Her voice put the last two words in quotation marks.

"Really?" I said. I wanted to encourage her to gossip about New Life.

"Well, he's thirty, and he's not married," Joy said. "I think there was a woman somewhere. You know what they say, 'cherchez la fèmme.' I don't know if she left him, or if she died. Or maybe she just broke his heart. I think Reverend Armbruster knows, though. Somebody will snatch him up one of these days. I think he's handsome, don't you? He's so good with Evie, you can just tell he'd make a good father."

The phone rang, and she caught her breath.

"Here I am, chit-chatting about people you don't even know, when you've come about your grandson," she said. "And me with so much work to do! That Evie can sure stir things up when she wants to. I'd better get that," she said in apology, and rushed for the phone.

I settled down on the couch again, taking care to maintain a good grip on my purse.

"New Life—," she said into the phone. "I'm fine, just fine. How are you? That's good. No, I haven't seen him. Yes, now we got a postcard—. Uh-huh. Uh-huh. That's right. No, I know who you mean. He's discipling that new boy, Seth. Uh-huh. Uh-huh. No, that's all right. I'll tell him. I know you do! I know he is! Well, bye, now."

To me, she said, "I'm so sorry, Mrs. Caliban! This place must seem like a three-ring circus to you. Anyway, as I was saying, the person you really need to talk to is Reverend Ted, and he won't be in till—what's today? Thursday? He'll be in on Saturday."

"Oh," I said, "does he meet with the kids on Saturdays?"

"That's right," she said. "Saturday mornings with the younger kids, and Sunday afternoons with the older ones."

"Oh," I said, trying not to sound disappointed.

"You think this place is busy now, you should come around on Saturdays and Sundays," she said. "There's so many activities I can't keep 'em all straight."

That cheered me up.

"You know," I said, as if I were making up my mind about something, "you really seem to have your hands full, with Margie out sick and all. Maybe I could stay a while, and help you out. I mean, if there are things I could do."

"Why, Mrs. Caliban!" she said.

"Catherine," I said.

"Why, Catherine!" she said, and laughed. "Do you know, I believe my prayers have been answered."

Chapter Fifteen

TAKE IT FROM me, Cat Caliban: if someone who looks and sounds like me, with or without pick-locks, ever shows up in answer to your prayers, you'd better have a serious heart-to-heart with your maker.

Me, I was mentally paging the patron saint of private dicks, who, as far as I could tell, was sleeping on the job.

Three hours later, there I was, my bum planted in a chair that was too low, working at a conference table that was too high. The chair got harder by the minute. My back ached, my shoulders ached, my elbows ached, and the ears under my clip earrings had passed through the stage of numbness to a painful throb. Shut up in an enclosed space, I was feeling nauseous from the combined scents of my cologne and the printer's ink. At lunchtime, I'd been treated to a Big Mac and fries, which had done nothing for the general state of my health, and nothing to further my mission, since Joy had returned to her desk to eat and work.

And what had I learned about New Life Ministries? Only that they were sponsoring a major area-wide youth rally in May, at which thousands of teens would be asked to dedicate, or re-dedicate, their lives to Christ. The keynoter would be, of course, the Reverend Vernon Armbruster, the Right Arm of God. I didn't even know whether they had anything at all to do with Peter's death, black-and-white bracelets, or the disappearance of two teenagers. I hadn't spotted a single black-and-white bracelet. But then, I hadn't seen anybody. I was stuck in the conference room. I'd managed to position myself to catch sight of people passing the door, but that only gave me glimpses of the activity at New Life. What was I doing here?

My job, apart from folding the flyers and stuffing them into envelopes, was to write, at the top of every sheet, "Hope to see you there! Love, Jesus." I felt pretty weird about the whole thing, to tell you the truth, even setting aside the glaring inaccuracy of making Jesus speak in contemporary English. Impersonating Jesus didn't seem like the kind of job that should just be handed out to the first person to walk in off the street and volunteer. By the twenty-fifth "Hope to see you there!" I had writer's cramp, so my normal scrawl deteriorated. The lines appeared to have been written by Evie after she'd had a go at the communion wine. I just hoped none of the addressees owned a book on handwriting analysis. I expected to be blasted by a thunderbolt at any moment.

I was sucking on a paper cut when a man appeared in the doorway. He was a barrel-chested man of medium height with a full head of bushy gray hair receding at the temples. He wore a conservative, well-cut navy suit, and his tie tack was a gold cross with a diamond at its center. He bestowed a radiant smile on me.

"A new volunteer! Marvelous! Marvelous!" he said, and advanced into the room. "I don't believe we've met. I'm Vernon Armbruster." He held out a hand.

I removed the finger from my mouth and shook hands. "Catherine Caliban. It's a real pleasure, Reverend." As I withdrew my hand, I said, "Sorry about the blood."

He looked down at his own hand, and then at mine. "You've cut yourself? Oh, I think we can fix that." He turned his head toward the outer office and called, "Joy! We have an emergency in here. We need a Band-Aid."

Joy hurried in with a box, and the Reverend Armbruster himself knelt, held my hand, and applied the Band-Aid to the bloody digit. I noticed that he had not, however, fetched the Band-Aids himself. Nor did he offer to apply any healing power he may have had by kissing it and making it well. But maybe the Rev wasn't the healing kind. I'd have to find out more about him.

He stood up and handed the crumpled wrapper to Joy. "You see, Catherine? Joy here has cast her bread of human kindness upon the waters, and it has been returned to her a thousandfold in you, a new volunteer in her time of need."

"I probably have folded a thousand," I said, "but I tried not to get any blood on them."

The reverend placed his hand on my shoulder and gave it a hearty squeeze. "I'm sure you're doing a fine job," he said. His smile was broad but his eyes had the look of a man whose mind had moved on to other things.

"Catherine has a grandson she wants to talk to Reverend Ted about," Joy said.

"Wonderful! I'm sure Ted can get him straightened out," he said. "That young man has a gift. And you be sure to take him one of those flyers, Catherine. In fact, take a handful, why don't you? Give them out to his friends."

"Thanks, Reverend," I said. "I'll do that."

He beamed at me again, and departed.

Joy lingered. "My! You surely are a fast worker! Look at all you've done."

"Yeah, but, Joy," I said, "my handwriting—."

Joy picked up a flyer. Her eyebrows flickered, but she wasn't about to look a gift horse in the hoof. "Now, it's perfectly legible. It's the spirit that counts, Catherine! Nobody really thinks that Jesus wrote this, anyway. It's just a little personal touch. You're doing fine!"

The Band-Aid did nothing to improve my handwriting.

At two-thirty, David stuck his head in. "Need a hand?" he asked. "I have fifteen minutes until I have to meet with Reverend Armbruster about our Web site."

"A hand is just what I need," I confessed. "How's your handwriting?"

"Tolerable," he said. "I learned from the nuns, but once I got out from under their thumbs, it went to hell in a hurry." He sat down and picked up a pen.

"Well, I don't want to put any pressure on you," I said, "but you have to write the way Jesus would have written if he wrote late twentieth-century English cursive."

He grinned at me. "No problema."

"So is that the secret of your dark past?" I asked. "You were once Catholic?"

"One of them," he said. "Although for the record, I have to point out that you didn't have to be Catholic to go to Catholic school."

"But it helped."

"Oh, yes," he admitted. "It helped."

"So what's Evie up to?"

"Last I looked, she was playing with her dolls."

"She has dolls?" I asked in surprise.

"Oh, yes," he said, "lots of them. And a baby carriage to wheel them around in, and a little plastic tub she gives them baths in. And when she gets mad at them, she makes them go to Time Out."

"Oh," I said. "Does Evie respond well to Time Out?"

"Not nearly as well as the dolls," he said, and grinned.

We worked for a few minutes in silence.

"Tell me something about your youth group," I said. "Do you plan activities? Because that's the only way I'll get my grandson involved—if he likes the kids and if the group does stuff that he likes to do."

"Sure," he said. "We know that. They have a lot of fun, actually. Skating parties, movie outings, concerts—."

"Really? Concerts?"

"Sure. Christian music is very popular with young people right now," he said. "What is your grandson into?"

I made a face. "The less said about that, the better," I said, "and I probably don't know the half of it. He is interested in computers."

He nodded. "We have several kids like that. He'd probably get along well with them. Do you think he enjoys camping? With summer coming, we have several camping trips planned."

"Well," I said, "I don't know how he feels about sleeping in a tent. He likes the water, though. Do you ever go boating as a group?"

"Sure," he said. "I wasn't here last summer, but I understand that the kids went canoeing, sailboating, and windsurfing."

I needed to find out more about marine rope, I reflected. I wasn't sure it was something used on canoes, but sailboats sounded promising. I didn't even know what windsurfing was. Peter probably wasn't murdered at a church outing because whoever was in charge would surely have noticed he was missing. But just to be sure, I needed to dig up an old calendar of events from the fall, something that would tell me whether any events had been scheduled around the time of his disappearance. Boating didn't seemed possible in November, but could the group have gone hiking at a park on the river?

I caught David regarding me with curiosity, and realized that I was reacting strangely to his comment about boating and windsurfing. "Does Evie get to go on these outings?" I asked, trying to keep my voice light.

He smiled. "Not usually. It's too bad, too. I'd love to see her windsurfing. But the water would probably freak her out."

"You're really fond of her, aren't you?" I said.

He grinned. "I love her like a sister."

I thought about Jason and Franny, and wondered if he and Evie bickered as much as my own children had. So far, I hadn't seen any signs of hostility between David and Evie, but maybe a minister's kids weren't allowed to clobber each other—or, at least, not in public.

I needed to know more about the computer connection between Peter and the missing kids. I said, "So, this Web site. Does that have something to do with computers and the Internet?"

"Something to do with it, yes."

"What is a Web site?"

"Well, everybody who has a computer and a phone line can tap into this worldwide system called the Internet. One of the places you can go on the Internet is the World Wide Web. A Web site is like—oh, a place you can visit from your computer. Individual people can have Web sites, or companies can, or organizations, like ours. Few people have access right now, of course. It's a developing communication system. But it's the wave of the future—or so I'm told. Our Web site explains what New Life is, what services we offer, how to contact us, how to join the church, stuff like that. Plus, we reproduce some of Reverend Armbruster's sermons, and different pages of advice on particular topics."

"Pages?" I frowned. "I thought you said this was on the computer."

"They're called 'pages,'" he explained. "Web sites have a structure, kind of like a book. You can go to different parts of the book depending on what topic you're interested in."

I had stopped folding. "So, when you say individuals can have Web sites, what are their books about? Do they give advice, too?"

"They can," he said. "An individual person's Web site really expresses that person's individuality. They could write about their favorite hobby, or give their favorite recipes, or give instructions for something they know how to do. They can include pictures of themselves, or their dogs and cats—anything they want."

"Wow." I mulled this over. Did Peter, Paul, and Jen have Web pages? "So then their friends and family go visit this Web site?"

"Anybody can visit it who has access to a server," he said. "Like I said, that doesn't include many people right now. There are only about five thousand hosts—a host is kind of like a publisher. But one day Internet access will be kind of like ordinary telephone service."

"Wow. So it's like publishing a book? Does it work like that? You know, it goes out of print or it gets released in a new edition or whatever?" I was wondering if any of the computer club kids had created one of these Web sites, and if so, if it would still be there.

"People update their Web sites all the time," he said. "Some of them get updated daily, but most are updated a lot less frequently. As for going out of print, that depends. Somebody has to host the site. Some hosts are free, and some cost money. But it's pretty much true that a site stays up forever if it's free or if the author keeps paying the host."

I tried not to show my rising excitement. "Suppose I wanted to find out if my grandson had one of these sites," I said. "Could I find out without asking him?"

"Maybe. It would depend on whether his real name appeared anywhere on the site."

"But he'd be the author. Wouldn't it have to?"

He shook his head. "Lots of people have pseudonyms on the Web or for e-mail purposes. It's kind of like a CB handle. You know what those are, right? Or like Mark Twain. I'm not sure how the copyright works, but if 'Samuel Clemens' didn't appear on the copyright page, there wouldn't be anything in the book to connect Clemens with Twain."

"So you must know a lot about computers, huh?"

"Not really," he said. "Compared to some of the kids, I'm a novice. They taught me everything I know."

A little while later, he excused himself for his lesson with Joy.

Some ten minutes later, another helper appeared in the doorway. She was trailing pink sash ties like downed power lines and carrying a purse, though whose purse I couldn't say. She grinned at me.

"Evie," I said. "How's your handwriting?"

Chapter Sixteen

AT FIVE I hobbled out to the parking lot, folded myself painfully into the driver's seat of my car, and headed for Mt. Adams to meet Tony Frank. I'd promised Joy I'd return the next day, if I could get out of bed. I didn't see how anybody could sit for eight hours a day doing anything, much less the same thing. When I raised my arms to the steering wheel, my shoulders and elbows joined the protest my back was making. When I turned my head to make sure I wasn't backing into a car with "Jesus on Board," my neck creaked. Cat Caliban, super spy.

I'd realized too late that I hadn't left myself time to go home and change clothes before meeting Tony Frank. Or, to put it more accurately, I realized what I was wearing and what a sixteen-year-old boy would make of it. What were my chances of wresting any secrets from him in my grandma get-up? But maybe I was wrong. Maybe I'd look more trustworthy than usual.

Mt. Adams is a trendy, artsy little neighborhood overlooking Eden Park, the Art Museum, and the Playhouse in the Park. Some buildings are still shabby and low-rent, but these are becoming less common than the rehabilitated upscale houses and condos running to security company decals rather than fashion geese. The streets are steep and narrow and not intended for crabby, arthritic old ladies to navigate.

The Frank house was a restored Italianate townhouse with a wrought-iron fence around what looked to be a well-tended garden. I opened the gate, negotiated the stone walk without falling and breaking a hip, and climbed three steps to a heavy front door of natural wood. When I pressed the doorbell, chimes rang inside the house.

The Franks were an affluent family. The Baers were an affluent family. What connection did these two families have, if any, to the Deemers, who were several tax brackets down from them?

The door was opened by a skinny, shaggy-headed teenager in an oversized sweatshirt. She was licking something chocolate off of a wooden spoon. She continued to lick and looked at me.

"I'm looking for Tony Frank," I said.

"Not here," she said.

"He said he'd meet me here at this time," I said.

She shrugged.

"He said he had to stay home and look after his sister," I said. I did not think I'd said it accusingly, but I wasn't in the best of moods, and teenagers are always on the lookout for affronts to their maturity.

She rolled her eyes. "Do I *look* like I need looking after? I don't *think* so."

"So do you know where he is?"

Shrug.

"If you were me, and you wanted to go looking for him, where would you look first?"

"Pool."

She stopped licking long enough to examine the ends of her hair for chocolate. Her eyes crossed as she studied them.

"Pool?" Just the word sent a shiver through me. The sun was out but it was low in the sky now, and the temperature wasn't warm enough to encourage me to take a refreshing dip. But since she didn't correct me, I added, "What pool?"

"School," she said.

"Which one?"

"Walnut Hills," she said.

"On—?"

"Victory Parkway."

"I wanted to talk to him about a friend of his, Peter Baer," I said.

She looked at me. "And—?"

"Did you know Peter Baer?"

"Never heard of him," she said. Then, as an afterthought, "Cute?"

I shook my head. "Dead," I said.

I figured that was the most I'd get out of her, so I retreated, eased myself into the car again, and studied a city map. I wasn't all that surprised that the reluctant Mr. Frank hadn't kept our appointment. He hadn't been eager to talk to me, and that's what I was counting on.

Walnut Hills High School was an impressive building, massive for a high school, or so it seemed to me. It was Romanesque, with lots of arches and even a domed roof off to one side of the main building, which was fronted by a circular drive and walkway. Inside, I looked for someone to ask directions of, preferably someone who didn't have the authority to give me the bum's rush.

I found a kid with damp red hair regarding his open locker with what appeared to be consternation. He was dressed only in a t-shirt and sweatpants; a medium-weight jacket lay in a heap on the floor next to a gym bag from which the contents were attempting to escape. I saw a towel, a sleeve, a sock, and a jock strap reaching for the scuffed linoleum.

I stood next to him. We both regarded his locker with sadness. It was one of those bonding experiences we detectives cultivate when we are looking for assistance.

"I know it's here somewhere," the kid said. "It's *got* to be."

A wave of nostalgia washed over me. I hadn't seen such a concentration of chaos since my son moved out of the house. His account books may be tidy, his business correspondence impeccable, but like most teenaged boys, he'd been a slob at heart. And since I'd never been too keen on cleaning myself, I'd longed for self-cleaning offspring, or, failing that, kids with a knack for a certain superficial tidiness.

"What color is it?" I asked.

I thought at first he was ignoring me, but no, he was just thinking. "Kind of orange, with purple letters."

Ignoring protests from all of my aching body parts, I squatted and rummaged.

"It's *gotta* be here!" he said, flinging his arms wide in a gesture of frustration. "It's got all my notes and stuff for my lab report."

I saw no trace of orange and purple. "Maybe," I suggested, "you left it in the lab."

I saw his face working up to one of those expressions teens affect when preparing to tell grown-ups how clueless they are. And then, it passed.

"Hey, yeah!" he said. "I bet that's where it is."

Cat Caliban, girl detective. Now if I could persuade one of the cats to ride around in the car with me, I could be another Judy Bolton, specialist in cracking tough cases at high schools all over Greater Cincinnati.

In the meantime, I was clinging to the locker door, trying to drag myself to a standing position. About the time I'd managed it, I felt a tentative hand on my elbow.

"Hey, thanks!" he said.

He snuffled, and withdrew his hand to raise the tail of his t-shirt and wipe his nose. This procedure seemed to clear his nasal passages enough to catch a snootful of my cologne, and he backed off a step.

"Are you somebody's grandmother?" he asked.

"I'm looking for the swimming pool," I said. "Can you tell me how to get there?"

He told me, then added, "But there's nobody there. They got a meet today. I know 'cause my sister swims for St. Ursula."

Was it possible that Tony had deliberately chosen a day when he knew he'd be anywhere except the places I was likely to look for him? Or had he just forgotten? Had I given him my phone number? I couldn't remember. What I could remember was that teenagers live in the present. Advance planning must be a cognitive skill that emerges at a later developmental stage. So it was plausible that he'd put me off until the unimaginable future, and then forgotten about me.

"I'm looking for a kid named Tony Frank," I said.

My informant was busy rearranging the contents of his gym bag. "I think I know who you mean. He's a freshman, so he might not've gone with the team, but probably he did."

I was ruminating on the resiliency of the young when I pushed open the door into the pool area. If my own olfactory nerves hadn't been so deadened by my cologne, I probably could have smelled my way there, because now the sour odor of chlorine rolled over me in a warm, steamy cloud.

I could see at a glance that no one was swimming in the pool. Pools, I should say. There were two, side by side. They looked to be the old-fashioned kind, with tiled walls, and I found myself wondering why there were two of them, exactly the same. The water was so still in both that it seemed unlikely that anyone had swum there in the past hour or so.

It was the double pool conundrum that led me closer. Was one pool shallower than the other? I looked down.

The swimmer lay face down on the bottom of the pool.

My heart lurched. I was dead sure I'd found Tony Frank.

I pulled off my shoes and jumped in. The water foamed and I couldn't see him, then spotted again the dark shape against the bluish white of tile and water. His arms extended in front of him, rippling with the disturbance I'd caused. I dove. I blinked my eyes against the burn of the chlorine. He was a small kid, even smaller close up without the magnifying effect of the water. He was wearing swim trunks, but no swimmers' goggles. I reached around his waist, bent my knees, and pushed hard against the bottom of the pool. I broke the surface coughing and sputtering, my lungs half-flooded. I didn't have enough wind left to yell for help.

But I heard a sound over the splashing and wheezing, and then somebody else was yelling. At the side of the pool, my locker buddy crouched. "Hey, over here!" he called, extending an arm. Then he shouted, "Hey! Somebody! In here! Help! Hey!"

He had a surprising grip for a skinny kid with a runny nose.

"Get him out first," I gasped.

I didn't have any strength left to help him lift the swimmer's dead weight out of the water, but I felt the body rise and let go. With the last of my strength, I raised and dragged my own considerable weight over the side and onto wet concrete.

"You know CPR?" I asked.

He shook his head.

"Go find someone who does," I said. "And tell somebody else to call for an ambulance."

The swimmer lay on his back, eyes closed, skin like wax. I rolled him over on his stomach with some vague notion of letting the water drain out of him, and maybe to prevent him from getting any wetter. By now, I was crying.

"God damn it!" I kept saying under my breath. Why hadn't I learned CPR? Been more cautious in approaching Tony? More sensitive? Was I responsible for this death? Had I screwed up? Too fucking excited about my new fucking career, and oblivious to the mistakes I was making?

I sat and cried and held the swimmer's cold hand. On his skinny wrist was a black-and-white woven bracelet.

Chapter Seventeen

"So tell me what you know about this Tony Frank," Rap Arpad said.

I was finally warm. A hot bubble bath and a gin and tonic had worked their restorative magic, but my joints still ached and I didn't have the strength to push my recliner back.

Mel handed me a piece of pizza. Mel had yet to encounter a health condition that couldn't be improved by an emergency pizza.

"Whyn't you let Cat eat while you tell us about this computer," Moses said, a little irritably. He was irritated because of his genuine concern about me, and also because he felt responsible for my screw-ups.

"Did you find it?" I asked.

"What computer?" Al asked.

"Peter Baer's," Moses said. "It wasn't in his room when Rap searched the place."

"Yeah, we found it," Rap said. "Dear old Dad had it at the office, just like the sister said. But it didn't tell us anything because it had been— what do you call it?—re-programmed."

Al, the only one of us who could tell a CPU from a pizza box, said, "Did a computer programmer look at it for you? Because sometimes you can recover—."

"Yeah, one of the lab techs looked at it," Rap said, sighing. "Nothing. Maybe 're-programmed' is the wrong word. It has something to do with the operating system."

Al nodded. "Probably re-imaged. That's where you start from scratch and reinstall the operating system. But it would be an odd thing to do if you planned to continue using the computer, unless you wanted a different operating system."

"Explain," Mel said.

"Well, hard-core hackers hate IBM systems, for example," Al said. "But lots of business environments use IBM. If Peter was more than just a kid fooling around with computers, if he was a hacker, he might have been using an OS like ITS or UNIX. So I could see where somebody might want to convert to an operating system compatible with the other machines in the office."

The rest of us exchanged blank looks. At Moses's feet, Winnie the beagle heaved an audible sigh and resettled herself on his shoes without opening her eyes. Sadie, who was sleeping on his lap, opened hers and shifted her head to look down at Winnie over his knees.

"Yeah, but that don't explain the timing," Moses said. "You got a kid missing, and you call in the cops, you might tidy the room just so the cops won't think your kid is a slob—yeah, I've seen that happen. But you don't start removing important pieces of evidence, not if you want your kid found. Parents got to have known the kid wrote letters on the computer."

Arpad shrugged. Sophie had settled in his lap and he was petting her. "It's a little hard to tell what these parents knew and what they didn't know. They aren't the attentive type. And as far as I can tell, the father doesn't know much about computers." He lifted a piece of pizza to his mouth, then hesitated, looked down, and grimaced. He set the pizza down, took hold of his necktie, already loose around his unbuttoned collar, and flipped it over his shoulder. "But I'll admit, it looks suspicious."

Sidney trotted in, chirping, from whatever kitty business he'd been attending to outside. He took in the scene and focused on the pizza box sitting on the coffee table. He crouched and leapt, then paused a moment, ears back, waiting for someone to scold him. When nobody did, he approached the pizza box with caution and sniffed. Then he pawed at it, trying to get it open. His frustration might have mounted if he hadn't been distracted by a stray pepperoni. He sniffed it, picked it up in his mouth and dropped it. He poked it. Then he took a swipe at it and watched it glide across the table like a hockey puck and disappear over the side. He gave a satisfied little grunt.

"So, what've we got?" Moses said.

"We've got two dead kids and two missing kids," I said. "Three boys, one girl. They all wore black-and-white bracelets. At least three of them had some computer knowledge." I turned to Arpad. "Was Tony Frank interested in computers?"

He fished a notebook out of his pocket, licked his fingers, and found a pen. "I haven't asked yet. Family's not too coherent right now."

"You got a preliminary cause of death?" Moses asked. "Suicide note?"

D.B. Borton

"Nope, not yet," Rap said. "But there was an empty prescription bottle in his backpack—valium. His mother's prescription. She said it was old, doesn't remember how many tablets were left in the bottle. Might mean something, might not. No way to tell how long it's been in his gym bag. You want to know the truth, Foggy, my money is on accidental death. Kid was having a bad day, took one too many valiums to mellow out, passed out and drowned. Kids these day are way too casual about using prescription drugs—any drug, anybody's prescription, long as it calms 'em down, makes the stress go away. Or it could have been an undiagnosed heart problem. You see a lot more of those than you do suicides involving swimming pool drownings. Or murder, either."

I sighed. Maybe Tony had taken the valiums in case he had to talk to me. But had he expected me to follow him to the pool?

"I like that theory better than the alternatives," I said. "And I guess the timing could explain the stress. He didn't want to talk to me, which made me think he knew something about Peter's death. But why didn't he go to the swim meet with the rest of the team? Just because he was a freshman? And he was wearing that bracelet."

"What is it with this bracelet?" Rap asked, sounding frustrated. "You keep talking about this bracelet. What's it for?"

"I haven't been able to find that out yet," Cat said, "which is strange in itself. Some of these woven bracelets mean something, some don't, but given what we've got now, I think you should go back through the missing persons files looking for teenagers who wore black-and-white ones. You said that when Peter's body was found, there were two kids on the books with those bracelets. You'd better look to see if there've been any more since."

"Yeah, all right," he said. As he made a note to himself, Sophie batted at his pen. She snagged it with her claws and began chewing on it.

"You think it's connected to this New Life Ministries, Cat?" Al said.

"I don't know," I said. "I'm looking for a way to connect all these kids from different neighborhoods. It could be through computer clubs and competitions, but why the bracelets? And aren't woven bracelets a little low-tech for teen computer junkies? And why doesn't anybody else know their significance? Other kids, I mean. Peter told Monica his was a good luck charm, but I'm not sure I believe that. Originally, they had some political significance. To some people, they still do. So what if there's some connection to the teen ministries program at New Life, which apparently recruits all over the city? They go around to the schools and do these anti-drug programs. One girl told me hers was like a memorial to a woman who'd died from domestic violence. The black-

110

and-white ones could serve a similar function, but if they memorialize some teenager who died from drugs, why wouldn't the kids come right out and say so? Wouldn't they want other kids to know that?"

Arpad was leaning forward. He'd extricated his pen from Sophie's grasp and pointed it at me now. "So you think—?"

"What if it was tied to some kind of anti-drug support group?" I said. "Maybe all the kids who wear the bracelets were users at one time."

"Peter Baer doesn't sound like the type of kid to use drugs, Cat." Mel frowned.

"Hard to say," Moses added. "Lot of pressure on a perfect kid to stay perfect."

"Who knows? Maybe he only took one hit off a joint, and feels so guilty, he's joined this group," I said.

"I had his parents, I'd be on drugs," Rap said. "No question."

"It would explain why the kids wouldn't want to advertise the significance of the bracelets," Al said.

"Or maybe the bracelets identify kids who are, like, drug counselors," Mel proposed. "You know, like trained peer counselors. Wouldn't even have to be drugs, it could be anything. You call the teen hotline, and they tell you that if you need someone to talk to at school, you should find a kid with a black-and-white bracelet."

"And if it's tied to this ministry, it could be a combination of counseling and ministry," Al said. "And maybe they figure teenagers in trouble wouldn't want to be seen talking to someone that everybody knew was a peer counselor, so they came up with the bracelets as a way of identifying the kids you could talk to."

"So, you spent the day at this place, Cat, this New Life Ministries," Moses said. "You see any bracelets?"

I sighed. "No. But I didn't see any teenagers, either. I'm going back tomorrow, though." I sat up with a realization. "Oh, shit!"

"What?" Al said.

"I ruined my grandma get-up," I said.

"We'll borrow something," Al said.

"Long's she don't have to go undercover at the computer club," Moses said.

"Yeah," Arpad agreed, grinning. "That would be hard for Cat to fake."

I ignored them. "But I need to be better prepared," I said. "I need to know more about this place. I wasn't really expecting to land a job there."

"Yeah, we need to know something about their reputation," Al said.

"These days, you can never find a good redheaded gossip when you need one," Mel complained.

It was true. Working at a bar frequented by everybody from city council members and attorneys to academics and artists put Kevin in the thick of things whenever any rumors were buzzing about. And he had ears like flypaper.

I sneezed. Three cats and one beagle jumped. Then Sophie and Sadie both flattened their ears to register disapproval, turned their backs on me, and lay down again. Sidney thought the sneeze deserved comment. He headed toward me across the coffee table, chattering. Winnie was still looking around, trying to figure out what was going on.

"But I really need to be there on the weekend," I said, "when all the teen activities happen. I told them my grandson was living with me, so I may be pressured to produce him. And I could really use a teenager to go undercover."

"But not Leon," Al said.

"No," I agreed with regret. "Not Leon." I don't like to call Leon "mentally handicapped" or "mentally challenged," because who isn't? Menopausal old ladies do not use these words lightly. Take now, for example. I was sure I'd forgotten something I'd learned that day, and I had a persistent sense that there was something I'd meant to do. But my mental files were waterlogged and hormonally deprived. Anyway, unlike me, Leon more than met his challenges with his personal charm and his entrepreneurial spirit. But there was no way he could convince anyone that he was a juvenile delinquent. He could never sustain the attitude.

The phone rang and Al went to answer it. She was gone a few minutes, then returned and announced, "It's Del, Cat."

I struggled to my feet, and picked up my empty glass. Aspirin just couldn't kill the pain like gin could, and it was time for another dose. I hobbled to the phone.

"Congratulations, Cousin Cat!"

Delbert Sweet belonged to my Texas cousin, and he had the accent to prove it. I assumed that Al had told him about Moses's P.I. license, either on the phone just now or by e-mail, since I knew they corresponded. Delbert was a teenaged computer geek. He had once stayed with me for a few weeks, and left me a roomful of computer equipment, which intimidated the hell out of me, and which, as a consequence, sat unplugged and gathering dust in my office. I think Sidney had shredded most of the instruction manuals, which was as good a use for them as any.

"So what I was thinking," Delbert was saying, "was that maybe I could come up there for a few days to design your Web site. I'm out of school next week for Spring Break."

"Our Web site! Del, I don't think we need a Web site," I said. "We're not really in business yet. We haven't even printed business cards."

"That's good, Cat," he said, with some urgency. "You don't want to print cards till you've got a Web address."

"But what would we—," I started to protest.

"Cat, I'm telling you, it's the wave of the future," Del insisted. "Ten years from now, nobody's going to look in the Yellow Pages when they want to hire a detective. They'll look for one on the Web. Only lusers will depend on the Yellow Pages."

"Oh," I said. Then a thought struck me. "Where is it your parents want you to go?"

"The Ozarks," he said, despondent. "Can you believe it? They've rented some crufty cabin in the Ozarks, and they think we should all go spend a week hiking and fishing and communing with nature." He made "communing with nature" sound like a blind date.

"Well," I said cautiously, "that sounds nice."

"Cat!" he said. "It's not even *wired*!"

"Oh," I said.

"I can't believe my brain-damaged father wants me to spend my vacation on this bogon in the middle of the fucking Ozarks! What a moby loss!"

"I see your point."

"So, what I was thinking, you could tell him you needed me to put in some tube time working on your Web site."

"Del," I said, "I think you may be the answer to my prayers."

Chapter Eighteen

I WOKE UP sneezing. Every sneeze jolted my joints, as if a squad of ponderous Lilliputians were using me for a trampoline. I felt a ripple through the mattress under me and concluded that my sneeze had dislodged a cat or two. When I raised my head, it throbbed. I swallowed several aspirins, which I'd had the foresight to place within easy reach the night before, lay down again, and contemplated my future, immediate and otherwise. It was one of those dark moments that come to every senior citizen who has contemplated embarking on a new career—even those filling out the lunch crew at your local Taco Bell. Trust me on this. But not every senior has found a dead teenager, especially one to whose death she may have contributed.

Had Tony Frank committed suicide to avoid telling what he knew about Peter Baer's death? Or been murdered for the same reason? If his death had been a suicide, that meant he'd probably overdosed on valium before going for his final swim. But even that could be faked, I supposed. It occurred to me, of course, that Tony might have been the one who'd killed Peter Baer, but I was having a hard time coming up with a scenario that made sense. Under what circumstances would a teenaged boy use a ligature to strangle another boy? The anger I could understand; I'd seen enough teenaged males who couldn't control their tempers to imagine Tony Frank in a murderous rage. And Peter Baer had been older and bigger; Tony had been slight, his swimmer's shoulders out of proportion to the rest of his physique, and based on the photographs I'd seen, Peter had definitely been large enough to earn his place on the football team. So a ligature might have helped Tony overcome Peter's size advantage in a fight. But where does a kid come up with a marine rope on the spur of the moment? It had to have been close at hand when the fight broke out.

Then there'd been the comments from a friend and a neighbor on the evening news. People don't speak ill of the dead, especially the young and especially on the news, but Tony had sounded like a nice, ordinary kid, not a killer. A nice, ordinary kid whose death I'd probably precipitated, even if it had been an accident.

Moses had given me a pep talk the night before. He'd made some inroads on my conscience, but I wasn't feeling very peppy in the cold light of morning. Moses had told me that Peter Baer's murderer had to be found, and that as an investigator, I had to believe in that necessity. Until we knew the truth about that death, we couldn't be sure that other deaths wouldn't follow.

"Yeah, but they *have* followed, Moses," I'd objected. "Or at least, one has. And it might not have followed if I hadn't gone looking for Tony Frank."

"You can't know that, Cat," he'd said. "Not even if it was suicide."

I'd seen the logic of his argument, but logic didn't comfort me. I was, however, a little comforted by his insistence that he wouldn't have handled Tony Frank any differently than I had. I couldn't afford to gain investigative experience at the cost of a life, and I'd been haunted by the possibility that my bumbling had cost Tony Frank's.

The phone rang, echoing inside my skull. It was Moses.

"You awake?" he said.

"Barely," I said.

"You up?" he said.

"Not exactly," I said.

"Take your aspirin yet?"

"Uh-huh." I sneezed.

"Then it's time to get moving, Cat," he said. "You got a couple of missing teenagers and a couple of dead ones depending on you to sort things out."

"God, let's hope they're missing," I said. "If I find another body, Moses, I'll—."

"Find out why," he finished. "That's what investigators do."

He hung up. I cranked myself up to a sitting position. Sophie and Sidney sat in the doorway regarding me, Sophie disapproving and Sidney curious.

"Hell," I said to them. "I'm not even sure I can bend over far enough to lace up my gumshoes."

Breakfast did little to restore my health or my humor, especially since it was accompanied by a front-page story in the *Enquirer* on the tragic death of Tony Frank, beloved nephew, neighbor, friend, and student. The body, according to the official story, had been found by one Andrew McCarty; I had Arpad to thank for that little bit of prestidigitation.

"Yeah, I was, like, just cutting through the gym from chem lab," McCarty was quoted as saying, "and there he was, just laying there on the bottom of the pool. I jumped in right away and, like, pulled him out." I pictured it in my mind, and found that it made a lot more sense with Andrew in the starring role than with a sextuagenarian in a polyester pantsuit.

The grandmotherly outfit my friend Mabel Hofstetter picked out for my continued undercover surveillance of New Life Ministries did nothing to improve my mood.

"It's purple," I objected.

"Yes, Cat, and it just sets off your white hair wonderfully," she said.

She brought out some clunky jewelry she'd made in her Fimo clay class. If I hadn't known better, I would have mistaken it for one of Ben's Play-Doh creations.

"Don't you have any lighter earrings?" I asked. "My ears still hurt from yesterday." I rubbed one lobe and it responded with a throb. At least my antihistamine was starting to kick in.

"These are the earrings that go with this necklace and this outfit," she said firmly, fashion cop to the over-sixty crowd.

At New Life Ministries, I parked next to "God Is My Co-Pilot." I eyed myself sternly in the rearview mirror. "You're a granny," I said. "Grannies are supposed to be good-natured and even-tempered. Don't you dare fucking blow your cover by behaving like you feel instead of like everybody thinks grannies are supposed to behave."

The purple pantsuit may have set off my white hair beautifully, but my earlobes, which had turned a bright red, were spoiling the effect. I ditched the earrings.

I was afraid that Joy would notice that I looked and moved like a Body Snatcher, but she had her own troubles today. Her nose was pink and her eyes were puffy and underscored by black lines where her mascara had run. David sat in a chair next to her desk, looking grave. My pulse quickened.

"Is something wrong?" I asked.

"Oh, it's just—. That boy, you know. The one they found in the swimming pool over at the high school?" She glanced up at me over her handkerchief.

"Oh, yes," I said. "I saw it on the news. What a tragedy."

"You knew him?" I added.

She nodded. "He was one of ours." She glanced at David. "Just the nicest boy! So polite. Everybody loved him. He was real sweet with the younger kids."

"When you say, 'one of ours'—," I said carefully, "do you mean he attended church here?"

"Sometimes," she said. "I think maybe he went to services with his family, too. But he came Sunday afternoons, too, for the youth meetings. And he wanted to train for our teen crisis line. He would've done that this summer."

"So he worked with Reverend Ted?"

"Yes," she said, "and with David here, too. He helped out sometimes with the younger kids on Saturday mornings."

"I'm so sorry," I said, and looked at David. I was just in time to catch a flash of something like anger in his face. Then it was gone, and when he returned my gaze, I saw only sadness.

"Thanks," he said. "It was quite a blow."

"You just never expect them to die so young," Joy said.

And there it was again, that flash of anger in David's eyes. But anger at whom? At Tony?

"What was he like?" I asked.

"Oh, like I said, just as sweet as he could be," she said. "And helpful, you know. He used to carry heavy boxes for me, though he wasn't so big. He had a swimmer's body, real lean. But he had muscles, because he handled those boxes okay."

"The paper said it might have been suicide," I said with caution. I didn't want them to think I found a teenager's death a suitable topic for idle gossip.

"Oh, I'm sure that's wrong, Catherine," Joy said. "Tony was a good Christian boy. He'd never do anything like that, would he, David?"

She looked to David for confirmation, but David surprised her. "I wish I knew," he said. "Teenagers can be so volatile."

"But Tony wasn't like that," Joy insisted. To me she said, "He was very mature for his age. Very responsible. He would never do anything to cause grief to his family and friends. I'm sure they'll find out that it was some kind of accident."

"What kind of accident?" I asked.

"Oh, you know—," she said, waving a hand to indicate the vagueness of her imagined possibilities. "Like one of those heart defects that kills athletes young. Or a brain aneurism. Or a serious cramp while he was swimming."

"Was he on any kind of medication, do you know?"

David reacted with surprise, and I decided I'd better back off. My curiosity was becoming too specific for credibility.

"Lots of kids take medicine these days for all kinds of things," I said. "I read about it in *Newsweek*. But when you said 'accident,' it reminded me of this friend of my niece's, who was an epileptic. I think they had a hard time getting the dosage right and he had a seizure one time at the beach and almost drowned."

"I don't think Tony had anything like that," Joy said. "But I still think—."

Her phone rang, and she excused herself. David said he had work to do, and left. I went to the conference room to put in a few more hours ghostwriting for Jesus.

Joy's theory had given me something new to think about, though. Was it possible that a support group existed for teens who had some kind of chronic illness? Any condition that teenagers would find especially embarrassing to acknowledge to healthier peers? So far, no one had mentioned such a condition in connection with any of the kids I'd been investigating, but I hadn't asked. Surely, though, if Peter had suffered from anything like that, Gussie would have told me. But Peter didn't have to have suffered from such a condition himself in order to serve as a counselor, or teen minister, to others. And then, it was always possible that only Peter's parents would know of a sensitive medical condition that wasn't obvious to other people. Or that the condition was only sensitive to Peter himself, but not considered to be worth mentioning by anyone else. I remembered all too clearly my own kids' teenaged years. It was a miracle they'd survived the daily humiliations to which they'd been subjected, by their parents' conduct in public in particular. But two out of three of my children had fought long battles with acne, and the acuteness of their pain had wrung my heart.

My ruminations made me lose track of time, and before I knew it, I'd folded the last flyer and sucked dry the last paper cut. Now, if only I could snag a job that would move me out of isolation and permit me greater access to the secrets of New Life.

"Can you type?" Joy asked, after appropriate heartfelt expressions of gratitude.

"I'm not very fast . . ." I said, crossing lacerated fingers behind my back, although this understatement was true, as far as it went.

"Have you ever typed on a computer?" she asked.

"Once or twice," I said.

I did not tell her that Del had threatened to confiscate my Publishers Clearinghouse Sweepstakes entry and subscribe me to every magazine from *Car and Driver* to *Golf Digest* unless I sat down at the computer and let him instruct me on a few of the basics, which, I might add, I'd long since forgotten. What I remembered was that they didn't put the On-Off switch in a conspicuous place. I couldn't remember where they did put it, only that you had to look hard for it. But the computer was out in the main office, where the action was, and working on it would afford me more opportunities of eavesdropping. And I knew enough about computers to know that I might want access to some of the information stored on this one, and that I might need some kind of security code to get it. My goals were modest, appropriate to my expertise. If I learned the security code, Del could do the rest. Hell, he could probably do it without the security code, but I didn't want him to think I wasn't pulling my weight in this investigation.

"Oh, good," Joy said in obvious relief. "Well, I don't know much about it myself. But the typing part is pretty easy, really. It's the other stuff that's tricky. But if you're willing to give it a try, I'll have you enter names on our mailing list, okay?"

"I'll give it a try," I said, trying to repress my excitement. Willing to be helpful, but not too confident—that was the note I was attempting to strike.

She smiled at me. "You know, I believe in the power of prayer, don't you?"

I smiled and nodded, even though I didn't have any idea what she was talking about. Did she expect me to drop to my knees right there in front of the computer and ask God for a little help on the keyboard? Or would bedtime prayers be presumed to cover this contingency? I was pretty sure He knew where the On-Off switch was, but I wasn't convinced that He would drop whatever He was doing to show me. Maybe this was a job for my guardian angel, assuming that guardian angels were kosher at New Life.

Joy turned on the computer herself. Then she walked me through the procedure. I had a rubber-banded pile of index cards, each with a name, address, and phone number on it, as well as a series of letter codes. The program I was using gave me a blank form to fill out on the screen. I filled in the slots on the form, pushed the Enter key, and went on to the next form. The work appeared to be straightforward and tedious. But at least I was out of isolation. And I was especially interested in the codes.

"See these letters here?" Joy said. "Those are codes we use to sort the big mailing list into smaller ones. You know, like 'A' is for 'adult,' 'Y' is for 'youth,' and 'C' is for child."

"Not 'chimpanzee'?" I asked.

She laughed. "No, Evie is all by herself in that category, thank the Lord!"

"What about these other letters?" I said, pointing. "What do they stand for?"

"Oh, all kinds of things," she said. "People's interests, mostly. Like 'M' means they're interested in our men's group, or 'L' means they want to participate in our pro-life activities."

"Like picketing abortion clinics?" I asked.

"Well, we don't do much picketing, but we sometimes have letter-writing campaigns," she said.

"Some of them have colors," I observed. I edged one out of the pile. Along the top was a band of green magic marker.

"Oh, that's the old system," she said. "You'll still see some of that. But since we're putting everything on the computer now, we've switched to letter codes. Plus the letters give us more options. I swear, Catherine, sometimes I get so mad at this machine! But really, the things it can do! Like, if we want to have a special program on parenting, say, we can pull up just those people who are interested in parenting. Isn't that amazing?"

I agreed. I couldn't wait to find Tony Frank's entry and find out how he was coded.

She left me to it, and I muddled along. It was fortunate that computer keys make less noise than typewriter keys, so she couldn't judge my speed without listening for it. And she had too much to do to give me any thought. The office was a busy place. Her phone rang every thirty seconds, the mail carrier brought mail, the UPS carrier brought two packages, and several people wandered through who appeared to be working in other parts of the complex. A woman stopped by to discuss a menu for some event. A young man brought a publicity poster that he wanted Armbruster to approve. An electrician appeared and was directed to the television station. Two young women and their five young children came together to ask about services. A well-dressed older man brought a check, a donation of some kind. By listening in, I learned that New Life was planning a memorial service for Tony Frank the following Wednesday night. Eavesdropping did nothing for my typing skills, but it did take my mind off my aching back and shoulders, my clogged sinuses, and my tender fingertips.

One of the phone callers was Margie, who, from Joy's end of the conversation, appeared to be in better health than her replacement. Joy cried some more over Tony, reassured Margie that New Life could survive without her service for one more day, and praised me far beyond my worth.

Nothing suspicious happened. Joy was good at her job—adept at handling people with competence and compassion. As the front woman for New Life, she was a knockout. Only Tony's death had put a dent in her unflappable good humor. She made you wish you had her secret. The other people who worked there all seemed pleasant but ordinary. If something nefarious was afoot, surely none of these people was involved.

About eleven forty-five, the office began to get more crowded. The troops were gathering to discuss the memorial service. The first arrival was the Reverend Ted himself, a young man of less than medium height, medium build, light brown hair combed back from his forehead and intense blue eyes framed by eyelashes so light as to seem almost invisible. He wore jeans, a turtleneck, and sneakers. His grip was firm, but in an odd way, as if he were a surgeon feeling the bones of my hand for possible breakage.

"Catherine here wants to talk to you about her grandson, when you get time, Ted," Joy told him.

"Oh?" He turned those intense blue eyes on me, and I tried to hold his gaze.

"That's right," I said. "He's pretty wild."

"Let's talk about that," he said. "I'm sure we can help." His voice expressed energy, confidence, reassurance. I could see why he'd be a hit with parents. I didn't yet see why teenagers might be attracted to him, apart from the jeans and sneakers. "We'll do that," he said.

David entered with another man, who was introduced to me as Reverend Harald. He was a big man, bald on top, wearing glasses and an air of superiority that I disliked. He gave me a limp handshake, and a squeeze of the shoulder in recognition of my volunteer work. I was going have a nice set of bruises on my shoulder if they kept up the encouragement.

"Will we be seeing you and your husband at services, Catherine?" he asked.

I bit off the comment about resurrection that rose to my lips, swallowed it down, and said, "I'm a widow, Reverend."

His eyebrows rose. "Oh, I'm sorry to hear that. Then you'll be interested in our group for older singles. I believe there are quite a number of men in that group." He actually winked at me.

I did not say, "'Single' is not synonymous with 'lonely.'" I did not say that one husband in a lifetime was more than enough. I did not say that I was too busy with my new career as a private investigator to have time for bridge-and-footsies with the seniors. I just smiled.

A short, well-dressed bearded man bustled in. Joy introduced him as the Reverend Doctor Maynard Clay. He fairly bristled with energy.

"Maynard is both a minister and a medical doctor," Joy said. "We're very lucky to have him."

"I do what I can, Mrs. Caliban," he said. "Where there is great need, the Lord's work is waiting to be done."

Next to arrive was the Reverend Armbruster himself, in close conversation with two men, who were introduced to me as Reverend Higginbotham and Mr. Johnson. Reverend Higginbotham was the first black person I'd seen on the premises, which were located in a predominantly black neighborhood, so I was curious about him. Both he and Mr. Johnson were around my age or older. Armbruster wore an expression of solemnity appropriate to the occasion. In fact, everyone looked solemn, but the only person who looked something more was David Green, though I couldn't put my finger on the emotion.

Two women entered next. One, an attractive blond in her thirties wearing a silk suit and high heels, held Evie by the paw. The second woman was older and heavier, with black hair and sharp eyebrows that gave her a look of determination. Evie was wearing a yellow dotted Swiss dress with a smear of something brown across the front and a strip of hem hanging down. In her free paw she carried something that looked like a plastic dump truck.

I happened to catch Rev Armbruster's reaction to this apparition, and he was not pleased. He frowned at Evie, then at his wife, who wasn't looking at him. He gave a perfunctory nod to the man he'd been listening to, touched him on the elbow, and crossed the room to his wife, whom he extricated from her conversation with a smile and took aside. I didn't need a script to understand what they were saying. They were speaking quietly, but their body language communicated annoyance and exasperation, and I'd participated in many such conversations myself in my younger days. He was asking the kinds of questions that push a woman's buttons. Why did you bring the baby? We're trying to have a meeting here. What were you thinking? And why can't you keep her clean at least? Why is her dress torn? If you're going to bring her out in public, can't you at least make her presentable? And she, I hoped, was giving it right back to him: if you ever spent half an hour with an average two-year-old, you'd know why I can't keep her presentable for more than five minutes. If the Rev was anything like Fred had been, he'd never even changed a diaper, much less tried to dress a wriggling toddler.

Evie, meanwhile, was pulling on the woman's hand. At last, she yanked free, dashed across the room, and scampered up the back of my chair. Though I was startled, I cried out more in pain than surprise as Evie leaned forward to study the computer screen and four little plastic wheels bit into my shoulder, adding a new set of bruises to my growing collection. I had an impression that all conversation and movement stopped, and then I was being rushed. Joy was the first to reach me, scolding, her voice thick with mortification as the truck was transferred to the top of my head.

Joy's attempts to dislodge her only caused Evie to take a firmer grip on the part of my anatomy most convenient for gripping from her position on my shoulders, and I felt warm, furry fingers close around my throat. It occurred to me that the last sound I was destined to hear was the screech of a chimpanzee. Then the fingers loosened and air rushed into my lungs. The shooting pains in my shoulders ceased and the weight on them lifted. My vision cleared and I could see faces, Joy's anxious, Armbruster's angry, the blond's long-suffering, the other men's concerned, and finally, David's, some unreadable combination of sternness and amusement, as he balanced Evie on his hip.

But a glance at them reminded me who was the only person present who was my kind of person.

"Eve, you're a *very* naughty girl!" Armbruster was saying. "Papa is *very* disappointed in you." To me, Papa sounded more angry than disappointed.

"She's just curious about the computer, aren't you, Evie?" I said to her. "If you'll sit on my lap instead of my head, I'll show you how it works." I held out my arms to her, and she leaned into them like a sociable baby. Cat Caliban, computer whiz and tamer of wild beasts.

"Oh, Catherine! Are you all right?" Joy asked. She was patting my head, and it took me a minute to realize she was trying to smooth my tousled hair, not making some kind of placatory gesture. My hair doesn't get a hell of a lot of attention from me, so it was unused to the sensation of being smoothed.

"I'm fine," I said and turned back to the screen. I had to lean around Evie to see it, since she was, in point of fact, standing on rather than sitting in my lap and I was getting a noseful of dotted Swiss and baby powder.

"Betsy, will you please—?" Armbruster said.

"I don't know what you want me to do," the blond said tartly. "Her cage is being cleaned. It won't be dry for another half hour." She turned to me. "She seems to be getting on so well with this very kind lady. Perhaps you—?" She smiled encouragement at me.

I supposed if I could survive four hours with my grandson, I could manage half an hour with a rambunctious chimpanzee, even in my current state of diminished capacity. "Half an hour?" I said. I wanted the terms clear.

She nodded. "Joy will help you," she promised. Past her shoulder I saw Joy's smile slip.

"Okay," I said. I sneezed, dislodging a yellow barrette clipped over Evie's left ear.

Something calculating in the blond's eyes told me what she was thinking: perhaps Evie and I were well matched.

"I'm Betsy Armbruster, by the way." She offered me a manicured hand, which Evie took. "I'm—."

"Evie's mother, I presume." I shook her hand when Evie was finished with it.

"How did you ever guess?" she asked.

David stood a minute after the others had turned toward the conference room.

"You sure this is okay?" he asked me.

"No problema," I said. "Any advice?"

"Yeah," he said. "Don't turn your back on her for a second."

Chapter Nineteen

EVIE AND I spent a rollicking half-hour together. First, we tried to see how many nonsense commands we could make the computer try to compute at one time. This was a great joke on the computer, but Joy didn't appreciate its humor. Evie danced in my lap, her sharp little toes digging into my thighs as she extended her lips and emitted little "ooh-ooh"s of enthusiasm.

"If it breaks," she said, "we'll have to re-enter the whole mailing list."

"Every party has a pooper, that's why we invited you," I hummed into Evie's ear. Evie swatted at the tickling sensation. Probably, she hadn't recognized the tune. People often have that difficulty when I wax musical.

But I didn't want the mailing list to disappear before I got a better look at it. Still, the truth was, Evie's refusal to be intimidated by a mere piece of machinery, no matter how smart, expensive, and technologically advanced, was an attitude I aspired to. I wanted to be liberated from intimidation.

"They've probably tested it on small children," I said to Joy, "don't you think?"

"I doubt it," she said. "How many small children do you think work at IBM?"

She was right, of course. Male product designers rarely considered the dangerous or destructive possibilities that children introduced.

Evie's eyes were on the tall bookshelves again. She followed them up to the ceiling and looked at the light fixture.

"Show her the screen saver," Joy suggested. "That should make her happy."

"Screen saver?" I echoed. I hadn't realized that the screen needed saving, but it occurred to me to wonder whether, from a New Life perspective, everything was in need of salvation.

But it turned out that screen savers had nothing to do with prayer and preaching, and everything to do with pixies, as I understood from Joy's explanation of screen strain. It turned out that the screen got just as tired of looking at me as I did of looking at it; you had to keep moving things around to avoid burning out your pixies, according to Joy. Not wanting to contribute to pixie burnout, I was eager to learn about screen savers. Joy showed me how to call up different ones, and Evie and I sat mesmerized by the colored patterns for another five minutes. My favorite was the shooting stars, but Evie liked the one where the little colored crosses flew out from the middle of the big cross against a background like the aurora borealis. I guessed that was her religious upbringing coming out.

Joy needed to deliver a script to the television station, and asked if I'd be all right alone with Evie. I thought of saying no so that she'd take Evie with her and leave me alone to search the mailing list, assuming I could figure out how to do that, but Evie gave me a conspiratorial grin, so I said yes.

She hadn't been gone a minute when a young man entered the office. He wore a nice overcoat and carried several notebooks in a gloved hand. He looked around for somebody he recognized, but Evie, after giving him the once-over, went back to punching keys.

"Joy or Margie around?" he asked.

"Margie's out sick, and Joy just stepped out," I said. I didn't offer to help him. Apart from my unfamiliarity with the New Life operation, I had a lapful of chimpanzee.

"I just brought over some of the log books," he said, holding up the notebooks. Then he added, "I'm Michael."

Michael of Youthline? That Michael?

"Mrs. Caliban," I said primly, though it's a hard act to pull off with a chimp bouncing in your lap.

"Good to meet you," he said. "Well, I can see you have your hands full. I'll just leave these on the desk, okay?"

I nodded, unwilling to give away any additional samples of my voice, on the off-chance that he'd recognize it. He dropped the notebooks on the desk and departed. I eyed them, wondering where the old ones were stored, and how I could get my hands on them.

Evie and I got tired of playing in two dimensions, and Evie rediscovered her dump truck, which had fallen to the floor. She climbed down to retrieve it, and noticed my purse again. She picked up the purse and slung the strap over her head. She marched around the room, dragging it along. She looked back at me over her shoulder to see if I'd noticed. Then she sat down on the floor and looked inside. She uncapped the lipstick, which was part of my disguise, and sniffed at it. Before I had a chance to think of all the surfaces she could deface with lipstick, she discarded it, capless, in favor of the pick-locks, which I'd forgotten to remove. She frowned in concentration as she examined them. Finally, she raised her eyebrows in my direction—or, to put it more accurately, she raised that expressive ridge of skin that framed her eyes.

"Pick-locks," I said. "For opening doors."

I glanced at the door through which Joy had exited, but saw and heard nothing to indicate her imminent return. I went to the outer door of the office and crooked my finger at Evie. "Come here, Evie," I said.

I studied the lock, an old one with a keyhole on either side and a button embedded in the door where the door met the jamb. It was just as well, I thought, for future reference, to know what kind of lock I'd be up against if I needed to break into the place. On the other hand, the age of the lock suggested that there was nothing inside worth hiding, a consideration I found discouraging.

Evie watched with interest while I locked the door, which I propped open with my foot, and then chose a pick and inserted it into the lock. Thanks to my practice session at the Catatonia Arms, I had the door unlocked in less than two minutes. The little button popped out with a satisfying click, to Evie's delight. I repeated my trick, having her try to turn the handle before and after, then offered the pick to Evie.

Just as I had suspected, Evie was a natural at breaking and entering, if a bit impatient as a learner. Her first try took her almost five minutes, and occasioned some hopping up and down and whooping to vent frustration. But once she got it, she was elated. I held out a hand, and to my amazement, she slapped it with a simian high-five. Maybe this was some kind of ancient tribal gesture, embedded in our genes.

I retrieved my purse and made to put away the pick-locks, but Evie protested loudly, so I gave them back to her before someone came running to investigate. Fearing that Joy would return at any moment, I sat down at the computer again, and lay my purse on its side on the floor. Behind me, I could hear noises that told me that Evie was happily locking and unlocking the door.

Then I realized that I couldn't hear her anymore. I turned my head to see what she was doing, but no Evie. Panic rose in my throat. I'd ignored the only piece of advice David had given me. Evie could be anywhere. She could be out directing traffic on Auburn Avenue by now, flashing motorists with her white lace underpants.

I vaulted from my chair and raced into the hall. It was empty. Which way to go? Up the stairs? Or down the hall? I was relieved to see that the front door was closed. Somehow, Evie didn't seem the type to take the time to close it after herself. I ought to know. I'd raised kids and cats, and all of them took offense at closed doors.

I stood still and listened. I heard a faint scraping noise, its source too near to be coming from upstairs. The first two doors off the hallway stood ajar. I pushed each of them open, and called softly for Evie, but she wasn't in either of these offices. The first, according to the name plate on the door, belonged to the Reverend Theodore W. Settles. I had an impression of green plants and untidiness, but my panic didn't permit me to linger and investigate further. The second office, starker and tidier than the first, belonged to a Reverend Ralph Higginbotham. I noted that these two offices had probably been made by dividing an old withdrawing room or parlor. The third door, the door to Reverend Vernon Armbruster's office, stood wide open.

From down the hall I heard coughing. Someone was there? Was that the source of the noise I'd heard earlier? But no. Arriving at the doorway to Reverend Armbruster's office, I saw, on the other side of a small anteroom, a short brown figure in yellow dotted Swiss, busy picking the lock to the reverend's inner office. Before I reached her, the door swung open.

Evie caught sight of me and grinned, pleased to have an audience. She was disappointed by my reaction.

"No, Evie," I said, hurrying toward her. I reached out, pushed the button to lock the door, and pulled it shut. "You can't go around breaking into people's offices. It isn't polite." Then I reflected that politeness wasn't Evie's strong suit, and amended, "It isn't legal."

Nice to know that it could be done, though, if the occasion arose. But I might have to bring Evie with me.

I dragged her out into the hall, and she allowed herself to be dragged, possibly because she'd grown bored with picking locks and hoped that I had plans for further hilarity. I was bending over, scrutinizing Reverend Dr. Clay's door lock for telltale scratches, when a woman emerged from the last office on the hall. I switched my attention to Evie, and said, "Now, Evie, you'll have to give me some help here. I can't find your dump truck by myself. Where were you playing with it?"

The woman, an attractive middle-aged person in a plaid wool skirt and sweater, gave me a sympathetic smile, but she kept her distance as she slid past us in the hall. Evie watched her with keen interest, and I guessed that she'd been on the receiving end of some of Evie's jokes in the past.

I managed to get all the doors re-locked and persuaded myself that nobody would notice a new set of scratches. Caught off guard by a sudden sneeze, I relaxed my grip on Evie's hand for an instant, and she made a break for freedom. She raced up the stairs, clambered up on the banister and stood erect and swaying, toes curled around the handrail and eyes on the chandelier.

"No, E—." A second sneeze cut short my admonition, but it startled Evie, who lost her balance and tumbled over the rail. Aghast, I ran, only to find her dangling from one of the balusters. I opened my arms and she dropped into them with a force that almost sent me sprawling. I now felt the pick-locks bite into one of my shoulder blades.

Back in Joy's office, Evie pulled free and ran straight to Joy's desk. She dropped the pick-locks, which I hadn't been able to pry loose from her grip, and I took the opportunity to slide them back into my purse. By the time I caught up with her, she was rummaging in Joy's bottom drawer. She brought out a bag of jelly beans.

I'd already deduced that it was no good talking property rights with Evie, so I let her keep them, and we spent a good while loading the dump truck with jelly beans and then dumping them out on the coffee table. Evie discovered that if she smacked the table with her hand, she could make the beans jump inside the truck. Meanwhile, Joy swept into the room as if she'd stayed away too long, and asked if Evie had been good. I didn't have to answer, because her phone rang. Evie smacked the table, and Joy jumped along with the jelly beans. But Joy only did it once, which gave her limited entertainment value.

Joy laughed and shook her head. "That little monkey is too smart for her own good! Not everybody appreciates your jokes, Evie."

"She sure is smart," I agreed. "I read once about a chimpanzee who'd been taught sign language. Has anybody ever tried to teach Evie?"

Joy cut her eyes at the closed door of the conference room. "No," she said. "And don't let Reverend Armbruster hear you say that."

"Why not?" I asked, surprised. "Doesn't he think she's smart?"

She sighed. "It's got something to do with evolution," she said, her voice lowered in confidence. "God made man in His own image, and gave him dominion over all creatures."

"So they're not allowed to learn sign language?"

"He says that language expresses the soul, and animals don't have souls," she said. "He says that animals don't have the intellectual capacity to learn language, only to respond to stimuluses—stimuli, I guess you'd say. He says that the people who write those books about chimps learning sign language are all evolutionists trying to trick the public into rejecting Scripture."

"Oh," I said. I flashed back to Reverend Armbruster in the role of Papa, telling Evie that he was disappointed in her. If she was only an animal with no soul, how could he be disappointed? For that matter, how could he be "Papa"? It was very confusing.

"Is that what you think?" I asked Joy.

She glanced nervously at the closed door again. "I don't know," she said. "Evie seems pretty smart to me. Sometimes I wonder. But you know what you should do? You should check out Reverend Armbruster's sermon on evolution, and take it home and watch it. He can explain it so much better. You got a VCR?"

"You have a sermon on video?" Now that she mentioned it, I remembered seeing some videos on the shelf in the conference room.

"We've got lots of 'em," she said. "You can check out whichever ones you want. But Evie's in the evolution one, aren't you, Evie?"

Evie had climbed onto the sofa and sat with a picture book open on her lap. She gave every sign of being engrossed in her reading. Then she looked up at us and grinned.

By the time Evie's mother returned to claim her, she was sitting on my lap on the couch, demure, and we were reading a picture book of Bible stories—at least, I was reading them while Evie prodded the pictures as if she expected them to emit sounds. I had no doubt that I looked every inch the perfect babysitter, grandmotherly, religious and sweet. Cat Caliban, master of disguise.

I had my second opportunity to play around with the mailing list when the meeting broke up and Reverend Armbruster took Joy and David to his office to discuss arrangements for the memorial service. I studied the typed list of "DOS codes." I didn't know what it meant, but I had a feeling it wasn't related to the "Dos" in "Dos Equis." I tried typing, "display list." My finger hovered over the return key, but what the hell? I hit return. The screen went blank for a long time—so long that I was sure I'd just screwed up. In a panic, I scanned the code list for anything that would tell the damn machine I was just kidding.

"Never mind, goddamn it!" I said under my breath. "Never mind, never mind, never mind!" Up to this point, I'd done an admirable job of suppressing my natural tendency toward profanity. "Don't you dare croak on me!"

Then, lines began to appear on the screen. Not just lines, the mailing list, in alphabetical order, with phone numbers and letter codes for each entry.

I hit the "page down" key and scoured the B's. No Peter Baer. No Baer of any kind. Could he have used a pseudonym? If a kid from a prominent Catholic family had started hanging out at New Life, would he have given a fake name? I doubted he'd change his first name, but I couldn't see myself searching the whole bloody mailing list for kids named "Peter." Then I remembered that the counselor from Youthline had emphasized that the crisis line only asked for first names when kids called in. So maybe the mailing list wasn't the best place to find kids in trouble. And, I realized, it was in the process of being transferred from cards. I wondered whether I could find the original cards.

But I paged down to the D's anyway. And there she was: Jennifer Deemer, a student at Aiken High School, coded "Y" and "NC." The "Y," I assumed, stood for "youth." But what, I wondered, was "NC"? Not committed? Not Catholic? Or did "C" stand for "church"? Or "Christ"? She was also labeled "Inact." Was she inactive because she'd gone missing, or had she become inactive even before that, when she'd stopped wearing her bracelet? I checked for Paul Whitney with rising excitement. He was there—a student at Mt. Healthy High School also labeled "NC" and "Inact." Paul, the card noted, played the organ.

Tony Frank was there, too: "Y," "NC," and "YL." Nobody had yet taken the time to add "Inact."

Three kids, from three different schools. What they had in common was a connection to New Life. But where was Peter Baer? I needed more time with this list. My eyes slid to the printer that sat beside the computer.

Over my left shoulder, a voice spoke. "Shall we have our talk now, Mrs. Caliban?"

Chapter Twenty

REVEREND TED FIXED his intense blue eyes on me, but he didn't ask why I was looking at Tony Frank's entry on the mailing list. I was hoping he thought I'd been asked to add the notation, "Inact.," although to do so just now seemed to exceed the bounds of decorum in the name of efficiency. Probably he thought, however, that I was satisfying an unseemly curiosity about a boy whose death had made headlines.

The play sessions on the floor with Evie had affected me more than I'd realized, as I discovered when I tried to stand up, and I was reminded why I had given up similar activities with my grandson Ben. Reverend Ted put out a hand to steady me.

"My office is just down the hall," he said. "Do youthink you can—?"

He didn't want to ask if this gimpy old lady could hobble down the hall and arrive at his office without collapsing.

"I'm fine," I lied.

"Can I get you some tea or coffee?"

Some gin and a hot tub would have been welcome, but I didn't suppose he'd offer those, and he didn't look like the kind of guy who was carrying a couple of spare Darvons in his back pocket. I declined and made an effort to square my shoulders and straighten my back.

He apologized for the state of his office and waved me to a comfortable high-backed reading chair. He sat in its mate, not behind his desk.

I looked around. On the wall across from where we sat was a large colorful poster, which read, "Jesus Is My Rock and My Name Is on the Roll!" Beneath this heading was a high-angle photograph of a large, diverse group of happy young teenagers, raising their hands above their heads. The poster had been signed by a number of people, often with inscriptions, but from this distance I couldn't read any of them. There were several plants scattered about the room, and the light streaming in from the tall windows kept them green. On a credenza behind the desk, against the window, was a hot plate and coffeemaker. The rest of the space was filled with bookshelves overflowing with books, and I thought of the Whitneys' Christian bookstore. Business must be booming. But on the table between us, in addition to several brochures ("Take Jesus with You on Your Date," "God Wants You to Know the Facts of Life," "Why God Hates Drugs," and "Why Does Death Hurt So Much?"), there was only one book, a Bible.

He crossed his legs and leaned back against his chair. "Tell me about your grandson," he said. "What's his name?"

"Del," I said. "Well, Delbert, really. We call him Del."

He nodded in a way that was supposed to seem encouraging, I thought, but it made him look instead as if that was the answer he was expecting.

"How old is he?"

"Sixteen."

He made a little face. "Difficult age," he observed.

That, too, seemed part of the script. What age could I have picked that he wouldn't have pronounced "difficult"? If I'd said "seventeen," would he have dismissed me as a whiner?

"Where are his parents?" he asked.

"Divorced," I said, trying to look disapproving. "After the divorce, his mother went back to work as a flight attendant, and Del was supposed to live with his father. But his father travels a lot on business, too, and, of course, Del is, like you said, at a difficult age. So I offered to take him."

He tented his fingers and stared off into space. He seemed to find so many moral failures to comment on in this narrative that he decided not to take them all on just yet.

"What kinds of things does he do that concern you?" he asked.

"Oh, well—." I'd given this some thought. I had to cast Del in a role I thought he could play. I'd decided on general recalcitrance. In my experience, most teenagers could do general recalcitrance, and if my memory served me, Del could do it as well as the next teenager. "He's just so darned ornery. Like, if I said it was raining, he'd say the sun was shining. And he'd say it like I was the stupidest person in the world. And then if I told him to wear his windbreaker because it was raining, he'd just flat out refuse. What can I do? He's too big to spank."

He nodded, but didn't comment.

"What he really likes to do is play on his computer," I said. "Day and night. I ask him if he doesn't want to go out with his friends, but he says all of the kids in his classes are stupid, and he doesn't like any of them.

Then he goes out sometimes and doesn't tell me where he's going or what he's up to. His father wasn't like that."

This part wasn't true. From what I remembered, his father, my cousin Buddy, had been just like that, minus the computer.

"So he doesn't have friends, or you think he has friends that you don't know?" Reverend Ted said.

"That's it," I said. "I think he has friends I don't know. I think somehow he meets other kids who like computers. He belongs to this computer club at school, and sometimes he goes to these—well, I don't know what they are, really—contests. And he meets kids that way."

"Are there signs of negative influences?" he asked. "For example, some parents find images on their kids' computers that are—well, let's say, x-rated. That's often how they discover what their kids are up to."

I would have blushed if I could have, but I didn't think I could raise a blush even if he'd whipped out an x-rated sample. So I dropped my eyes instead. "Well, I don't know much about the computer. It's mostly for Del. But I think that he trades, um, pornographic pictures," I said. This part, at least, was true, though the pictures I'd seen I'd categorize as soft-core at most.

He nodded as if his suspicions had been confirmed.

"And, well, computers are expensive," I continued. "It seems like he's always adding things or changing things. He says he's not spending money, but is that possible? And if he is spending money, where is it coming from? He gets an allowance, of course, but I don't think it's enough to pay for—well, computer gadgets."

In truth, apart from the initial assault on my credit card, Del hadn't spent much money on my computer. He'd had a good two weeks after the initial purchase to add more equipment, but he seemed to consider it beneath him to spend more money. He claimed that all of the programming modifications he'd made were "freeware" or "shareware," paid for by the aforementioned pictures of space bimbos. He told me that he considered the prices for computer hardware and software "the height of bogosity," whatever that meant, but I could tell from his expression of disdain that it wasn't good.

But the Reverend Ted's knowledge of teen computer culture, or at least of hacker culture, was pretty shallow. He seemed to have a bee in his bonnet about cyberporn. "These pictures," he said. "Would you say he shows an unhealthy obsession with them? Does he, for example, print them out and take them to his room and spend a lot of time there alone with them?"

Fucking unbelievable. He wanted to know if Del was masturbating or not, and didn't want to come right out and ask me. I caught my jaw on the way down, closed my mouth, and looked away. This was no time to burst out laughing.

But this line of questioning I took as another sign that he didn't have a clue about hacker culture. Del wouldn't be alone in his room unless he had a computer there. And the good reverend should have been more worried about hacking than whacking. The world faced more danger from kids who could hack into the Defense Department's, local power station's, or Bank of America's computers than from a teenager doing what normal teenagers do.

"I don't know," I said, trying to look like I was giving it some thought. It was on the tip of my tongue to tell him what kind of real trouble a teen hacker like Del could get into, when I realized that I didn't want him enlightened. "Maybe."

"Have you tried restricting his computer use?" he asked.

"It's hopeless," I said. "He just gets angrier and less cooperative."

"Violent?"

"Oh, no," I said. I didn't want him greeting Del with a straight jacket and syringe.

"Well, maybe you need to stand firm," he suggested. "He's manipulating you through his behavior. He knows you'll back down."

"That's probably true," I conceded. "Does that mean you can't do anything to help?"

"I didn't say that, Catherine," he said, giving me a broad, beneficent smile. "No, I think we can do a great deal. You see, most teenagers want some authority in their life. They often recognize that, with all of the hormonal changes they're going through, they can't control their own behavior. They want to, but they can't. So, deep down, what they really want is someone to take charge."

"You?"

He shook his head.

"Me?"

He shook his head again.

"God," he said.

"Oh." I'd flunked the test. "Like 'God Is My Co-Pilot'?"

"Something like that, sure," he said. "We ask teenagers to let God take over their lives." He leaned forward. "God is more than willing, we tell them, because He loves you and wants you to be happy."

"Don't they resist?"

"Of course they do," he said. "But if they come here and see other kids who have been where they are, and made the decision to let God take over, and they see how happy those kids are, why, they want that kind of happiness. And our kids are happy, Catherine! You can't imagine what a relief it is to them to turn everything over to God." Then he gave me a slight smile. "Or maybe you can."

If he was expecting a confession out of me, he was barking up the wrong Cat. Still, what he said made a lot of sense, except that it made God sound like a tranquilizer. I thought of Tony Frank and the bottle of valium in his gym bag. Not all of his kids were happy. I wanted to know exactly how God told the kids what He wanted them to do. This seemed to me a crucial question, but I couldn't figure out how to frame it.

I tended to think that you usually knew what God wanted you to do, or what was right, in any situation, you just didn't want to do it. But Tony Frank's death had unsettled me. I believed that it was right to find out who killed Peter Baer. I believed that it was wrong to endanger other innocent lives in the process. But was it possible to do one without the other? In spite of what Moses said, I still suspected that it all came down to my inexperience, and that was a painful thing to admit.

I'd let the silence stretch too long, I knew. But I still couldn't figure out how to ask what I really wanted to ask. I smiled. "Sorry," I said, dotty old lady in ascendance. "What were you saying?"

"I'll tell you what, Catherine," he said. "Why don't you bring Del in to see me some time next week?"

"Oh, that would be great," I said, trying to look relieved. "But I was hoping I could maybe bring him to the youth group on Sunday. Is that possible?"

"Certainly," he said. "We'd love to have him. And perhaps, in the meantime—." He rifled through a stack of brochures on a nearby shelf and plucked one from the pile. He handed it to me. "Maybe you'd like a little reading matter," he said.

The brochure was called, "You and Your Troubled Teenager: God Is on Both Your Sides."

I smiled. It was as if I'd cracked open a Chinese fortune cookie and read, "You and your second cousin will succeed in an important joint venture."

Chapter Twenty-one

THE DAY WORE on, and the next time Joy announced an errand to the television studio, I begged her to let me go.

She was all sympathy. "Well, sure! I guess you're getting pretty tired of being cooped up in here, pounding away on that computer. Just take this envelope to Hank, would you? But put on your coat. It's cold out there!"

She was right about the cold. The wind put the finishing touches on my hairdo as styled by Evie and re-styled by Joy. Beneath purple polyester, my legs turned to ice in three steps. I gritted my teeth, hugged my coat to my body, and made my way down the cleared sidewalk, hearing, but not feeling, the crunch of salt beneath my shoes. The sun, when I stepped into it, proved to be brighter than I expected. I looked down, partly to shield my eyes and partly to watch for treacherous patches of ice. Women my age know that one broken hip can be the end of you.

Joy had directed me to the smaller of two buildings behind the Victorian house where I'd spent the day. This one was low, flat, and functional, unlike the one with the cantilevered semicircular auditorium. A young woman wearing corduroys and t-shirt nearly collided with me as I entered, then directed me to studio A. A tall, lanky man descended a ladder, where he'd been setting lights, and took the envelope from me.

The set he'd been lighting was decorated like a cozy private office or library, with two leather chairs fronting full bookshelves. The set contrasted with the electronic equipment surrounding it—cameras, lights, microphones, and a dark soundproof room where I could make out the shapes of monitors and headphones hanging on the wall.

Hank clearly wasn't one for chitchat, so I nodded at him and left. From the doorway of the studio, I studied New Life's world headquarters. My eyes climbed the fire escape to second and third floor windows. I wondered what was upstairs, and decided that the fire escape might come in handy if I needed to find out without being seen. I didn't think I could jump high enough to catch the ladder and pull it down—at least, not without re-injuring the ankle I'd injured during my brief basketball career.[†] But I could reach it standing on the shoulders of my partner, the same guy who'd let me take his charge.

Now I turned to look at the fairy-tale cottage behind the parking lot. A winding brick path led from the walkway between the buildings to its front door. The cottage itself was just brimming with ye olde English charm—stone walls, mullioned windows, a chimney, and, unless my eyes deceived me, an honest-to-God thatched roof under the melting snow. Picturesque icicles tickled the brown outline of what must be a climbing rose that hung over the arched portico. A quaint little mailbox stood on a post halfway up the stone walk. "Evie" it said in large, black, crooked letters that looked as if they'd been printed by a five-year-old on Thorazine.

Fascinated, I detoured up the walkway. The stones were slicker than the cement. A sudden sneeze sent me skating, and I fetched up against the mailbox. I stood clinging to it like a drunk, catching my breath and taking in the view.

Why a chimpanzee would live in such a house I couldn't fathom. Surely no house like this one ever existed in the rain forest. The thatching would rot, for one thing, if it survived the abuse of dozens of little chimp feet dropping out of the trees overhead. I'd read somewhere that the chimpanzee's natural habitat was fast disappearing, and here was the living proof: the most unnatural habitat humankind could devise. It made me wonder if Evie wore a dirndl around the house.

The closer I came to the house, the stranger and more distorted it seemed. The proportions were off; it wasn't a classic English cottage, it was a classic English cottage that had been stretched and elongated to something like two stories. Up close, I could see that the thatching covered a more modern roof. And standing sentry in what looked like dead geraniums by the front door was a security system sign.

Ruffled curtains hung in the windows, blocking my view of the interior. If I stood in a flowerbed and pressed my nose against the glass, I might be able to see something, but I'd have to fight off some tough-looking juniper bushes to do it. I stepped up to the front door, cupped my hands around my face, and tried to look through the fanlights over the door. I could dimly see a hallway opening into a room beyond.

[†] See *Two-Shot Foul.*

I heard steps on the walk behind me and turned just in time to be knocked against the door by an enthusiastic chimp. David ambled along behind her, smiling and inscrutable as ever.

"Want to see the inside?" he asked.

"I sure do," I said. "Does Evie really live here?"

"These are her digs," he confirmed, fitting a key into the lock.

Evie, by this time, was sitting on my shoulders, so when the door swung open I saw everything through a curtain of dotted Swiss. Her toes found the little ruts in my shoulders left by her truck tires.

I didn't want to take a step until I could see, so I stood still until David plucked her from her perch and settled her on his hip. I followed him down an entry hall whose walls were painted yellow and whose floor was tile. A door opened off the hallway to the left, and he opened it, and gestured.

"Kitchen, bathroom, and laundry room on the left," he said. He opened a door on the other side of the hall, and said, "Formal dining room."

I didn't know what to ask first. I knew I wanted to inspect the kitchen more closely, so I turned to the formal dining room. Sure enough, there was a polished mahogany dining table, eight chairs, and an elegant antique high chair. This room was carpeted.

"So, what?" I asked. "She gives dinner parties?"

"Sometimes," David said. "She's quite the little hostess. Practices with her tea set."

I couldn't tell if he was pulling my leg or not.

Evie pulled away from him and reached for the doorjamb at the entrance to the kitchen.

"Not our favorite room, is it, Sis?" David said. "It's a best-behavior room, and we don't much like best-behavior rooms." Evie frowned and shook her head vigorously at the sound of the words, "best-behavior."

"I'm with you, Toots," I said. "A girl should be able to eat in comfort."

David set Evie down and she led the way into the kitchen. It was a cheerful room, if a bit too clean for my tastes, and ran to tile, polished metal, and glass. On the other hand, several brightly colored samples of what must have been Evie's artwork decorated the refrigerator, and they almost made me miss the keyed lock on the refrigerator door. Meanwhile, Evie was dragging a high chair—the everyday high chair—out from against the wall. When she was satisfied with its position, she clambered up and stood in the seat, watching David.

"Time for her snack," David said.

I noticed now that the knobs had been removed from the stove.

He fitted a small silver key into a locked cabinet door, opened it, and extracted a banana from inside. He handed it to Evie, who swung round and offered it to me, emitting polite little grunts I took to be invitations.

"Sorry, you're right," David said to her. He held up another banana and cocked his head at me. "Banana?"

"No, thanks," I said. The burger I'd had for lunch was sitting in my stomach like a bowling ball. "Is that really her favorite snack?"

Satisfied, Evie had swiveled around, planted her padded bum on the high chair seat, and addressed herself to the peeling of her banana. The tray on her high chair had apparently been removed to permit her to hold the banana between her toes while peeling it.

"No," David said, "I'd say Twinkies were her favorite, but she's not allowed to have them, and bananas run them a close second."

"So she eats mostly fruit?" I asked.

"She eats whatever she can get her mitts on," he said, setting a child's sipping mug on the counter. "Like us, she's an omnivore. She likes almost all fruits, most vegetables, leaves and nuts. But she's not a vegetarian. She likes chicken and pork. She's not much on seafood or beef. And I haven't noticed her eating any termites around here, but I wouldn't put it past her." He'd removed a small pitcher from the refrigerator and was now pouring a yellow liquid into the cup. The small room filled with the pungent scent of pineapple.

I was watching Evie, who seemed absorbed in her banana. Then I saw her glance up at something over David's head. I followed her gaze to a clock on the wall. Evie stood suddenly, knocking over the cup David had just placed on the counter next to her. She leaned over and made anxious sounds, staring, as far as I could tell, at a cabinet across from her. She made some curious hand gestures, which she seemed to repeat several times.

David glanced up at the clock, too, and said, "Yeah, okay, okay. Keep your pants on."

He unlocked the cabinet on which her attention was focused, and turned on a small television set. The screen turned bright green with glistening rainforest foliage.

"Her favorite nature show," he said by way of explanation. He turned the sound down, but she started to protest, so he turned it up a little. She watched him from under her brow, and then subsided, like a child who knows she has just gotten the best deal on offer.

"How does she react to the sight of other chimpanzees?" I asked.

"She seems intrigued," he said. "Sometimes she gets excited. But sometimes she looks bored, as if she's being forced to watch somebody else's home movies. She'd rather watch cheetahs and elephants and gazelles. Want to see the rest of the place?"

I noticed that he locked several locks before leaving the room, even though Evie didn't seem to be paying any attention.

He took me down the hallway to the heart of the little house: a tall open room entered through a door in a floor-to-ceiling set of iron bars. Here there was no coy faux English charm, no floral wallpaper, chintz curtains, or deep-pile rugs, it was pure primatial utilitarianism. Late afternoon sunlight entered through a skylight that was invisible from the outside. It fell on a tree that dominated the center of the room. On closer inspection, I could see that the tree was artificial, with a massive trunk to anchor it to the floor and a network of trunks no doubt designed by a primatologist for maximum chimpanzee entertainment. Artificial leaves provided occasional screens among its branches. Hanging from some of these, and from hooks in the ceiling, were heavy ropes, one rope ladder, and a tire swing. Under my feet as I entered Evie's inner sanctum I felt something both hard and slightly yielding—a floor tiled in a hard rubber surface I'd noticed in zoos.

Once I'd taken in the splendor of Evie's artificial tree, I noticed scattered about the more normal accoutrements of human childhood—enough dolls to throw a Tupperware party; a small table and chairs boasting a tea set in disarray, as if someone had dropped on top of it from the tire swing; a baby carriage on its side; a small wagon carrying a load of blocks; a reading corner, with bookshelves and large floor cushions; a child's boom box in Strawberry Shortcake pink; and in the distance, a large toy box overflowing with toys. Against the far wall was a sleeping loft, with steps leading up to accommodate those who were vertically challenged.

"Go on up," David urged. So, joints protesting, I did. My clogged sinuses combined with the height made me a bit giddy.

The far wall of the sleeping loft was glass, and looked out on woods. In the two corners formed by the inside walls of the house, two hammocks, one low and one high, had been suspended.

It was a cage, I thought, a glorified cage that separated its occupant from freedom by the width of a wall of heavy shatterproof glass. And yet it was a beautiful cage, lovingly constructed.

I felt David's presence behind me just before he spoke.

"Yeah, I know," he said softly. "But what chance would she have in the wild? It's a dangerous world for kids out there."

Behind us a series of whoops rose in volume and I caught a glimpse of brown and pink flying through my line of vision.

As if to prove David's point, three-thirty saw the beginning of a parade of teens and pre-teens through the office, all of them looking for a shoulder to cry on. On Joy's red blouse, dark splotches soon erupted where tearful faces had been pressed. Joy held them, they held each other, and I sat by and thought of the still, soggy corpse I'd pulled from the pool. The more the kids talked about Tony Frank, the more I wished I'd known him.

My heart caught when I spotted a black-and-white woven bracelet on the thin wrist of a quiet girl with long, light brown hair that looked steam-pressed. I studied her face, but all I saw there was misery. Although I saw bracelets in other colors, three other kids showed up wearing the black-and-white combination: a tall, athletic-looking boy with Asian features, a chubby pale-skinned boy, and a petite girl with delicate features and the awkward grace of a colt. Whatever they had in common apart from their grief over Tony, I couldn't tell. None of them appeared to be on drugs—or at least, none appeared spacier than the average teen.

Rev. Ted breezed in around four, passed out hugs, squeezed a few shoulders, and invited them to an impromptu group session in the library. I thought a group session was what they'd been having, and that they'd been doing a fine job with it, but my uncharitable thoughts flung in the direction of Rev. Ted's retreating back no doubt had as much to do with my general aversion to psychotherapy, which dated back to before my daughter's psych major period, as it did with the man himself. Some of the kids followed him, others announced to Joy their intention of retiring to the "Clubhouse."

"The Clubhouse?" I echoed when they'd gone.

"Oh, that's their name for the homework room upstairs," she said, blowing her nose on a handkerchief limp with salt water. "Well, it's supposed to be a homework room, and some kids do go there to do homework, and some kids play games. Some kids call it the computer room."

The tips of my little Cat ears quivered. "The computer room?" I said.

"Yes, we have quite a lot of computer equipment up there." Her eyes lifted to the ceiling for emphasis, and in fact, I could hear the old floorboards creaking under the weight of a herd of teenagers. "Thanks to some very generous donors," Joy added, as if reciting a mantra.

"My grandson will love that," I said. "Is there some kind of computer club the kids have?"

She was studying herself in a compact mirror. "My goodness, just look at me! I'm a fright!" She poked at her hair as if that could erase the ravages of emotion on her face. "No, it's not really a club—not officially, anyway. But there's a group of them who spend a lot of time up there together."

"And Tony was one of them?" I asked.

She nodded. "I think he enjoyed the company, really," she said. "His father's a graphic designer, and I got the impression he had fancier equipment at home. But he liked to come here and hang out with the other kids. He was always showing them things on the computer. Lord only knows what he's programmed them to do." She laughed with the air of someone determined to recover and live up to her name. "The computers, I mean, not the kids. Of course, I don't think anybody can program kids. Not mine, anyway."

I nodded. "I know what you mean."

"Go on up and take a look, why don't you?" she offered.

"All right, I will." One step outside the office door, I decided to try that Columbo trick. I stepped back inside the office. Joy had perched her reading glasses on the end of her nose and was reading some paper she held in her hand.

"By the way," I said, keeping my voice casual. "I noticed that several of the kids were wearing black-and-white bracelets. What's that about?"

The little chains attached to her glasses swayed as she looked up at me.

"I'm sorry, Catherine. What?" she said.

I repeated my question.

She shook her head, and the chains danced. "Lord, Catherine, I don't know. It's just some fad the kids have. We just thank the Lord it isn't something worse, like—you know—black and white hair or something." She smiled at her own joke but she was already reading again by the time I shut the office door.

I found my way to the room above the office. It was a large room, bright with artificial lighting now that the sun was low in the west. A well-worn carpet in industrial gray-green covered the floor, but there were some colorful posters on the walls. Bookcases stood on either side of the door and along part of one wall. Along two walls stood computers. Some, though not all, appeared to be the same model, at least to my unpracticed eye, which suggested that the generous donors in question had not simply donated used equipment, but had instead financed the purchase of new equipment. I was again struck by the amount of money invested in New Life Ministries.

The kids, however, were not busy at the computers, they were congregated around a large oak table that might indeed have once served as someone's dining room table. They were speaking in low voices, and turned toward the door when I entered the room.

"Sorry," I said into the silence. "Didn't mean to interrupt. It's just that I'm bringing my grandson here on Sunday, and Joy suggested I come take a look at the computer room." When they made no response, I added lamely, "He's pretty interested in computers." This was the understatement of the year. "I'll have to unplug him to drag him down here" is what I should have said.

"What's he got?" asked the chubby kid I'd noticed downstairs. He pushed his glasses up on his nose to get a better look at me.

At first, I thought they were expecting me to name a disease, maybe a psychological condition of the type that led parents to religion in desperation. And I wondered if they'd all been brought here under circumstances similar to the ones I'd been inventing for Del. But conjuring Del's name gave me a flash of insight. The kid meant, what kind of computer?

"Um, I don't exactly know," I said. The chubby kid's interest deflated, and he turned away. As Del's advance man, I was a miserable failure. "I . . . I . . . just know he hacked into the computers at the Department of Justice." My voice, which had risen in desperation at the beginning of the sentence, dropped to an embarrassed whisper.

"What part?" somebody asked.

"The FBI," I admitted. This was true. Del loved a challenge.

"He's a phreak?" The petite girl asked.

"He's a little strange," I admitted. "But he's a very accomplished hacker," I added.

"Lady, if he hacked the fibbies," said a burly kid, "he's a fucking guru." There were nods and murmurs of assent that encouraged me to think that Del would be welcomed with open arms here.

I left then, thinking how very young and sad and vulnerable they all looked. And frightened.

Chapter Twenty-two

I'D JUST PLANTED my bum on a barstool at Arnold's downtown when Kevin set a gin and tonic in front of me. What are friends for?

Maybe he'd noticed my grimace of pain when I hoisted myself onto the stool. Or maybe it was the angle at which I held my head to reduce the throbbing in my neck and shoulder. Red eyes? Runny nose? Any of these could have tipped off someone less observant than Kevin.

"Thangz," I said, blowing my nose. Through clogged ears I heard my speech thickening. "By drugs are weading off."

I fished in my bag and brought out a bottle of aspirin, shook out two, and downed them with a swig of gin. I felt around in the lint at the bottom of my purse and came up with a smooth green tablet that looked like an antihistamine, so I downed that, too.

"I feel bedder awready," I said.

"That's the spirit, Mrs. C," Kevin said. He took a sip of his own nonalcoholic drink and studied me over his straw. "Case getting you down?"

I confessed that I didn't think I was cut out for undercover work.

I told him what I'd been up to, and what I'd found out so far. He'd already heard from Al about my plunge into the Walnut Hills pool. While he went off to wait on some customers, I put my head back, closed my eyes, and enjoyed the sensation of my sinuses draining. It was the first time all day that gravity was working to my advantage.

"You ever watch *Sea Hunt?*" Kevin was back, and he seemed determined to add to my misery by tormenting me with non sequiturs.

"Yeah," I said, returning my head to its upright and locked position.

"You know when Mike Nelson came up too fast and he got the bends?" Kevin said. "It had something to do with pressure. I used to wonder if it was like a really bad cold."

I leveled my gaze at him. "Whatever happened to your enthusiasm for my new career? Whatever happened to, 'I'm behind you, Mrs. C., every step of the way'? To 'You need anything, Mrs. C., don't hesitate to call'? I'm trying to solve a murder case here, maybe two murder cases, maybe more, and you're speculating about some wacko water sickness Lloyd Bridges used to get in the sixties."

Kevin patted my hand. "I'm all ears, Mrs. C. But you know as well as I do that television is never irrelevant. You can learn a lot from watching television."

"Well, unless Mike Nelson taught you something about marine rope, I'm not interested," I said.

Kevin looked at me. "You know, there was this one episode where he had to rescue three people and make sure he got them up safely, so he tied this rope around all of them, the way mountain climbers do, and —."

"Was it marine rope?" I cut in. "Because unless it was, I'm not interested. Read my lips—not interested."

"It might have been what passed for marine rope in the sixties," he said. "What kind are you interested in?" He waved at a group that was headed out the door.

"I don't know," I said. "How many kinds of marine rope are there?"

"Well, you said the kid was strangled, right?"

"Yeah. What's that got to do with it?"

"Well, look. There are different types of rope. Two of the most common are nylon and polyester. If you knew which one of those it was, you might have some useful information."

"Why?" I didn't ask him how he knew this stuff. I never asked.

He got called to the end of the bar to fill a drink order. It was still early for the after-work crowd. I sucked on my lime wedge and tried to remember if I'd seen anything in Evie's house that might be classed as marine rope. I hadn't. I didn't think it could be disguised, either.

Kevin resumed our conversation without missing a beat—a trick that turns forgetful old ladies like me more surly than envious. I can't remember the beginnings of my own sentences half the time.

"Polyester has less stretch than nylon," he said. "Nylon is stronger, but it has more give to it, too."

"So you're saying—."

"I'm saying that if you wanted a rope to take some weight and not stretch, which might apply in a strangulation, you don't choose nylon," he said. Then he added, "So long as you know what you're doing. And of course, assuming that it was premeditated. So if the rope was nylon, which certainly isn't impossible, it could tell us that either the killer doesn't know anything about boats and boat ropes, or wasn't planning to use one to strangle Peter Baer. Or it might only tell us what he or she had available. Nylon is much more common. But it's also more expensive."

"Gosh," I said, "that explains everything. Good think I asked." But he had given me something to think about.

"Are ropes color-coded?" I asked, thinking about the different colors Arpad had reported—yellow in the Baer garage, orange on the body.

"Not really," he said. "Ropes used for tow lines and ski lines usually come in bright colors, so you can see them in the water."

"So would the average boat owner be as likely to own nylon as polyester?" I asked.

He shook his head. "Nylon's more common. Polyester might be used to tie stuff down with. I think maybe they use it to tow water skiers, too."

"So I couldn't just go to K-Mart and buy a polyester rope."

"Oh, they probably carry both nylon and polyester," he said, nodding at someone behind me. I wasn't about to unlock my neck to turn around. "Nylon's more common, but polyester isn't uncommon. Let me refresh that drink for you, Mrs. C." He took my glass and winked at me. "I'll just double the lime to pump up your vitamin C intake."

He returned with my drink, went off again to fill some orders, returned.

"So, Kev," I said. I lowered my voice and leaned toward him. "What do you know about New Life Ministries?"

"New Life, New Life," he repeated. He tapped his chin with an index finger. "Who's in charge?"

"The Reverend Vernon Armbruster," I said. "The right arm of God."

Kevin raised his eyebrows. "Say no more. I know the one you mean. I don't know much about him except that he, like all those fundamentalist yahoos, is rabidly homophobic."

"Come on, Kev," I said. "You must know something."

"No, really," he said. "He believes in curing homosexuality through prayer and meditation. Though I think he's got some kind of bogus doctor of aberrant sexuality on the payroll."

I thought of the man introduced as Dr. Maynard Clay. Since Joy had mentioned his ministerial credentials, I hadn't questioned the relevance of his medical ones. Did New Life have a particular need for a medical doctor on the payroll?

"What else?" I prodded Kevin. "Armbruster does a lot of anti-drug programs in the schools. Is he dealing on the side?"

"Hah! Don't I wish," Kevin said.

"Bilking widows out of their pensions? Distributing kiddie porn?"

Kevin shook his head over crossed arms. "Don't know. Isn't he the guy with the chimp?"

"Evie."

"Yeah, that's right. Eve. I caught his act one Sunday when I was channel surfing. That Evie, she's a pistol, as my grandmother would say."

"She certainly is," I agreed. "So, okay, Kevin, theologically speaking, where would you put Armbruster and his organization?" Kevin had begun his education in Catholic school, so I always referred theological questions to him.

"Probably a few steps right of the Pope, and you know how I feel about the Pope," he said. "You know what you should do? You should talk to Linda DeGenova. She's the pastor at Seven Hills Methodist. She's in the next room, killing time before a rehearsal dinner. Let me see if she's got a minute."

I let slide my opportunity to ask about the seven hills.

Kevin returned on my side of the bar with an attractive middle-aged brunette with a glass of white wine in her hand. She wore a dressy pantsuit of woven silk in muted violets, purples, and grays. Kevin introduced us, and she sat down next to me at the bar.

"Sorry," I said. "I know this is an imposition. I don't know how much information you can give me in a short time."

"What's it about?" she asked.

I told her that I was investigating the murder of one, maybe two, teenagers and the disappearances of two others. I explained that the only connection I had between them was a possible link to New Life Ministries.

"I'm not saying that New Life is involved in any way other than as a point of contact, you understand," I said. Or if I was, I wasn't saying it to her.

She nodded. She had wide-spaced dark eyes beneath fashionable large-framed glasses and broad cheeks decorated with faint freckles. "How can I help?" she asked.

"I just need to know something about New Life," I said. "What their reputation is, for example. I've actually worked there for two days as a volunteer, and I don't even know much about their take on religion, other than that they're fundamentalists."

She'd been looking down at the bar, as if to concentrate on what I was saying, but at that she looked up and shook her head. "They're not fundamentalist, they're evangelical," she said. "Most people confuse the two."

"What's the difference?" I asked.

She flashed me a smile. "In a nutshell? Most fundamentalists believe that the Bible, in its original state, is the Word of God and therefore inerrant. Most evangelicals believe, as other protestants do, that Christ is the Word of God incarnate. Most evangelicals will allow for the possibility of some errors, but not on spiritual questions. They believe, as we do, that the Bible requires interpretation."

"Because Jesus spoke in parables," I said.

"Yes, that's one reason," she said. "Jesus told the disciples, 'Unto you it is given to know the mysteries of God, but to others in parables, that seeing they might not see, and hearing they might not understand.' The fundamentalists are extremely anti-intellectual; the evangelicals, to varying degrees, less so."

"So the Moral Majority, Reagan's supporters, which are they?" I asked. "They seem pretty anti-intellectual to me."

She nodded as Kevin set down another glass of wine in front of her and picked up her empty glass.

"It's all relative, Cat," she said. "For example, Falwell was broad-minded enough to form that coalition, which included lots of other conservative Christians, even Catholics. That's why they had such a big impact on the elections last year. The fundamentalists would never do something like that. The neo-evangelicals trace their roots to Billy Graham, who appealed to a broad spectrum of Christian denominations. The fundamentalists regard the neo-evangelicals as sell-outs."

I thought of Evie. "You say the evangelicals aren't anti-intellectual. But they oppose evolution? Armbruster does."

She nodded. "He's kind of a maverick in that regard. Many evangelicals are willing to interpret the Bible loosely enough to allow for evolution. But Vernon Armbruster doesn't. He has some kind of bee in his bonnet about Darwin. Or at least he claims to. It makes for a good show."

"You've seen Evie perform?"

She smiled. "Oh, yes. I'm a great fan of hers. The odd thing is, he intends to use her to ridicule the idea that chimps and humans are related. But you only have to watch her for five minutes to be persuaded that they are. At least, if you're watching with an open mind. And behind the scenes, he treats her very much like a human child."

"Do you think he's insincere? What kind of person is he?"

She thought for a moment, drawing a finger through the ring left by glass on the bar.

"I can't make up my mind whether he's insincere about evolution," she said at last. "I don't think he's insincere about his religious beliefs generally. He's certainly ambitious, and he's a genius at promoting his church. He's quite successful."

"Is he well respected? By other clergy, I mean."

She laughed. "You're really pinning me down, aren't you? He's pretty well respected, I think. But he wouldn't be elected chair of any interdenominational groups because he wouldn't be trusted to put the needs of the group ahead of his own church and his own agenda. If you want to know what I think of him, I can't say that I like him, but he's meeting a lot of needs with his various special ministries, like the youth ministries."

"But how does he manage to get into the schools to put on these anti-drug assemblies?"

She made a face. "Oh, Cat, I don't know. He probably has church members on the various school boards. I wouldn't put it past him to target school boards for membership recruitment."

"So what's your take on these youth ministries of his? Are they legit?"

"I'm sure they are, depending on what you mean by 'legit,'" she said. "If you mean that spiritually needy kids find a place to get their needs met, meet other kids, and have some fun, then I'm sure they're effective."

"So it's not a cult?"

She laughed. "A Reverend Ted cult? I won't say that the kids don't idolize him, but I wouldn't call it a cult."

She was getting to the bottom of her glass, and I didn't want to detain her much longer. "Okay, so, bottom line. If I'm a kid, why should I join a youth group at Seven Hills Methodist instead of at New Life Ministries?"

She leaned back against her barstool and regarded me, still smiling. "Because we're more interested in moral development, in helping to shape young people who think for themselves, who use their God-given reason and imagination in conjunction with their faith to solve moral dilemmas. We have fewer rules."

"You don't want God for a co-pilot?" I asked.

"For a co-pilot, yes," she said seriously, "but not for a pilot. The problem with having God for a pilot is that one day you turn around to see who's flying the plane and it isn't God at all but some ordinary Joe who claims to be speaking for God."

"God's right arm," I said.

"Oh, please," she said, and grinned. "Don't get me started. You'll make me remember all the jokes I've heard about that. I have a colleague, who shall remain nameless, who calls himself 'God's big toe.' Which reminds me of two other reasons why you should join our youth group instead of theirs."

"Yeah? Why?"

She winked at me. "We have a better sense of humor and we give better parties."

Chapter Twenty-three

MOSES AND I were sitting on his couch, our feet on the coffee table in defiance of Charisse, with a beagle and a bowl of popcorn between us. On my other side was a growing mound of used tissues.

"I gotta admit, he's got something," I said, as the preacher emerged from behind the podium as if propelled, by the force of his words closer to his audience.

"Yeah," Moses said. "A forty-dollar haircut and a four hundred-dollar suit."

The preacher's voice rose and fell like a roller coaster. Now it was hushed. "But having created all of this beauty, all of these wondrous and amazing things out of the sheer exuberance of His imagination, God had one thing more to create. One thing. And that would be the most beautiful and most wondrous thing of all because it would mirror the beauty and wonder of its creator. This one thing that He would create would not merely suggest His power, like the lightning bolt, or His glory, like the sun. It would not merely imply His majesty, like the mountains, or His vastness, like the oceans, or His grace, like the rainbow, or His mystery, like the rose."

The preacher's voice picked up speed and volume. "No!" He flung an arm wide. "This one thing that was yet to be created would allow all of creation to gaze upon the face of God Almighty Himself! For the Book of Genesis tells us, 'And God said, Let us make man in our image, after our likeness.' And then it tells us, 'So God created man in his own image, in the image of God created he him.' That's four times we're told that man was created in God's likeness! Four times! And yet we're not told what the sun looked like, or the stars, or the oceans. The grasses and herbs, the fruit trees, the moving creatures, the fowl, the whales—none of these creations merits the kind of specificity devoted to man. Why? Because none of them was created in the image of God!"

Up to this point, the Reverend Armbruster seemed to be oblivious to the camera, speaking to an audience visible in wide shots and cutaways. But now, he raised his head to make eye contact with the camera. He spoke more conversationally.

"Now, I know that there are those who would say that man was only part of a long-range plan of God's—that God didn't create Adam 'out of the ground,' as the Bible says, in the way we think of it, like a sculptor creating a statue." Here he scooped an imaginary handful of dust. "'No,' they say, 'that's not the way it happened at all.' We're not intended to take literally this account in the Book of Genesis. No, the way it happened, they say, is that God created amoebas, and over time, the amoebas turned into fish, and the fish turned into lizards, and the lizards turned into birds and horses and apes, and the apes turned into man. Anyone who believes differently, they say, is confusing fairy tale with reality. Now, you all look like reasonable people." He scanned the audience beyond the camera. "I ask you to consider this account of lizards turning into men, and then compare that image with the one of a magisterial God sculpting a man out of clay. Tell me, which one do you think is the fairy tale?" He opened his arms wide.

The audience exploded with laughter and applause.

He let the commotion continue for several minutes, then held out his hands, palms down. "All right. All right. I know. They tell you that they have scientific evidence that the lizard became the man. Scientific evidence! As if that settled the matter! Well, my friends, I need only remind you of the past errors of so-called scientific evidence to start you wondering. I don't deny that they have fossils recording the presence of creatures now extinct. I don't deny that some of those creatures may be difficult to classify according to our modern systems of classification. I'm content to recall the infinite creativity of the Creator who called forth from his mind such a magnificent abundance of plants and animals. I don't deny the skeletal remains of apelike humans or human-like apes." He shrugged dismissively. "I believe that God created many wondrous creatures, among them moths that look like birds, lizards that look like leaves, flowers that look like butterflies. And yet, we can distinguish each of these from the other."

He paused, as if thinking. "The evolutionists, for we might as well call them that, believe that when the Bible says 'day' in the Book of Genesis, it doesn't mean 'day' at all but decades—indeed, millennia. Why Moses, its author, he who received from God Ten Commandments quite remarkable for their clarity—why Moses should choose to give us such a slippery account of the single most important event in the history of creation—creation itself—is a mystery they cannot sufficiently explain." He rubbed his chin, as if pondering this enigma.

Then his mood changed again. "But friends, don't take *my* word for this reading of the Book of Genesis," he said, eyes twinkling now. "Let God enlighten your own hearts and minds. Use your own eyes. I give you—." He made a sweeping gesture with his arm, his voice pitched like a carnival barker's. "—The e-volutionists' Eve!"

Evie scampered out on all fours, white lace underpants prominent under a stiff, gathered slip and a bright red dress with a Peter Pan collar, puffed sleeves, and a sash tied in a bow at the waist. She wore anklets trimmed with lace, and they didn't look like they would survive another sixty seconds of abuse. She was dragging a boxy little red purse.

The audience went wild, shouting, clapping, and hooting. Finally, the racket resolved itself into a chorus. "E-vie! E-vie! E-vie!" they called.

Evie capered over to a bright red box at stage right, dropped her purse, opened the box, and extracted a tambourine. Leaving one sock behind, she ran upstage, raised up on two legs and danced a little hoochie-koochie, beating the tambourine and grinning at the audience over her shoulder.

"Very nice, Eve," Armbruster said. The audience quieted. "You dance divinely. And that's a very pretty dress."

Evie mugged for the audience, opening her lips and showing her teeth.

"Did Adam buy you that dress?"

Evie shook her head with emphasis, still grinning.

"No? Is he still mad at you?"

Evie's head bobbed in an exaggerated affirmative.

"Well, I can see why." Armbruster's voice took on a sterner tone. "You mustn't disobey God, you know."

Evie shook her head.

"I hope you've learned your lesson."

Evie showed her teeth—an ambiguous response, I thought.

"That's a very nice purse you have."

Evie scampered to retrieve her purse.

"What do you have in there?" Armbruster drew closer to Evie and looked down on her.

Evie opened the purse and removed a powder puff. She dabbed at her nose, causing a visible cloud of powder, and laughed along with the audience.

"What else do you have?"

Evie rummaged in the purse and removed a lipstick and mirror. She set the purse down, uncapped the lipstick, held the mirror up, and drew a kind of clown's mouth around her own.

"Very pretty," Armbruster said. "Is that all you have in your purse?" He pretended to be trying to see inside the purse. Evie turned away from him, blocking his view, and the audience tittered.

Evie made a big show of searching her small purse, then finally turning it upside down and shaking it. A bright red apple fell out and rolled to the edge of the stage. She went after it and sat down to eat it.

The crowd roared as Armbruster folded his arms and shook his head in disapproval. When the laughter died down, he said, "You know, Evie, you're setting a very bad example for your grandchildren here." His gesture swept the audience. "All of these good people are your grandchildren and they look to you to teach them to walk in the way of the Lord."

Evie dropped the apple, galloped back to the box, and returned with a large black leather-bound book, on the cover of which the words "HOLY BIBLE" were prominent. She sat down, turned the book upside down, opened it, and, holding it between her toes, pretended to read.

Armbruster gave an exaggerated sigh, bent, and turned the book right side-up. "I'm afraid, Evie, you're not doing a very good job of persuading these good people that you're one of them. Isn't there anything you can do to convince them that you're a creature with intelligence and reason, heart and soul?"

Evie appeared to consider this, dropping the Bible and working her hands rhythmically as she thought. Then she ran back to the spot where she'd dropped the tambourine, and reprised her hoochie-koochie dance.

Armbruster turned to the audience with an elaborate shrug. "I guess that's the best she can do." With the bluff heartiness of a talk show host, he gestured toward Evie, and said, "Your grandmother, friends! Let's hear it for Evie!"

The crowd applauded. Evie made an awkward curtsey, then exited on all fours, stage right.

Armbruster had more to say, but I'd heard enough. I picked up the remote and hit "Stop."

"I kept wishing she'd brain him with the tambourine," I said.

Moses caught my wrist. He was leaning forward. "Wait, Cat. Run it back a little ways. I want to see something."

I handed him the remote, and he played the tape backward, stopping at the point when Armbruster was challenging Evie to demonstrate her humanity. Moses replayed the tape, then hit "Pause."

"There!" he said. "See that, Cat?"

He started the tape again, then paused it again.

"And that?"

"What am I supposed to be seeing?"

"Well, I'm no expert," he said, "so I can't be sure. But it looks to me like she's signing."

"What do you mean?"

"ASL," he said, pointing. "It looks to me like Evie's using American Sign Language."

"No shit!" I leaned forward too. "What's she saying?"

He shook his head. "I don't know much. But the only thing I recognize looks like 'I love you.'"

Chapter Twenty-four

I PUT IN a few hours of surveillance on Saturday afternoon, sitting in the parking lot at Christ Hospital with a pair of binoculars, just me and my head cold. At the end of three hours, all I had to show for it was a sore butt and a mountain of damp tissues on the seat next to me. Kids had come and gone, some of them teens but most younger, and a few of the usual suspects had put in an appearance—not only the Reverend Ted, whom I'd expected, but also the Reverends Armbruster, Harald and Higginbotham and Reverend Dr. Clay. But the most suspicious thing I'd seen was a littering incident. The perp was Evie, and I guessed she'd been scolded, because I saw her waddle back to where she'd dropped the banana peel and pick it up.

There were no cars left in the parking lot at New Life, and I was turning the key in my ignition when a red Toyota turned into the lot. I hadn't been paying attention, so I hadn't seen the driver, and now he or she was only a dark shape, even in the binoculars. A teenaged girl came out of the building wearing a backpack. I could see that she was blond, and dressed in a bright pink parka, but when she stood talking to the driver, the car cut her off from my line of vision. They didn't talk long. She abruptly reappeared behind the car, walked to the passenger's side, and got in. I saw her slump down in her seat, pushing the hair back from her face and then resting her hand on the back of her head.

I pressed the binoculars to my forehead. Was she wearing a bracelet? Damn, I just couldn't see.

She talked, and the car didn't move for a minute or two. Then, it backed up, and drove out of the parking lot, turning right on Auburn.

As soon as I saw the driver, I ducked. It was David Green.

I slammed the gear shift into reverse, and took off in pursuit of the red Toyota.

I trailed it onto I-71 to the Norwood Lateral. It exited at Reading Road. Half a mile later, it turned into a Wendy's drive-through lane.

This was a cheap date, I thought, if that's what it was. I parked and waited, then followed again as the red Toyota exited and turned down Reading. A few blocks later, it turned into the lot of an apartment complex—not one of the originals that dotted this older neighborhood, but not a new one either. Not that I cared about architecture or landscaping in my business; no, all I cared about was the level of security and the age of the locks. I pulled into the lot of a convenience store across the street.

I snapped a few pictures of the happy couple with the small camera my daughter Franny had given me for my birthday, along with a lecture about respecting people's rights to privacy. And there, through the telephoto lens, I glimpsed a small band of black and white just below the bright pink of the parka sleeve: the girl was wearing a bracelet.

In truth, the couple didn't look all that happy. The kid wore a sour expression familiar to any mother who's had the misfortune to live with teenagers, and David Green looked downright grim.

I checked my watch. It was time to go to the airport and collect Del. In fact, it was now past time to go to the airport.

I hesitated, indecisive. Was the girl in any danger? There was no reason other than my naturally suspicious nature and the trend of recent events to think that she was.

I rummaged through my handbag and came up with a folded piece of paper. I flattened it against the steering wheel, and ran my finger down the list of names and addresses I'd culled from the personnel files at New Life the day before, until I came to David Green's address: 2260D W. Glenview. I wasn't exactly sure where that was, but I was sure it wasn't where we were now.

So was it the girl who lived here? A friend of hers or his?

With another glance at my watch, I opened the car door, unfolded myself, and then sprinted across the street, dodging traffic. I checked a set of mailboxes whose general appearance did not inspire confidence. On 2260D was a name, hand-printed in fading purple letters: D. N. Green.

My eyes followed the cracked cement walk up a rusted wrought-iron banister to the second floor. The curtains in the window of 2260D, colorless in the twilight, were firmly closed. The scent of meat frying and the sound of canned laughter from a television set gave the place a benign, domestic air. I must be crazy, I thought, to consider that somebody might be contemplating murder in 2260D.

And anyway, what could I do? Even if I showed up at the door with a good story, the best I could hope for was an introduction to the kid and a plausible explanation for her presence, which might or might not be true.

Why couldn't a nice young man like David take one of the New Life kids home for a visit, after all? What was wrong with that? And if he was offering her a shoulder to cry on, well, that was what ministers did, wasn't it? Even ministers' sidekicks should be commended for taking an interest in the kids, shouldn't they?

The only person who could infiltrate the ministry and tell me what was really going on there was at that moment touching down on a runway at the Greater Cincinnati International Airport. I dialed the cops, reported a domestic disturbance at 2260D Reading Road, and gave my name as Eichenbaum, who, according to the mailboxes, lived at 2260A Reading Road. Then I drove to the airport.

Planes were never late at the Cincinnati airport. They could even be early. But this one had been routed through Atlanta, and that gave me a little breathing time.

Del was the last one off the plane. He loped along, both arms wrapped around a large attaché case. A duffel bag hung from one shoulder.

He gave me an awkward hug and launched into a diatribe about some bagbiter in cowboy boots who kept kicking the case during the flight.

I smiled. "Nice to have you back, Del."

He flashed me a rare smile, and gave me the full benefit of his Texas drawl. "Nice to be back, Cousin Cat."

On the way home, I filled him in on the case, knowing that I wouldn't be accorded much "face time," as he called it, and wanting to take advantage of his almost undivided attention. This was a technique I'd practiced for years with my own kids, whose attention had been no easier to capture than Del's. If I'd ever divorced Fred, my kids would have heard about it in the car between the orthodontist's office and the ballpark.

He only interrupted to ask questions which he considered crucial. I couldn't answer any of them. I couldn't even translate them.

"Look, Cat, if I'm going in there, I need to know whether the stuff they've got is hardwarily reliable and if the software is crufty or not," he said.

"I couldn't tell you," I said. "You'll have to figure that out for yourself."

"Okay," he said. "Control Q."

At the last minute, I remembered that his favored meal while he was working was a bowl of cereal, so I pulled into the UDF for some milk. While I was there, I cruised the drugs, and decided to try a new antihistamine that promised me instantaneous relief.

Standing in the checkout line, I heard Leon before I saw him.

"Sh-she a nice g-g-girl," he said, "b-but we just f-f-friends."

"That's not what *I* heard," a male voice said, insinuatingly. "I heard she was your girlfriend and you were taking her to the junior prom."

Leon was washing the windows in the ice cream parlor section of the store. Leon was a man with many irons in the fire, and you never knew when you'd run into him on the job. The boy who was talking to him, a broad-faced kid in a letter jacket who was taking up more space than he was entitled to, sat at a nearby table with three friends, two boys and a girl. The boys were egging their buddy on with laughter. The girl was making feeble protests and giggling. I took in the whole situation in an instant, and the blood rose to my temples.

"Leon!" I spoke more sharply than I intended, and adjusted my tone when I added, "Got a minute?"

"S-s-sure, M-Miz Cat," Leon said, looking relieved to be extricated from the conversation.

I scanned the teenagers, and then nodded at the table farthest from them.

"Over there," I said.

When Leon had joined me at the table, I leaned toward him and spoke in a low voice that I hoped was just loud enough to carry. "Got a little job for you tomorrow," I said.

"Is it one of th-them st-st-stake things, M-Miz Cat?" he asked.

I shook my head. "It's a little more dangerous than that." I let my voice caress the word "dangerous." I could sense the stillness that told me the four teenagers were tuned in. "It's an undercover job."

Someone at the other table made a remark, and a male voice said, "Hanson, you're so queer!" General laughter followed.

I leaned in closer to Leon and dropped my voice. "My cousin Del's in town. He's going undercover at New Life Ministries. Ever hear of them?"

He nodded, excited. "Th-they got a m-m-monkey," he said.

"That's the one," I agreed. "Del knows what to do, but I want you there as back-up."

"B-b-back-up," he said, committing the phrase to memory. I could expect a phone call from his mother later. He frowned. "W-will it be after ch-church? Momma don't like me to m-miss no ch-ch-church."

"Just ask her if you can go to a different church tomorrow," I said. I glanced with exaggerated suspicion at the group of teenagers, which reacted as if I'd touched their collective antennae. "Better yet, I'll talk to her."

I stood up, hoping the carton of milk, swollen nose, and puffy eyes weren't ruining my street cred, hoping I just looked like the spy who came in from the cold. "And Leon," I said, in a voice just loud enough to carry, "don't bring your gun. I don't want you packing."

He stared up at me in confusion. "I d-don't have no—," he started. I cut my eyes in the direction of the teenagers. He turned his head to look at them, then looked back at me. "D-don't worry, M-Miz Cat," he said in a voice clear as a bell. "I'll leave the g-gun at home."

I left the store satisfied. I'd be sending Daniel into the lion's den tomorrow, but I really did believe that in crucial matters, God was looking out for him. Apparently, God thought either that a little teasing was insignificant in the grand scheme of things, or that it built character. Me, I thought Leon already had all the character a person could need.

Quite often, God and I didn't see eye to eye.

I climbed into the car, blew my nose, and tossed the tissue into the backseat, where I'd moved the rest of them to make space for Del.

Del looked at me in the dull light coming through the store window.

"You got a cold or something?" he asked.

I managed to get Del to go out for dinner, but only because I took him to the China Chef for what he called "laser chicken," though the menu called it Kung Pao chicken.

Over dessert at the DQ, Del dug around in his attaché case and produced a crumpled box, haphazardly wrapped in baby shower paper and sporting a mangled bow. "Just a little something I crufted together," he said. "For your new business."

I unwrapped a thin, rectangular piece of flexible plastic about the size of a cocktail napkin.

"Gee, Del," I said. "You shouldn't have." I turned it over on my palm, thinking that it looked vaguely familiar. It was labeled on one side, and on the label was what I took to be a set of instructions, printed by a myopic spider.

"Okay, look," he said. "Say you have this J. Random Bagbiter whose files you want to snoop into."

"Yeah," I said. I envisioned a set of army surplus file cabinets like the ones in my office, and I wondered it this object would do for a set of locked files what a credit card would do to my back door.

"But say these files are protected by a password, see?"

He'd lost me but I was damned if I was going to admit it. I pretended to study the object over my chocolate-dipped custard.

"So to unlock the files, you need to know which foos of all the possible foos got assigned as the password. So, you run the app on this floppy." He took it from me and waved it in the air for emphasis. "Cruncha, cruncha, cruncha, and in no time—moby win— automagically."

"So, what you're saying is, I put this thing in the computer?" I asked.

He narrowed his eyes at me, and shoved the last of his cone down his throat.

"Let's go home," he said.

At home, he stood in my office door, surveying all the equipment he'd installed there, and muttering imprecations. I didn't know what he was complaining about; it was just the way he'd left it, only furrier. I retreated, knowing that he wanted to be alone to commune with the digital gods.

I called Gussie Baer to give her a report, and to tell her I was undercover at New Life.

"Peter's name doesn't appear on any of their lists," I told her, "but several missing kids who wore the same bracelet he wore are there, and I want to find out if there's a connection."

"I don't know, Cat," she said. "George and Vanessa are more Catholic than God. But I guess if he'd jumped ship, he wouldn't broadcast it within the family. Still, I like to think he would've told me."

Her feelings were natural, and I didn't comment. I promised to let her know what I found out.

I wanted to think about the case, but damn! 2260D Reading Road was calling me. When I couldn't stand it anymore, I called Moses, but he wasn't in. So I called Leon. He admitted that he didn't have anything planned for the next hour or so, and agreed on an outing. That gave me an opportunity to talk to his mother, who more or less gave me carte blanche, as long as her son didn't get arrested.

"I'll make sure he keeps a low profile," I reassured her.

I didn't see any red Toyotas in the lot at the apartment complex on Reading Road, but I wasn't going to take any chances. That's why I'd brought my secret weapon: Leon.

I'd had Leon bring his salesman's kit so he'd be on familiar ground.

"Start with 2260C next door," I instructed him, "so nobody will be suspicious. Just give them your usual pitch and show them your samples—you know, like you do with us. Remind them that St. Patrick's Day is coming up, and Easter, and make them worry about not having the appropriate greeting card on hand when the occasion arises."

That I bothered to instruct him at all betrayed my nerves, not his. Leon could sell Easter cards to the Chinese, Kwanza cards to the Arabs, and solstice cards to the Pope.

"B-b-but Miz C-Cat," he said, "how I'm g-going to d-d-deliver them? Momma d-don't let me ride out the n-n-neighborhood on my b-bike."

"I'll drive you," I said.

I hadn't expected it to take so long, but I'd forgotten how good a salesman he was. Leon disappeared inside 2260C and emerged twenty minutes later, clutching an order form and grinning. He waved at me and made an elaborate gesture in the direction of 2260D. I ducked back behind a bush I couldn't identify in the dark, and discovered that it had thorns attached.

He stood outside of 2260D for some minutes, then turned in my direction with an exaggerated shrug. I waved him on to the next apartment, glimpsing a new opportunity for cover in his presence.

But nobody answered the door there, either, so I waved him down.

I posted him at the mailboxes. "Stand here," I said, "and pretend that you're just hanging out, waiting for your mother to come pick you up. The guy you're looking out for is medium height and build, sandy blond hair, beard, and moustache, with glasses. You see him, you stop him and give him your best sales pitch. Raise your voice, if you can. Don't let him get past you without buying the deluxe collection."

He nodded. "B-but M-Miz Cat, somebody else c-come along, I c-c-can't sell them n-nothing?"

"Sure," I said. "Go ahead. Just don't let our pigeon get past you while you're putting the screws on somebody else."

I could see this was too metaphorical for Leon, who began looking around for pigeons.

"I mean," I said, "just don't let this one guy get past you. Oh, and Leon—."

"Yes, M-Miz Cat?"

"Anything goes wrong, remember, you've never seen me before in your life."

"Never seen you b-b-before in my life," he repeated, committing the line to memory.

At the door to 2260D, I glanced around, and then eased my pick-locks out of my pocket. These were my back-up set, since when I'd gone to retrieve them from my handbag earlier, I'd discovered that my regular set had been purloined. I was pretty sure I knew who'd purloined them, and I was trying not to imagine David's face in the morning when he went to fix Evie's breakfast and discovered the refrigerator and all the cabinet doors standing open and a trail of darkening banana peels leading from the kitchen to Evie's loft.

One soft click and I was in. A floor lamp provided dim illumination. First things first. I pulled on a pair of plastic gloves as I surveyed the living room, and spotted a long set of curtains across the room. The curtains proved to conceal a sliding glass door to a balcony, with a drop to the ground that would be bone-jarring but manageable. I thumbed up the lock on the glass door, in case I needed to disappear in a hurry, and slid the door open far enough to provide me with an emergency exit. Then I pulled the curtain back into place.

I turned back to the room, which looked more like a motel room than someone's residence. "Spartan" would be a euphemism for its décor. At a glance I could see everything but the bathroom—a sofa bed, a two-drawer nightstand/end table, an old Formica table with a couple of chrome chairs, one moth-eaten armchair, an army surplus footlocker that doubled as a coffee table, a small television set resting atop a bookshelf made from old boards and cement blocks, and a kitchenette so small that you couldn't open the oven door without backing into the refrigerator. No art prints or posters on the walls, no family photos on the shelves, not a single note stuck to the refrigerator—nothing to tell me who David Green really was and what he was up to with the braceleted girl in the pink parka.

I started with the bathroom, hoping to get a clue from a prescription bottle at the very least, or at best, a stash of drugs or pornography. I found neither.

Replacing the lid on the toilet tank, I swore under my breath. What kind of guy didn't have a single prescription drug in his medicine chest? He did have a contact lens container, but it didn't appear to hold anything more revealing than contact lens solution.

He also had two boxes of prescription lenses, which held—big surprise—prescription lenses. And I almost didn't notice the significance of them. My eyes had brushed the part of the label where the prescription was indicated and I was putting the box back on the shelf when my brain, working in that slo-mo so familiar to the elderly, snagged. Green? I examined the box again. The lenses were green. So what color were his eyes really? And why did he want green ones? To set off his blond hair? To match his name? To match a fake driver's license?

It was a small detail, but interesting nonetheless.

I went back to the living room and checked out the closet. I found a few shirts and sweaters hanging there, along with two pairs of slacks, two ties, and a jacket. A set of built-in shelves held neat stacks of underwear, socks, t-shirts, sweatshirts, and jeans.

The man travels light, I thought.

I continued my preliminary survey by looking inside the footlocker, where I found a few sweaters, one scarf, and a pair of heavy gloves, and the refrigerator, where I found a carton of milk, a loaf of bread, and a package of American cheese. The freezer compartment, kitchen cabinets, and oven were all equally unrevealing. Or rather, they revealed that David Green didn't cook and didn't eat at home much. I found the Wendy's bag and two crushed paper cups in the trash. What hadn't I found? I hadn't found drugs, pornography, condoms, love letters, forged papers, a family Bible, a firearm—registered or unregistered, a snapshot of any kind, a diary, a date book, a computer disk, a collection of black-and-white braided bracelets, an address book, a kidnapped teenager, or a postcard from anybody, saying "Wish You Were Here." But who's counting?

It was time to dig deeper, but as I was opening the closet door for another look, a high-pitched voice reached me from somewhere outside.

"—b-b-because lotta c-c-card c-collections, you only g-get b-b-birthdays and g-get wells," it was saying. "B-b-but we g-got Valentimes, and Easter c-cards, and S-S-Saint P-Patrick's Day, and even H-Halloween."

I was slipping through the door onto the balcony and sliding the door closed as I heard the scrape of a key in the lock.

I heard David Green's voice say, "That so?"

I was over the balcony rail and hanging by the bars when Leon said, "Uh-huh, p-plus we g-got this other c-c-collection, it's all f-family c-cards, like, M-m-mother's Day and F-father's Day and special c-cards for your b-brothers and s-sisters on their b-birthdays."

I hit the ground and rolled. Somewhere a dog began to bark.

When Leon rejoined me in the car, he was beaming. "I g-got t-two orders!" he reported. "That m-man you s-s-spying on, he s-so n-nice! I h-hope you ain't going to m-make no trouble for him, M-Miz Cat."

I brushed some mud off one knee and said, "I'll wait until he's paid you, Leon. How's that?"

But if I was planning to make trouble for David Green, I'd have to have more to make trouble with than I had now. The most suspicious thing about him was that he was living like a transient. That, however, struck me as extremely suspicious.

I dropped Leon off and went home.

I sat down on the living room floor to sort through all of my notes on the Peter Baer case and see if I could make some sense of them. I thought perhaps if I spread everything out in front of me, I'd see something I hadn't seen before.   The new antihistamines I'd taken seemed to be working like a charm, and my head felt clearer than it had in days.

Chapter Twenty-five

I WOKE WITH a start. I had a nice low-angle view of my living room. Sidney lay curled in an armchair across from me, sleeping. In the foreground, out of focus, was a small brown blob. I sat up, taking with me a small Post-it that clung to my cheek. My notes had spread to the far corners of the room, as if blown there by a small tornado. The brown blob resolved itself into a dead mouse. On the couch behind me, Sadie snored softly at one end, and Sophie twitched in her sleep at the other.

There was a tap on the door, and then it opened and Kevin walked in. With all of the piercing deductive clarity common to trained detectives on downers, I deduced that Kevin had knocked before and awakened me.

"I saw all the lights on, so I figured you were up," he said, studying me. "But you're not, are you?"

"I hope not," I said.

He squatted down and peered at the mouse.

"Shouldn't you have it in an evidence bag?" he asked. "It's organic matter."

"What time is it?" I asked, rubbing the back of my neck. I didn't want to risk standing up because I wasn't sure I could make it. My body ached all over.

"Around two-thirty," he said. "Del get in okay?"

I nodded in the direction of the office, where we could hear little chattering sounds reminiscent of tap-dancing chipmunks.

I began collecting paper, starting with the one decorating my face. He looked around. "Looks like you slept through the conga line."

"Looks like it," I admitted.

He pointed at the corpse. "Shall I—?"

"You're a real pal," I said.

He'd probably tossed out a few drunks earlier that evening, but now he took the mouse's tail delicately between thumb and forefinger, lifted it, and bore it away. I heard the back door open and close. He returned mouseless.

He got down on his hands and knees and helped me gather my notes.

"What's this?" he asked, frowning at a piece of notebook paper. From where I sat, I could tell that whatever was written on it was not in my handwriting.

He handed it to me.

"Oh," I said. "Peter's music collection. Quite a range, isn't it?" I handed it back.

He sat back on his heels and looked at me. "*This* was Peter Baer's music collection? The stuff he owned?"

"Well," I said, "the Baers have money."

"Cat, he was gay," he said.

"Oh, please," I said. "You see the world through lavender-colored glasses. He wasn't gay. He had a perfectly attractive girlfriend. And how the hell you think you can tell somebody's sexual preference from their musical tastes is beyond me. Give me that."

I plucked the paper from between his fingers.

"Orientation," he said.

"What?"

"We use 'sexual orientation,' now, Cat, not 'sexual preference,'" he said. "Nobody *prefers* to be gay." His face was serious. "You think I didn't have a 'perfectly attractive girlfriend' when I was his age? Her name was Mary Beth Zucchero. She was a cheerleader and homecoming queen."

I looked at him in consternation. Kevin wasn't the sensitive type. If he had been, we'd never have become friends, since foot-in-mouth disease is a chronic condition of mine. But I was bound to cross the line with him from time to time.

"Oh, Kevin, I—."

"She beat me out by three votes," he said with a straight face.

"It was the rented tux," I said.

He squinted, as if calling up the picture of himself at eighteen. The truth is that most straight people wouldn't guess that Kevin was gay. He liked to camp it up among friends, but in public, he seemed the same as any other guy, only better looking. "The pants were too short and the sleeves were too long," he said. "But the really cute guy at the tux rental place said I looked terrific."

"Plus, she got the corsage," I pointed out.

He sighed. "And all I got was a green carnation." He shook his head. "Girl never did have any taste in clothes. Her little brother always told her what to wear."

He sat crosslegged now, straightening papers.

"So where is she now, this Mary Beth Zucchero?" I asked.

"Somewhere in the Bay Area," he said. "She met the love of her life in college, and they've been together ever since."

"He anything like you?" I asked.

He considered. "In some ways, yeah," he said, "she is." Then he gestured at the paper he was holding. "But seriously, Mrs. C., the kid was gay. No straight male teenager owns Judy Garland and Barbra Streisand records."

"But, look. He owns the Beatles, Charlie Byrd, and Aaron Neville."

"And show music. *My Fair Lady. Camelot.*"

"Phil Collins, Huey Lewis, Elton John?"

He started laughing. "Elton John. Right."

I frowned. "What? You mean Elton John is—?"

"No, look, it doesn't matter about those guys. It's the divas—Garland and Streisand in particular."

"Are you telling me that certain musical tastes are programmed into the genes?"

He shrugged. "I can't explain it," he said. "But I know what I know. Some gay men can't stand them, of course. But a male teenager who likes them enough to add them to his collection? The kid is gay, whether he realizes it yet or not."

"You think it's connected to his death?"

"I don't know," he said. "But gay teenagers have a high mortality rate. Of course, most of it's suicide—probably a third of the total of all teen suicides."

"But this was murder," I pointed out. "You think he went out cruising and got into something dangerous?"

He shrugged. "I guess that's what you have to find out."

I felt overwhelmed. I stared into space while Kevin sorted papers. I was trying to adjust my mental image of the athlete, student government leader, computer whiz, good Catholic, model grandson, boyfriend and buddy to accommodate this new piece of information. And I still wasn't sure I believed Kevin.

Kevin broke in. "Look, Mrs. C., he's everything he was before—and then some," he said. "Whatever he was before, he could have been all of those things sincerely—even a boyfriend."

"You're saying he probably didn't know?"

He shook his head. "No, I'm not saying that. He was probably old enough and smart enough to have a good idea. Younger kids just know that something is wrong with them, but they don't know what it is. At Peter's age these days, it's hard not to know."

"But he must have been miserable!" I said. My chest ached, and for once, it wasn't a lung problem. "Kevin, his dad is some big muckety-muck in the Catholic diocese."

"Tell me about it," he said.

I reached for Peter's daily planner. "He used to go someplace on Saturday afternoons," I said. "Does that mean anything to you?"

"Saturday afternoons? No."

"I spent the afternoon watching the ministry, but it was hard to tell what was going on. Most of the kids were younger, though. Maybe I'm barking up the wrong tree. Maybe he was out cruising. Or—wait! Maybe he had a boyfriend he went to see." I flipped through the planner. "Here," I said, and offered the book to Kevin. "Every other Saturday afternoon, there's a notation: 'P.' Maybe 'P' was his boyfriend."

Kevin turned the pages, studying the entries. "Possible."

"What about you? Did you have a boyfriend?"

He shook his head. "I didn't have the guts," he said. Then he gave me a wry smile. "But I spent a lot of time with Father McCarthy."

My voice was shocked. "Fooling around?"

"Certainly not," he said. "Or at least, not quite. There was a lot of physical contact, which I explained to myself in various ways, and he probably did, too. He was a priest, after all. He was really devout and everything. But he was only about ten years older than I was."

"Shit," I said.

We sat in silence for a minute, Kevin lost in memories and I—well, I was handicapped by a sixty-one-year-old brain drained by motherhood and slow to respond appropriately to change. I wanted to ask if Kevin had ever considered suicide, but I wasn't sure I really wanted to know the answer.

I looked around. "Somewhere here, there's a note," I said. "Wait, there it is!" I picked up the small, accordion-folded slip of paper which now bore a tiny brown spot that might have been mouse blood. I unfolded it, and read it aloud. "'Can't do this anymore. Maybe I'll see you sometime. P.' Maybe the boyfriend broke up with him. If 'P' was a person he saw on Saturdays, Peter should have seen him on the Saturday he disappeared, but there's no notation in the planner."

"Yeah, and then what?"

"Shit, I don't know. Maybe he was so upset over the break-up, he went out cruising, and then—you know, got himself in trouble."

"Maybe," Kevin conceded.

"There's too fucking many 'maybes' in this story."

"Well," Kevin said, "let's play the Glad Game. Let's be glad you have such a challenging case to work on, because it will really build your investigative skills."

At this moment, a shadow fell across the papers. Cousin Del loomed in the doorway like the Thing from Another Planet, wearing that vacant look that the pod people got in *Invasion of the Body Snatchers*, after their brains had been drained.

"Del," I said, "you own any records by Judy Garland or Barbra Streisand?"

"Who?"

Chapter Twenty-six

IT WAS JUST as well we had Leon along. He was the only one of us with any recent experience with religious ritual. He looked natty in his Sunday best. Delbert wore jeans, sneakers, a t-shirt that said, "Heaven Is Just Another Mainframe," and the sour expression he always wore when he was forced to emerge from "hack mode," as he called it. But his truculence was overmatched by my own, and I felt sure that anyone who looked at me would know that I despise pale green polyester only slightly less than I despise pantyhose, which were even at that moment slowly descending toward my crotch.

"Y'all s-s-s'posed to look happy!" Leon admonished us, adjusting his tie. "You g-goin' to church!"

"You can be happy for all of us," I said. I checked my little Diane to make sure it was loaded, and zipped it into an inside pocket of my purse. I tend to carry purses the size of the Mormon Tabernacle anyway, and though the Diane gave me some heft, it wasn't nearly as heavy as the Bible that Kevin had loaned me. I just hoped I'd grab for the right weapon if I got into a tight spot.

Moses breezed in and his English Leather began waging war with Leon's Chaps. If even I could smell the encounter, it must have been pretty potent.

"Coming to church with us, Moses?" I asked.

He shook his head. "Promised Charisse. But I been looking at those kids' files, Cat. And I'll take another look at 'em this afternoon. We should talk."

I started the stiff-legged waddle familiar to those in my condition, reached the door, and turned back. "Hell, I can't do this!" I said. I retired to the bedroom, peeled off the pantyhose, replaced the green polyester dress with a pair of black wool slacks and a white shirt that made me look like an out-of-shape waitress, and topped off the ensemble with a demure white sweater with pearl buttons that smelled like the cedar chest I'd found it in. I laced up some black crepe soles, confident that nobody cared what old ladies wore on their feet. As long as we're upright and mobile and don't drop dead at their feet, people cut us some slack.

From the living room, I heard Leon calling, "Come on, M-Miz Cat! We g-g-goin' be late! God don't care how you l-l-look."

"That's a comfort to me, Leon," I said, and returned to the living room. "Let's go."

Sitting in a padded seat in the crowded auditorium at New Life, I was struck by the distance between that religious venue and the ones I was somewhat more accustomed to. It wasn't just the lights and the television cameras, although those were pretty distracting at first. It was everything—the comfortable seats, the boxes of tissues provided along with the hymn books, the keyboard, electric guitar, and drum set sitting off to one side, the comparatively unadorned stage with its minimalist altar. Everything seemed so—well, modern. I preferred to think of God as a woman most of the time, but if God *was* a he, I figured him for a pretty old-fashioned guy, more set in his ways than my late husband. Of course, I knew he didn't really speak in Elizabethan English, anymore than he spoke in Latin or Greek or Hebrew. But it was a little hard to picture a guy older than Methusaleh getting down to a reggae or rap hymn.

It had occurred to me to wonder what I'd say to David Green if he recognized Leon in my entourage. With other kids, I might have been able to bluff, but not with Leon. Leon was unique. So I decided that there was nothing to do but brazen it out. Leon's choice of territory last night could have been coincidental, after all, but I doubted David would see it that way. I already thought he suspected me of something, though of what, I didn't think he'd decided. Tying me to Leon would make him even more suspicious, but was that necessarily a bad thing? He wasn't exactly in any position to spread the word, given the address in his personnel records. I would await developments.

There was a choir, though, as it turned out, and they had a range only slightly narrower than Peter Baer's music collection. And there must have been an organ hidden somewhere, because it alternated with the rock group to provide the music. When Leon first elbowed me to pick up a hymn book and stand up to sing, something fell out on the floor. I bent to retrieve it and nearly lost my balance when I saw Tony Frank staring up at me. I handed the hymnbook to Del, who looked at it as if he didn't know what to do with it. I turned over the memorial card on my palm and read the all-too-brief biography of Tony Frank.

I felt Leon's steadying hand under my elbow.

Perhaps because I'd known that there was a special memorial service still to come, I wasn't prepared for how much postmortem influence Tony would wield that day. Reverend Ted talked about him until there wasn't a dry eye in the house except Del's, and I doubted that Del was listening. Then one of Tony's friends spoke briefly. Then Reverend Armbruster let loose with a sermon about the mystery of what we regarded as an intimely death, but which, he assured us, had been a death that came right on time—God's time. Then a single female voice sang an eerie rendition of "Amazing Grace," which was purported to be Tony's favorite song.

Then it was time for Evie's appearance, and this, I realized, was what the crowd had been waiting for. Cheeks still wet, they began chanting, "E-*vie!* E-*vie!*" And she emerged from the back of the stage, a lonely little figure in a dark blue dress, swaggering across the stage to hand Daddy Armbruster something.

He took it from her, and showed it to the audience. It was a crayon drawing in brown and black, a circle and a few squiggles. "We invited Evie to draw a portrait of her friend, Tony Frank," he said.

He sat down in a convenient armchair that had appeared while we were focused on Evie's progress across the stage. He took her on his lap. The lights in the hall grew dim, while the television spots held on him. He began talking in a quiet, conversational voice about Tony Frank's many virtues, punctuating his talk with, "Isn't that right, Evie?" and "You remember that, don't you, Evie?" Evie never answered him, but she kept her head on his chest, sucked her thumb, and remained so still that after awhile the hypnotic effect of his voice began to wear off and my suspicious nature began to reassert itself. Could she be drugged? I wondered.

Reverend Armbruster appeared to study the crayon portrait again. "Well, I don't know," he said at last. "Maybe it takes a lot of imagination to see Tony Frank in this picture. But maybe that's not really what Evie intended." He turned the picture outward again for the audience to study. "Maybe what she really meant to draw was how she felt now that Tony was gone—how we all feel now that Tony is gone. And you know, I think maybe she got it just about right after all."

The lights went out and the room was plunged in darkness. Above the sounds of sobbing and sniffling, someone started to clap and then others joined in. I clapped, too. After all, it was a pretty good show for the money.

And speaking of money, just before the lights came up again on the empty stage, and the collection plates were passed—proceeds earmarked for Tony's youth group—I found myself wondering whether the killing of the lights cued a commercial break for the television audience.

Del chose that moment to exit. I thought he was overplaying his role as a hard-boiled kid, and frowned at him to let him know I thought so, but he ignored my look as any normal teenager would.

He reappeared at my elbow as the young keyboardist was playing the introduction to the final hymn.

"Know a dude with a reddish blond beard and glasses?" Del said in my ear.

"Young?" I asked.

He shook his head, frowning. "Probably thirty at least," he said. "Old dude." When I nodded, he continued, "He's puking his guts out in the men's john."

I raised my eyebrows and nodded to let him know I understood. And wondered what the hell it meant.

In the crush that followed the service, I found myself being steered by Joy, and introduced to all and sundry as an angel in disguise. Leon seemed to be in his element, shaking hands all around and chit-chatting about the service. Del trailed me, a look of utter boredom on his face, until he was cut from the herd by Reverend Ted. I saw the latter give him an ingratiating smile, capture his hand in a hearty shake, and then put an avuncular paw on his shoulder. Del glared at it as if it was a swarm of head lice.

"Why don't you let me take charge of this young man?" Rev. Ted called to me.

I gave him my best imitation of a weary, grateful smile. As they turned away, I tapped Leon on the shoulder and nodded at the retreating figures.

"You're back-up, remember?" I hissed in his ear.

He nodded once, and headed after them, repeating "back-up" several times over to make sure he had his assignment straight.

I went looking for David Green. I found him with Evie in his arms, surrounded by kids. He squatted and set her on her feet so that the smallest kids could touch her.

"You okay?" I asked. He looked a little pale, and his eyes were a little red, but otherwise, I couldn't see any traces of the episode that Del had witnessed.

He straightened. "Yeah, sure," he said. "Why?"

"I heard you were sick."

"Not sick," he said, and gave me a rueful smile. "Not really. It was just—you know, the stuff about Tony. It upset me."

I nodded. "Me, too. And I didn't even know him."

He turned to answer a question from the peanut gallery.

"Reverend Ted took my grandson off my hands," I said.

He nodded. "You won't see him for hours, then."

"So I should go away and come back?"

He checked his watch. "Ted will probably talk to him for a while, then bring him in to meet the rest of the kids for lunch. The youth group officially meets from one-thirty to three. He won't get away before that."

"Will you keep an eye on him?" I asked.

"Sure," he said.

I felt a strong tug on my handbag. It was Evie.

I waited until David was distracted, then leaned down and said quietly, "Sorry, cookie, no dice. I don't trust you. Next time you'll steal my credit card and use it buy out Chiquita Banana."

She gave me a soulful stare, but I wasn't fooled. Then something else caught her eye and I made my escape.

I sat in my car and calculated. For the next three hours, if he made good on his promise, David would be keeping an eye on Del, who would in turn be keeping an eye on David. I'd never have a better opportunity to finish what I'd started last night.

Chapter Twenty-seven

Okay, maybe that wasn't true. Nighttime, for example, is the more traditional time for breaking and entering, and there is a reason for that. On the other hand, brazenness is also often rewarded with success. And concealment comes in many guises. Sometimes, it comes in the guise of white hair and a cedar-scented sweater with pearl buttons.

Besides, I hadn't practiced with those damn pick-locks for nothing. I was now so proficient that I could open the average lock as easily with a pick as with a key. And David Green's locks were not above average. So I smiled in a neighborly fashion at the woman coming down the stairs with a basket of washing, and stood aside to let her pass. Then I climbed the stairs myself, breezed past an open apartment door, and let myself in at 2260D.

I took the same precautions as the day before, and went to work.

Anything that would have been easy to find I would have found the night before, so I wasn't expecting an easy time of it. I slid my hands in pockets, felt the linings of the few items of clothing that were lined, shook the Cheerios box to satisfy myself that it contained nothing more intriguing than Cheerios, unfolded and refolded every t-shirt and pair of socks, opened the sofa bed and checked between mattress and box springs, and examined every book on the shelves—an odd mix of popular religion and sci-fi, in addition to Jane Goodall's *In the Shadow of Man* and *Through a Window*. It occurred to me that I should have come equipped with a cat, a small, nosy one like Sidney, who could find the smallest hidey hole in any given space.

More than half an hour passed before I hit pay dirt. I was pulling the drawers out of the night stand, and the bottom one stuck. I raised it a bit, and pulled again, and this time it came. The drawer itself was empty, so I turned it over. Three objects were taped to the bottom with duct tape. One was a plastic square—one of those computer things Del called a "floppy." One was a small key. One was a small package of some kind, wrapped in a black plastic bag.

I went for the package first, even though handling it made me nervous. What if I tore the damn thing and heroin went flying all over the place? I considered taking it into the bathroom to open it in the sink, but by the time I had it in my hand, I'd changed my mind about what it was. My next guess was cash. It felt like a stack of paper. I opened the bag with care, and withdrew its contents. My breath caught. It was a rubber-banded bundle of small brochures. On the front of the top one, I read, "God Loves You Just the Way You Are." Below the headline was a picture of a group of teenagers, laughing, their arms around each other's shoulders.

Whatever I'd expected, it wasn't this. I turned the bundle over. On the back at the bottom I read, "The Metropolitan Community Churches of America." This was what David was up to? Proselytizing for a rival church? Stealing members for a rival youth group? And for that he was living like a CIA mole? Boy, churches must really be hard up these days. I didn't get it.

I extracted a brochure from the bundle and opened it. At the top of the inside cover, it said, "Answering Teens' Questions About Homosexuality." I felt giddy with excitement as I scanned the text and the implications began to sink in. This was a brochure that told Christian teenagers that it was okay to be gay. The text reviewed and refuted the biblical evidence that God abhorred homosexuality, though it never used language as strong as "abhorred," it described the blessings of human love as expressed through the body, and it preached safe sex. It was illustrated with pictures of happy teenaged faces. It offered kids a national hotline number to call twenty-four hours a day.

I sat back on my heels and wondered whether Kevin had ever been offered such a lifeline when he was a teenager.

I thumbed through the stack and discovered that half of them had a different heading, though the text was pretty much the same: "God Made You, and God Doesn't Make Mistakes."

I turned my attention to the floppy thing. I untaped it and turned it over, but it wasn't labeled like the one that Del had given me. The key was small, and I was willing to bet my Adidas that it unlocked a safety deposit box.

I helped myself to a brochure. I doubted that David kept an inventory, and I might run into a teenager who needed one. I replaced the floppy. I considered that if I'd had a piece of wax in my pocket, I could have made an impression of the key, but if it was the key to a safety deposit box, a duplicate would do me no good without the right credentials. Of course, I could have some credentials manufactured, but I doubted that anyone would mistake me for a man in his late twenties or early thirties, even with a good makeup job.

I had a feeling that I'd found what there was to find, but I couldn't leave the job half done. I searched the footlocker, examined the worn carpet for loose spots, checked the top of every cabinet and inside the light fixtures, the lampshades, and the toilet paper roll. Nada. It was time to go.

I sat in a Burger King, ate a Whopper and contemplated my score. So David Green was a—what? A pro-gay missionary undercover at a homophobic youth ministry? But why? Couldn't this other church—the Metropolitan Community Church—find enough teenagers to help without stealing them away from New Life? Was he working on some kind of exposé? If so, maybe he knew something about the missing teenagers, and about Peter Baer's and Tony Frank's deaths.

Okay, I thought, what about this. A kid calls the national hotline. The kid knows that something bad is happening at New Life, something scary, but he can't tell the proper authorities—his parents, the cops, one of his teachers—because? Because he's gay. Because if he tells what he knows, everyone will find out he's gay. Or she. The caller could have been a girl—the girl in the pink parka, say. Maybe what's going on has something to do with the gay teens being counseled at New Life. And that brought me back to the bracelets. The bracelets, I speculated, are worn by gay teens, or teens who think they're gay, who are being counseled at New Life. I thought of Dr. Maynard Clay. No, not "counseled." "Treated." The bracelets were being worn by kids being "treated" for homosexuality by Dr. Maynard Clay. Maybe.

And meanwhile, back at the hotline, they're trying to figure out what to do with this information the kid has given them. They can't risk exposing the kid's identity, even if they know his or her name. They can't charge in and make wild accusations. They can't even depend upon the local police to be sympathetic or discreet. So they send an investigator: David Green. And in the eight months he's worked at New Life, David has uncovered a connection between New Life and a series of missing or murdered teens. Hasn't he?

So why hasn't he spoken up? It's all well and good to hand out brochures on the sly, but surely he hadn't been sent just to do that. The whole affair must be more complicated than he'd realized.

Or I was way off base and the Metropolitan Community Church had developed a radical new approach to missionary work.

It was time to pick up the kids, so I drove back to New Life with a dry lump of trepidation stuck in my throat.

Leon was sitting alone on the steps.

"Del say to t-tell you, he n-n-not ready to leave yet, M-Miz Cat," he said. "This g-girl Chris? She ax us t-to supper later. She's real n-nice. They up in the c-c-computer r-room. B-b-but I p-promised Momma I'd g-go to church with her t-tonight."

I saw David Green coming up behind him.

"You tell Del," I said severely to Leon, "to come down here. I want to talk to him."

No self-respecting mother, or even grandmother, let a teenager announce his plans in such a cavalier fashion.

Leon scuttled off and David came and leaned against the car.

"He's something else, that Leon," he said casually. "Quite the salesman."

I made a face. "Everybody in the neighborhood has bought something from Leon at one time or another."

"Other neighborhoods, too," he said. The sun was behind him, and squinting up at him, I couldn't read his expression.

I nodded. "I hear he's branching out."

"You don't have to worry about Del, you know," he said. "He's found a soulmate in Chris. They're up there now, probably breaking into the FBI's classified files. But don't worry. Every half hour or so I make the kids get up and run around the building five times. It rests their eyes and exercises the rest of them."

I squinted up at him. "You're good with kids, aren't you?"

He shrugged. "I enjoy them. I was a kid myself once."

Del appeared, followed by none other than the girl in the pink parka. She wasn't wearing the parka at the moment, and I hadn't seen her close up before, but I knew she was the one. As if to confirm it, she made that characteristic gesture of hers, brushing her hair back with a braceleted hand.

"Me and Chris are juggling eggs up there, Grandma," Del whined. "We don't have time for a bogus priority interrupt right now." He made a gesture of impatience and rolled his eyes.

"Mrs. Caliban, Chris Shellenbarger," David said. "Chris, Mrs. Caliban, Del's grandmother."

"Hi," she said.

Up close, I could see that she was cute as a bug. Fresh-faced, delicate-featured, and thin, with a permanent crease across her forehead, no doubt put there by thinking. And in spite of the soft-core space bimbo pornography that Del traded with other hackers, I was pretty sure that the only part of her anatomy that he'd registered was her mind.

She rested her arms on the frame of the open car window. "We don't live too far from here," she told me. "Me and Del can walk home later for dinner, and then come back and work some more. He's showing me some really cool stuff. He's convinced me that the way we've been cranking code is highly nonoptimal."

David Green was grinning at me.

"Does your mother know you've invited him to dinner?" I asked.

"Uh-huh," she said. "She doesn't care, honest. I do most of the cooking, anyway."

"Okay," I said, making a show of reluctance, and wondering whether, given my discoveries of the afternoon, I should yield to the real reluctance I was feeling. I looked at Del. "But if you don't behave yourself, I'll nonoptimize you—and highly, at that!"

Del didn't dignify this with an answer. But as he turned away, he deigned to say, "I'll call you."

Moses wasn't back yet when I returned to the Catatonia Arms, but I found Kevin sorting laundry in the basement.

"Gee," I said, "I just cram it all in together."

"That's because you're a straight lady of a certain age," he said with equanimity, "while I am a gay guy of a certain age."

"If you're trying to say you dress better than I do, I'm not even in the competition," I said.

I held out the brochure. "Ever seen one of these?"

He pushed the button to fill the drum, and rinsed his hands in the water. He dried them on the seat of his jeans, then took the brochure.

"Very nice," he said, looking it over. "I've seen some like it. Not this particular one, though. Where'd you get it? Not among the murdered kid's papers?"

"Nope," I said. "It was concealed underneath a drawer in the apartment of a young man who works at New Life and helps out with the youth ministry."

Kevin whistled and his green eyes opened wide. "I'll bet he helps out, if he's handing out this stuff on the side."

I pointed. "It's put out by the Metropolitan Community Church," I said. "Ever hear of them?"

"The MCC? Sure," he said. "It's a gay church."

"What do you mean?"

He shrugged. "It's a Christian denomination of, by, and for gay people. It's been around for a while. It's the one place where a gay

Christian like me can go to worship and feel totally accepted and welcomed."

"But you don't," I pointed out.

He sighed. "I'm a Catholic. I was brought up to suffer, and to embrace paradox. That's why I keep going back to the Catholic church, when I go to church, where probably more than half of the priests and nuns are gay, the organist is gay, and all of the best music was written by gay men. We like to get together and worship a virgin mother and a divine son rendered by gay male painters and sculptors as the most beautiful of men."

"And to be told that any sex outside of procreation is a sin?"

"That too, of course."

"I've heard that the Unitarians are pretty warm and welcoming," I said.

"I've heard that, too," he said. "I don't think you even have to believe in anything to join the Unitarians. But where's the drama? The color? The pageantry? The men in dresses?"

"The Spanish Inquisition?"

"Any religion run by ordinary mortals is bound to make a few mistakes," he said, then held up his hand. "I know, I know. I'd be far less forgiving if my mother had been burned at the stake."

"Or if you had."

"Or if I had," he admitted. "But look at it this way: being a Catholic really tests your powers of forgiveness."

"Tell me this, then, oh master of theology," I said. "Why would an MCC missionary go undercover at an evangelical ministry?"

"The same reason robbers go to banks?" he guessed.

"Because that's where they'll find the most people in need of conversion?"

I thought about that. I didn't buy it.

"I don't think there's been a noticeable drop in church membership since he's been there."

"Maybe he's no good at his job."

I shook my head. "I don't think so. I have a feeling he's very good at his job. If I can only figure out what his job is."

I told him my theory about the hotline tip.

"What do you think?" I asked. "Would the MCC send someone to investigate in a case like that?"

"Gee, Mrs. C., I don't know," he said. "They're a church, not an investigative agency. And I get the impression they're a kind of loose organization."

"That's just your Catholic bias coming out," I said.

"I don't think so," he said. "But I suppose it wouldn't be outside the realm of possibility that an individual church member—maybe even a church member who was trained as an investigator—might take it upon himself to investigate the allegations."

That gave me pause. What if David Green was just another private dick like me? If he was, I probably hadn't fooled him for a second. But he hadn't bothered with me because he had bigger fish to fry.

"Now I've got a question for you," Kevin said leaning his butt against the dryer.

"What?"

"Is he cute?" He raised a suggestive eyebrow.

"What do you care? You've got What's-his-name. The guy who writes mash notes on cocktail napkins before rushing home to his wife and kiddies."

Kevin turned away. "Yeah. Well."

"You had a fight?"

"Sort of," he admitted. He was folding a towel with exaggerated care. "It gets old pretty fast, you know—the wife and kiddies."

"You broke up?"

He whirled around, one hand thrust out in my direction. "Don't say it! Just don't say it, okay? I know what you're going to say."

"What?" I was bewildered.

"'Why can't we get rid of Charisse that easily?'"

Chapter Twenty-eight

MOSES DIDN'T COME home until seven, and I followed him upstairs.

"She wanted me to go furniture shopping with her," he grumbled. "Wanted my opinion. Don't ask me why. She's seen my living room, she knows what I like—Salvation Army Comfortable."

Furniture shopping? I didn't like the sound of that. But I had other things on my mind right now. I hadn't heard anything from Del, and I wanted Moses to talk me out of my anxieties.

We settled down at his kitchen table, with a stack of file folders between us, and I told him everything I'd found out. I told him my hotline theory, and I told him that Del was still hanging around New Life.

I glanced at my watch. "He'll never call me on his own. I should probably just go over there and drag him away, huh?"

Moses snorted. "You want him home, you should. Go unplug him, bring him home, plug him back in here."

"Well, what do you think of my theory? And what have you found out from the case files?" I nodded at the folders. "What'd you get?"

He put on his bifocals and pulled them toward him. "I got seven files here, dating back to last summer. I didn't go back any earlier, but I reckon I can if I need to. All these kids were fourteen and older, five boys, two girls. Five missing, two open deaths. They all wore black-and-white braided bracelets." He opened the top file, extracted a piece of legal paper, and handed it to me. The names on his list included Peter Baer, Tony Frank, Paul Whitney, and Jennifer Deemer.

He looked at me over his bifocals.

"I've got to tell you, though, Cat, the files look pretty ordinary. Except for the bracelets, and the ties we know some of 'em had to New Life, there's nothing to distinguish them from your average teen runaway."

"Any of them gay that you know of?" I asked.

One investigator notes a possible boyfriend, based solely on his impression when he interviewed the kid. But that's all."

"What do you think?"

"I wouldn't be surprised," he said. "In any group of runaways, you expect some kids who are gay, or some kids who think they might be, or some kids other kids have labeled that way. It's damn hard to live life as a gay teenager—or any teenager who doesn't fit the mold. That's why the suicide rate is so high."

"Does Arpad think that Tony Frank was a suicide?"

"That's what his instinct tells him now, and I've got to agree it sounds right."

"Even without a note?"

"Hard to know what to say," Moses said. "The one thing you can't say is why."

"But Peter Baer's death wasn't a suicide," I said. "It was murder."

He didn't say anything.

"Unless it wasn't," I added.

He just looked at me.

"Is that possible?" I asked. "It would mean . . ." I trailed off, unable to frame an account of everything it would mean. I shifted my eyes to the window and the darkness beyond, trying to picture what might have happened.

Moses sighed. "Cat, one thing I learned from being a cop, when you're dealing with the human race, anything's possible."

"But how do we find out for sure?" I asked. "Because we need to know. I mean, Gussie needs to know, of course. But we need to know. Because if Tony Frank was a suicide, and if Peter Baer was a suicide, and if the rest were just runaways, then I can stop worrying about Del. I can stop worrying about whatever's going on at New Life, and let David Green handle it."

My phone was ringing. I'd left the doors to both apartments open so that I could hear it, and now I raced down the stairs. Even before I picked it up, I could hear Del's voice on the answering machine, a frightened whisper.

"—don't know what to do, because Chris says he must be dead, and they're still in the building some—."

As I picked up the receiver, I heard a sound on the other end that I couldn't identify, and then the line went dead.

I was speaking to air.

Kevin appeared in the doorway. "Oh," he said. "You got it."

"Not soon enough," I said. Then I shouted for Moses as I ran for my gun.

Chapter Twenty-nine

THE NEW LIFE headquarters building was in total darkness when we arrived. Moses had been in favor of calling the cops in, without sirens and lights, but I vetoed that idea. If someone had attacked the kids, I didn't want to risk panicking that person with a visible police presence. We parked in the hospital lot, crossed Auburn Avenue out of view of New Life, and worked our way toward the New Life complex.

"The computer room is on the second floor," I told Moses, who had pulled on a dark sweater over his dress shirt. The air was cold, but not as cold as it had been. Moses had made both Kevin and me stop long enough to put on something dark. I'd grabbed a navy blue sweatshirt, never before worn, that said, "Happiness is Being a Grandma." Kevin was sporting a dark plaid sweatshirt that said, "Kiss Me! I'm Irish!"

"Somebody should check out the main building," Moses said, "'case the kids are there."

"What's that?" Kevin asked, pointing his chin at Evie's little storybook cottage, the only building in the complex that showed light at the windows.

"Evie's house," I said. "I'd better check the main building, since I sort of know my way around."

"Me and Kevin will take Evie's," Moses said.

I nodded and headed for the big house, my Diane in one hand, my flashlight in the other. Once inside, I stopped to listen. The stillness and chill in the air made the house feel like a crypt. I moved, all of my senses alert, trying to feel the floorboards through the soles of my feet.

A faint scent led me down the hall past the main office—a man's after-shave. I tried all the doors on the hall, and they were all locked, until I came to Reverend Ted's. That one swung open. I smelled the blood before I saw it, a faint metallic odor mingling with the spicy after-shave. I played my flashlight around the room and lit on an overturned chair and lamp. I located the blood in a surprisingly small stain where an oriental rug met an industrial carpet beneath it. The blood was still damp to the touch, and made a reddish-brown smear on my forefinger.

I backed out of the room and took the stairs as quickly as I dared. But one glance around the computer room told me that no one was there. From where I was standing, I could look down on Evie's house, and I thought I saw a shadow moving in silhouette against a curtained window.

Oblivious to the noise, I ran downstairs and out the door. Someone flashed a light and I joined Moses and Kevin at the edge of the parking lot by the woods.

"Find anything?" Moses asked.

I shook my head.

We all turned to look at the cottage.

"Place is like a fortress," Moses complained. "Door was bolted on the outside, but it must be bolted from the inside, too. Couldn't crack it."

I nodded. "And the mullioned windows are actually fortified with steel. Underneath all that Seven Dwarfs kitsch is a simian Alcatraz. But around back is a bigger window, if we want to see in."

A ray of light broke through one of the front curtains, and we instinctively stepped back, though it didn't reach us. A small, brown face appeared, backlit by the light from within.

"It's Evie!" I said.

"Could be worse," Moses observed. "Could be better."

"I wonder if she really does know sign language," I mused.

"You want to ask her what's going on?" Moses said.

"No," I said, irritable. "I want to ask her to open the door."

"You think she can?" Moses asked.

"You think she knows sign language?" Kevin asked.

"For all the good it will do us," I said, "yes to both questions."

"Only one way to find out," Kevin said, and he stepped forward into the light.

"Jee-zus!" I said, grabbing for air.

But Kevin was already in full view of the window. From where we were standing, we couldn't see what he was doing, we could only see that he was moving his arms.

"You know he could do that?" Moses asked.

"No. You?"

"No."

I shifted my attention to the small brown face in the window. We couldn't see her expression, and I was afraid she'd get excited and draw attention to the figure outside. Her head moved, and she appeared to have cocked it to one side. Then she disappeared.

Kevin waved us over, and we sprinted for the front door. Moses and I both had guns drawn, but as we stood waiting to see if our message had been received, a faint but pungent odor reached us.

"Smell that?" Moses whispered. "No guns, Cat."

I stuffed my gun inside my waistband. I didn't have to ask. If we could smell the gasoline fumes out here, they must be pretty strong inside, and a gunshot could ignite the vapors.

We heard some fumbling at the door, a small click, and then the sound of metal scraping metal. The door swung open, revealing the hall and Evie's retreating back. She turned into the kitchen, pick-locks dangling from one hand. We stepped inside, Moses in the lead.

A figure appeared at the other end of the hall. It was Clay, his face flushed, his comb-over plastered to the sweat that stood glistening on his forehead. No longer the jovial professional man, he was dressed in gray sweats that emphasized his bulk. His eyes were wide with panic. He was unarmed except for a cigarette lighter. He held it aloft, his thumb poised. We froze.

"Okay, now, let's all remain calm," Moses said in his most soothing voice.

My eyes were fixed on the lighter. If he panicked, we were all history.

Then, Clay's body jerked and rose in the air. His head snapped back. His arms flailed. The lighter popped loose. Kevin lunged and leapt into the air, catching the lighter in both hands like an end-zone Hail Mary. He collided with Clay in mid-air, and both crashed to the floor, on top of the hapless Evie, whose tackle had put the play in motion. She screeched in indignation.

Kevin was the first to regain his feet. He lifted the dazed Clay by his lapels, and delivered a quick combination that put his lights out. As he slid to the floor, we stepped over him and ran for Evie's quarters.

We found the kids there, tied to Evie's tree and gagged. I yanked the kitchen towel from Chris's mouth and said, "You okay?" I was already sawing away at her bindings.

"Goddamn sons-of-bitches!" she said, her voice shaking with fury. Tears sprang to her eyes, and as soon as I liberated one of her hands, she swiped at her cheeks. "I'm going to kill them! So help me God, I'm going to kill them both!"

She repeated this mantra over and over as I pulled her to her feet. I didn't object, since it seemed to me to exhibit a reasonable attitude under the circumstances. There are limits to Christian forbearance.

"Come on, Cat!" Moses was shouting. "Let's get out of here!"

Del grabbed Chris's hand and dragged her in the direction of safety.

"What about him?" I asked.

Moses, Kevin, and I turned to look at the still figure lying on his back on the floor nearby. David Green's green eyes were half-open, but we all knew they would never close again until someone closed them. One side of his head was crushed and bloody.

"I got him," Kevin said, and bending, he gathered the body gently in his arms.

Moses looked at me. "I'd do it," he said, "'cept for my back."

"Me, too," I said.

Moses grabbed my elbow and gave it a squeeze. We hurried out after Kevin.

We bumped into Clay in the hall. We exchanged rueful looks, then bent to seize hold of him.

"Bend your knees, now, Cat," Moses admonished me. "He's a heavy bastard. Don't use your back."

Moses lifted his shoulders and I lifted his feet, and between us we half-dragged, half-carried him over the threshold and into the crisp, fresh, night air.

As soon as we set him down, Chris went after him, her sneakered feet making audible thuds as they made contact with his torso. She rained curses, tears and blows on the inert form until Del pulled her off.

"You think she broke anything?" Kevin asked in a detached voice.

"I hope so," I said.

"Be a shame if she didn't," Moses said.

"Hey!" I said. I scanned our little tableau, counting noses. "Where's Evie?"

I ran toward the cottage, shouting her name. "Evie!" I yelled. "You've got to get out of there."

She appeared in the door, a small brown silhouette. I knelt and held out my arms to her. She scuttled to me in a three-legged run. As I picked her up, I noticed she was clutching something.

I heard a muscle in my back scream as I stood up. "What do you have there, smartypants?"

She unfolded one arm to show me. In the dim light coming from the cottage, even upside down I recognized the figures in the photograph. It was David and Evie, in profile, nose to nose and grinning at each other. With a pang, I turned it right side up, then I turned it over. Someone had written on the back, "Me and Sis."

I realized that Moses was shouting at me. He was dragging Clay by one foot. "Come on, Cat! You got to get back! You too close if that thing blows!"

I joined them on the other side of the parking lot, close to the house.

"Kevin went to call the cops," Moses told me.

"You okay?" I asked Del. His arms were around Chris's shoulders, and she had calmed down. Tears trickled down her cheeks but she ignored them.

"I knew you'd come," he said, the picture of teen cool.

"But you didn't know if I'd come soon enough," I added.

He shrugged.

"Moby win for the home team," I said.

He grinned and nodded.

I handed Evie over to Chris, who took her without comment. I turned to Moses.

"I need the car keys," I said, holding out my hand. "You and Kevin had better both stay here."

Moses started to protest, but then he nodded and handed over the keys.

"Don't do anything stupid," he said.

"You mean, don't do anything you wouldn't do?"

"I hope you smarter than that," he grumbled.

"Don't worry," I said. "I'll bend my knees."

Chapter Thirty

THE CURTAINS WERE drawn closed across the window at 2260D Reading Road, but a light was lit on the other side. I had left the place in darkness earlier.

I turned the doorknob, and encountered no resistance. Gun up, I leaned against the door and eased it open.

Someone was tossing the place. Books and clothing lay in a pile on the living room floor. I scanned the room and saw no one, but I could hear noises coming from the bathroom. I crossed the room quickly and stood in the bathroom door.

"Damn!" I said. "It must be my night for finding distinguished men in compromising positions."

The Right Arm of God, the Reverend Vernon Armbruster, was on his hands and knees in front of the open cabinet beneath the sink.

"What the hell—," he said, and sat back on his heels, staring at the gun in my hand.

Then his eyes shifted and I felt rather than heard the movement behind me. I whirled, slamming an elbow into the person who stood poised behind me. He grunted, and something fell, striking me on the head. I pressed my advantage and continued the turn, delivering a punch to the side of his head that I put the force of my hip into. He fell against the door jamb and went down. I stepped over him and backed away so that I could cover both of them. On the floor lay a cast iron skillet, which explained the painful lump swelling over my right ear. I glanced back at the kitchenette, hoping that nobody else was crouched there, examining the broiler, but I didn't think so. Still, it was best not to make the same mistake twice.

Armbruster was pale, but he'd spent a lifetime being in charge, and he wasn't about to give it up now.

"See here!" he protested in his most peremptory voice.

The Reverend Ted put an arm out to steady himself against the wall, and started to stand up.

"I wouldn't do that if I were you," I warned him.

But he just glared at me and kept moving, confident. So I shot him.

It wasn't much. A Diane makes a very small hole, hardly more than a pin prick, really, but if you aim for the right place, it can be very persuasive. I would have aimed for his shoulder, except that I didn't have a good angle on that, so I lowered my aim a few inches.

"Jesus Christ!" he yelped.

He clapped both hands to his groin and fell back to the floor. I didn't think I'd managed to hit him there, but I figured I'd come close enough to give him something to worry about.

I squeezed off another round at the ceiling, just in case everybody in the apartment complex had decided to ignore the first shot. Then I lowered the gun and pointed it at his head.

"I feel a sneeze coming on," I said, and panted a little, just for effect.

The remaining color drained out of Ted's face. Armbruster sat frozen in place.

"It's a funny thing about small caliber pistols," I observed. "I'm told they can be deadlier than the big guns because the bullets ricochet off everything instead of smashing through it."

"Knock, knock," a tentative voice called.

From where I stood, I saw the neighbor, an angel of deliverance in aqua stretch pants and hair curlers, standing in the doorway. She was taking in the mess, frowning in bewilderment.

"Are you having some trouble here?" She looked at me, then squinted at the gun.

"I am," I said. "Thanks for asking. Would you mind going to call the cops for me?"

"Aren't you David's mother?" she asked, uncertainty shading her voice.

"Just a friend," I said.

"And you want me to call the police?"

"Please."

"Well," she said, with another glance around the room, "okay."

"Hey," I said. "Thanks a million."

"Don't mention it," she said, and went away.

"Now, we wait," I said to my two companions.

"Who the hell are you?" Armbruster croaked.

"Why, Vernon," I said. "Don't you recognize me? I'm somebody's idea of an avenging angel."

Chapter Thirty-one

IT TOOK A few days for Arpad and his colleagues to sort out all the stories they heard about what had happened that night. But I got most of what I needed to know from the kids. Somehow, everyone ended up back at the Catatonia Arms later that night, or rather, very early Monday morning. I had tried to send Chris home, but she was too wired and eager to talk, and Moses had persuaded me to let her stay. She'd called her mother, who as far as I could tell didn't appreciate the gravity of the situation, and maybe that was just as well. She'd see her daughter's swollen jaw and black eye soon enough.

I do mean "everyone." Evie showed up sporting a new Cincinnati PD sweatshirt that came down to her ankles and an honorary police badge.

"She's running away from home," Chris told me.

"Oh," I said. But to Moses in private, I said, "Why here? Would you please explain to me why every kid who runs away from home in this town runs away to our house? I don't get it. What is this, Sesame Street? We still have a few holes in the wall from our previous pint-sized houseguests, not to mention the dent in my life savings caused by a certain computer geek in possession of my credit card.[‡] And I've never managed to get all the fingerpaint out of the hall carpet."

"I know, Cat, I know," he said. "But they don't all come here. We still got a few runaways we can't account for."

That sobered me up. He had a point. So I made hot chocolate, and we all got into pajamas, except Evie, who was too fond of her new sweatshirt to part with it, and sat around the living room talking.

"Can you talk about David?" I asked Chris.

[‡] See *Six Feet Under* and *Four Elements of Murder*.

She nodded. "I don't know everything," she began. "I mean, I know he was on this mission, and he was, like, undercover and all, but I don't know any more than that."

"A mission?" Kevin echoed.

"Yeah," she said. "He said that New Life was screwing kids up, I mean really hurting them. 'They play dangerous mind games' was how he put it. 'They get inside kids' heads and make them hate themselves'—that's what he said." She looked up. "Not all the kids. Just—."

"The gay kids," Kevin said.

"Yeah." She narrowed her eyes. "The gay kids. The New Covenant kids." Without looking at it, she fingered the black-and-white bracelet.

"What was the New Covenant?" Kevin asked.

"It was this, like, supersecret club for gay kids," she said. "Some kids joined on their own. Like, if they called the New Life hotline and talked to somebody, they were encouraged to come in and talk to Ted, and then Ted set them up with Clay. Or sometimes their parents made them come." She made a face. "Ted and Clay, they were supposed to cure us."

It was the first time she'd used the first person plural, but nobody responded to it.

"The bracelets were for members of the New Covenant?" Moses asked, pointing at her wrist.

She looked down at the bracelet. "The black and white symbolize good and evil—you know, opposites and all that. No gray areas. The only reason I'm still wearing this fucking bracelet is that David didn't want me to take it off yet." Her voice thickened, but I didn't think she had many tears left to cry tonight. "When you took it off, it was like being cast into the outer darkness, where you'd be damned for all eternity." She said this almost casually, like a catechism she'd memorized. "But as long as you wore it, you had a shot at a new life. You could grow up to be normal and get married and have kids and a house in the suburbs with a two-car garage. Otherwise, you'd die on the streets of some horrible disease only prostitutes and druggies get."

She looked up again, as if to gauge our reactions. "He was right about the mind games. It was part of the treatment. They called you up, or they handed you a note or a brochure or something. It was always about how God hates fags, or about the diseases queers get, or how Jesus was weeping over your impure thoughts—that kind of crap. Except that you didn't see it as crap when you read it, or at least, I didn't. And if they thought you were resisting, they threatened to talk to your parents."

"And David took you aside and told you they were full of shit," Kevin guessed.

She grinned at the obscenity. "Pretty much. And he was, like, this amazing talker—totally credible. He knew the Bible backwards and forwards. He'd been to seminary and everything. And he said there was nothing wrong with being gay and being Christian. He belonged to this church that was just for homosexuals, he said." Her voice dropped. "He liked to talk about love—all kinds of love. He believed that all love was sacred."

"He sounds like a wonderful guy," Moses said.

"Yeah," she said. She heaved a ragged sigh. "I'm going to miss him."

"Did this New Covenant group meet on Saturday afternoons?" I asked her.

She shook her head. "Sundays, after the regular youth group."

Of course, I'd never asked anybody if Peter had disappeared regularly on Sunday afternoons, I was too busy focusing on Saturdays.

"So Tony Frank was in this group," I said. "What about Jen Deemer, Paul Whitney, and Peter Baer?"

"Jen was in it for a while, but I don't know the second person you said," she answered thoughtfully. "I've only been going since early November. I saw Peter Baer there this one time, but that's all. I recognized his picture in the paper afterwards." She frowned. "We talked about it, of course. His murder, I mean. I don't know whether Rev. Ted came right out and said that Peter had probably been killed because he was cruising, but he sure made us believe it, and it scared us pretty bad."

"What were the meetings like?" Kevin asked.

She shifted. "Oh—you know. They were kind of—oh, I don't know. Ted encouraged us to talk about our sexual feelings, or anything we'd done that we shouldn't have. It sounds awful, but it was kind of a relief to confess stuff."

Kevin was nodding, well-trained Catholic boy that he was. Chris seemed to be speaking to him in particular, and it occurred to me afterward to wonder whether she would have been so open with us if one of us at least hadn't been gay.

"Dude was weird," Del put in. "Kept asking me what I did when I was alone in my room. I told him I gronked out when I wasn't hacking. He didn't seem to get it. Wanted to know what I was thinking about. What did he think I was thinking about? When you've got a head full of state, if you swap out, you're going to adger some code, commit pilot error."

We greeted this account with a few beats of silence. I wished I'd been a fly on the wall when Ted had tried to communicate with Del.

Chris continued. "I mean, Ted didn't, you know, yell at you or anything. He'd just ask you in this real quiet voice how you felt about stuff you'd done or thought. And it wasn't so bad because everybody else in the group felt the same way you did, and they all had stuff to confess. And so we'd, like, cry together and pray together. And you felt better afterward."

So Ted had made them feel that they fit in somewhere at last, I thought, and used that feeling against them.

"But in between times," she continued, "when you didn't have the group around you, you just kind of felt weaker than ever, and ashamed. I mean, I would try to pray and all, but I couldn't get over this feeling that God wouldn't listen to me because I kept thinking bad thoughts. I mean, I know his mercy is supposed to be infinite and all that, but I don't know anybody like that, you know? Everybody has their limits. Ted sure did."

"Chris, when you said David hadn't wanted you to remove the bracelet yet," I said, "what exactly did he mean? When would you be able to take it off?" Call me insensitive, but I could only take so much emotion. I wanted to get back to the plot.

She frowned. "I'm not sure, but I think he was planning something. I don't really know what it was, but he needed some of us to serve as his agents. That's what he called us. But whatever it was, I think it was going to happen soon. Tony's death really shook him. 'This has got to stop,' he said."

"I'm not really sure, either," I said, "but I think he was planning some kind of exposé. I think he'd been gathering dirt on the people in charge at New Life. I don't really know what he found, but he must have found something, or they wouldn't have risked going to his apartment tonight to retrieve it. Which reminds me—did you give him David's home address, Chris?"

She glanced at Del, then looked away.

"Ted threatened to rough me up," Del said. "He slapped me around a little—nothing serious. He's not nearly as tough as he thinks he is. But she told him."

Moses held up a hand. "Hold it! Back up. Let's get the whole story from the beginning. What happened over there tonight?"

"We went over to Chris's for dinner," Del said. "Then, we went back to the Clubhouse to work. That's what they call the computer room—the Clubhouse."

"We didn't think anybody else was there," Chris added. "The whole place was real quiet."

"If nobody was there, how'd you get in?" I asked.

The teenagers exchanged a look. "There's ways," Chris said. "We do it all the time."

"Security through obscurity," Del told Moses in an aside. "Highly hardwarily unreliable."

"Uh-huh," he said. "And then what?"

"We were twiddling this froggy program, and we heard voices," Del said.

"Coming from downstairs," Chris clarified. "And I said, 'Just keep quiet and they'll go away. They'll never glark that we're up here.'"

"Yeah, but after a while they started shouting," Del said.

"And they must have been right under us, 'cause it was coming up through the whatchallits—."

"Those frobs in the floor—you know, like where the heat comes from," Del said.

"And we could tell that it was Ted and David going at it," Chris said. "And David said something like, 'I'm going to see to it that you never get your hooks into another kid the way you did Tony Frank—you and that fat fraud Clay. Your days are numbered!"

"Yeah, geez, just like in the movies," Del affirmed. "'Your days are numbered'—just like that!"

"And Ted was just furious, you could tell," Chris said. "And he goes, like, 'Who the hell do you think you are?' And David goes, 'I'll tell you who I am, pal. I'm the guy who's going to push you off this gravy train.' He goes, 'What do you think would happen if a real psychologist or a real minister ever walked in here and took a good look at your so-called treatment? Or if somebody who'd been keeping track of your record told the truth about all those success stories you like to brag about? Or told the truth about your credentials, yours and Clay's?'"

"And Ted says something like, 'You son of a bitch! You'd better not start something with me!'" Del continued.

"Yeah, but then, David said something real quiet," Chris said.

"I still think it was something about 'your sexual preferences, Reverend Ted,'" Del said. "And I think he called Ted a 'pervert.'"

"But we don't really know what he said," Chris said. "All we know is that's when the fight started."

"And we were trying to decide whether to call the cops or call you, Cat, when we heard this huge crash," Del said. "And then it got real quiet."

"And I said I'd go see, because what if somebody was hurt down there? It got so quiet so suddenly. But I made Del stay in case we needed to call for help," Chris said. "Anyway, I knew the house. Del didn't. So, I went downstairs, real quiet, and I saw light coming from Reverend Ted's office. And so I crept up to the door and peeked in."

She took a deep breath. "It was the way he was laying. On his side, like he was watching the door, with his eyes half-open. But his head was all—." She took another shuddering breath. I leaned down and squeezed her shoulder. "It was awful. I guess I made a noise, because Ted turned around and saw me. So he came after me and caught me by the arm. I screamed, but I didn't scream for Del because I didn't want Ted to know he was up there."

She put a hand to her swollen jaw and winced. "He hit me, the bastard. He hit me hard, and I blacked out. He used to be a fighter, I think, and he always said he was pretty good."

I snorted. Anybody who'd sneak up on an opponent and raise his arms, leaving himself wide open for an elbow strike, wasn't ready for the Golden Gloves. And his technique ran more to hitting people with heavy objects, not punching their lights out with his fists.

"When she screamed, that was when I called you, Cat," Del said. "I thought you'd never answer. And I can't tell you what happened. I was on the phone with you, and then the next thing I knew, I was sitting there, tied to that stupid tree, with this moby headache."

"Dr. Clay was there by then," Chris told us. "He didn't seem too happy, but it was like he had to do whatever Ted said. And Ted was obviously going to just torch the place with all of us inside."

"I don't think Chris could see David lying there," Del said. "But Evie could." He spoke this last sentence quietly, and we all looked at Evie, where she was lying asleep on the couch, her bottle of apple juice tucked under her chin. "Evie just freaked."

Chris nodded. "She was making so much noise, I was afraid they'd hurt her. And she was running all over the place, and climbing, and screeching. But Ted just ignored her."

Another of his mistakes, I thought. Never underestimate old ladies and chimpanzees.

"Then Ted left, and the other guy, the doctor, he stayed to finish throwing gasoline around," Del said.

Chris sniffed at her damp hair. "God, I'll bet I still reek! I'll probably totally smell like gasoline for the whole rest of my entire life! If I have to go to school tomorrow smelling like this, I'll just die!" She said this with the self-consciousness of the young.

"We'll use vinegar or something," I said, and anticipated her when she opened her mouth to protest, "some nice apple cider vinegar, and then wash out the vinegar smell with shampoo. We'll get it out."

"He didn't actually throw it on us," Del said, "but he was kind of panicky and it splashed all over the place."

"He was meant to die, too—the doctor," I said. "Ted had him bolt the door on the inside when he left, but then Ted went back and bolted the door on the outside. Clay wouldn't have made it out alive, once he'd started the fire."

"Ewww, that's so creepy!" Chris said. "And they would have killed Evie, too—an innocent little animal."

Evie did look innocent, now that she was asleep. You'd never guess that she had a career as a safecracker ahead of her.

"So tell us what happened at Ted's place, Cat," Kevin said.

I told them.

Chris's eyes widened with mixed horror and delight. "You shot him? Awesome! I hope you shot his nuts off!"

"Not exactly," I admitted. "But I gave him something to think about."

Sidney chose that moment to make his entrance, chattering and swinging his tail. Evie's eyes popped open, and she sat up, a look of fascination lighting up her face. Surely, I thought, she's seen a cat before. But if she had, she gave no sign of it.

Sidney, meanwhile, had spotted her. He sat down and studied her, then approached her warily, leading with his nose. Evie bent down and put out a tentative finger, which Sidney sniffed. Satisfied, Sidney turned his head and butted Evie's hand for a pet. Evie made a sound I couldn't interpret, and before anyone could stop her, she snatched Sidney up, climbed the nearest curtain, and hung from the curtain rod, crowing with pleasure.

We were all on our feet, scolding her, warning her, pleading with her, and reaching for her, but we were all afraid she might crush the wriggling Sidney, who was adding his squawks of protest to the melee, so nobody grabbed hold of her. I expected the curtain rod to pull free from the wall any second.

But Evie seemed to consider Sidney's objections, and find them reasonable. She boosted him up to her shoulder, and he scrambled to his new perch, digging in his claws to find purchase. I was sure his razor-sharp claws were penetrating the sweatshirt, but Evie just grinned at us.

Sidney, having found his balance, looked down at us, and appeared to find his situation as amusing as Evie did. He strolled to Evie's ear and butted it playfully. We could hear his purr. Evie reached up with her free hand and gave him a gentle poke. He crouched, fitted his head into her palm, and taught her how to pet a cat.

With Sidney safe, I could afford to look away. Del and Chris were grinning, joining in the discussion of Sidney's prospective stage career as Evie's assistant.

"I don't think there were any cats in Eden, though," Chris was saying.

"No cats in the Bible at all," Moses put in.

"Yeah, that's why they used to be considered agents of Satan," Kevin said.

I was happy to see the kids laughing again, relieved to know that the Reverend Ted Settles and Dr. Maynard Clay were behind bars tonight. The Right Arm of God might also be there, but I doubted that they'd hold him overnight on a simple B&E—not if he had a competent lawyer. And David Green's computer disk and key were in the right hands.

But my heart ached every time I thought of David, who had held in so much for so long, only to lose control when he was most vulnerable. Tony Frank's death had precipitated that final confrontation, and it pained me to think that I might have precipitated Tony's death. I hadn't caused it; I understood that. But I had played my part in it.

I escaped from the general merriment into the kitchen, where I stood at the window and looked out on the dark. The case I'd been hired to solve wasn't over yet, and there would be more grief to come. And somewhere out there, in another place, David Green had other friends and family and, perhaps, a lover.

I felt hands on my shoulders and turned into Moses's hug. I buried my face in the familiar scent of him and let the tears come.

"Damned unprofessional," I said into his bathrobe.

"What?" he asked.

I stepped back. "Damned unprofessional of me," I repeated. "But thanks."

"What are partners for?" he said.

Chapter Thirty-two

I SKIPPED THE memorial service for Tony Frank at New Life, but my inside source said that Armbruster had turned most of it over to the kids, and had seemed subdued when he had spoken. Evie had skipped it, too, but then, she was settling into temporary quarters in the form of a prefabricated house set up in the parking lot while her own cottage was sealed off by the cops.

Arpad came for a visit a few days later, after he'd pieced together most of the story. We sat at Moses's kitchen table, drinking beer. Arpad told us that David Green had assembled quite a dossier on New Life.

"Nothing really big, taken by itself," he said, "but taken all together, it would have done a lot of damage. Clay didn't have a medical degree, just a B.A. in Business. Which means he was illegally prescribing tranquilizers and other psychiatric drugs to keep the kids under control and make their parents happy, so they'd donate more money to New Life and, of course, show their appreciation to him personally. Of course, the drugs alone might not have worked without Ted Settles's intimidation games."

Arpad shook his head. "That bastard was a piece of work. He was a seminary drop-out, with no background in counseling. And it wasn't just the gay kids he fucked with, he did it with any kid who gave him trouble. And he recruited spies among the other kids, so he could keep tabs on everybody. Well, you know how vulnerable teenagers are, Foggy. You know the right buttons to push, you can really mess them up. Anyway, he had copies on that disk of some of Settles's little reminders to the kids—pictures of dead junkies, men in the terminal stage of AIDS, Jesus in the background, crying, stuff like that. 'Course, as far as I can make out, a lot of the kids liked him just fine—the good kids, that is. If you weren't a troublemaker, he could be real nice to you."

"And let the troublemakers see how nice he could be," I said.

"Oooh, girl, that's cold," Arpad said, shaking his head in mock disapproval. "Foggy, your partner's a cynic. She get that from you?"

"Uh-uh," Moses said. "She got it from her kids."

"So what else did he have on New Life?" I asked.

"Before I tell you that, let me tell you about these kids here," he said, pulling the stack of case files toward him. "We located the Deemer girl, and the Whitney and Lyons boy through a phone number we found in the safe deposit box. The number belonged to a national teen crisis hotline, with some kind of connection to a Metropolitan Community Church in San Francisco. You know who they are?"

We nodded.

"Using David Green's name—his real name, that is—got us connected to somebody who got us connected to somebody who coordinates a national network of safehouses for teens. We were told that any kids on our list whose whereabouts were known to them would be asked to contact their parents. Asked, not forced. They claim that they always try to get the kids to phone home."

"And I suppose it's in your best interest to cooperate with them," I said.

"Damn straight," Arpad said. "We take any of these rescue places to court, or go in there and throw our weight around, we risk putting them out of business."

"Which means more kids on the street," Moses said.

"It's a judgment call," Arpad continued. "Anything seems funny, we go after 'em. We're not in the business of supporting teen prostitution rings. But if they seem legit, we ask for their help and leave it at that. Two of the kids, the Deemer girl and the Lyons boy, called their parents within twenty-four hours. The Whitney kid called me."

"Did he know Peter Baer?" I asked.

"You way ahead of me, Cat," he said. "Peter was a friend of his. They met through this New Covenant at New Life, used to meet regularly on Saturdays and hang out together. Paul said they weren't lovers, just friends, and I believe him. Must have been nice for both of them to have one friend who knew the secrets they were keeping from everybody else. Paul said both of them went to the New Covenant meetings sometimes, but not regularly, because they were both worried their parents would find out that they'd been attending another church. Plus, they both had other church-related activities on Sunday sometimes.

"Paul said he'd started talking to David Green in September—or maybe David Green had started talking to him would be more accurate— and Paul decided to leave the New Covenant. He'd been thinking about running away from home for a long time, and now David arranged a place for him to stay. He wrote that note to Peter Baer and mailed it on his way out of town. Says David gave him the bus fare, but he had to call David when he got where he was going. He didn't know about Peter's death."

"So we don't know whether David started talking to Peter as well?" I asked.

"Nobody knows," Arpad said. "Or nobody's saying. Now, as for what else David Green had on New Life, to understand that, you have to know who David Green was."

He cocked his head at me, inviting me to guess.

I took a deep breath. "I don't really know for sure," I said, "but I think he was Armbruster's son."

Arpad raised his eyebrows and applauded. "Very good! Here I'm about to pull my rabbit out of the hat, and you and him's already acquainted. Tell me how you knew that."

I shifted, uncomfortable, and took a swig of beer. "You'll say it's stupid."

He raised his hands in protest. "Hey, you got the right answer! Any way you got it can't be too stupid."

"Well," I said, "what I couldn't figure out was the timing. David Green arrived at New Life last summer. He arrived with a clear intent, a mission of some kind. If he hadn't, he wouldn't have given them a fake address. And his apartment, which at least one kid I knew had visited, was Spartan. It didn't give away anything about him. That means he anticipated some curiosity, maybe even betrayal, and he didn't want to give anybody anything to betray.

"But now it's been, what? Seven months? The argument that the kids overheard between Green and Settles indicates that he had something on New Life—enough, at least in his mind, to, as you say, do some significant damage. But why hadn't he used it already? What was he waiting for? Maybe he thought he could get more if he hung around longer, I don't know. But Tony Frank's death really devastated him. That death was being considered a possible suicide from the beginning, unlike Peter's. So David probably felt he'd failed Tony, and understood that he couldn't go on rescuing kids one by one anymore. The service on Sunday at New Life actually made David sick. Del saw him throwing up in the bathroom. The sanctification of Tony by the very people David believed had driven him to his death infuriated David—at least, that's my guess.

"I don't know how David and Ted came to be together at New Life Sunday night," I said, and looked at Arpad, but he shrugged, so I went on. "But Ted must have said something that set David off. Otherwise, how long would he have waited to tell what he knew about New Life Ministries? I think he might have been planning to say something at Tony's memorial service, or maybe right after. But why had he waited so long?"

I looked down at the table. "Here comes the silly part. Evie brought one thing away with her when we escaped from the cottage. It was a photograph of her with David Green. On the back, in David's handwriting, it said, 'Me and Sis.'"

Arpad's eyebrows lifted again, but he didn't say anything.

"Before Mrs. Armbruster came to pick her up, I gave Evie the photograph, and Kevin asked her who it was."

Arpad opened his mouth to speak, but I anticipated him.

"In sign language." I circled my lips with my index finger. "Who? And Evie answered—." I held up my hand palm down, the way Kevin had showed me, and pressed my forefingers to my index finger. Then I dropped it to my other hand, and lining them up side by side, palms down, tapped my index fingers together. "'Brother.' That was her name for David. I remembered that he'd always called her 'Sis.' Not often 'Honey,' or 'Sweetie,' and rarely 'Evie,' but 'Sis.' And I began to wonder if it was some kind of inside joke they had together. He always struck me as the kind of guy who meant more than he was saying—so much so that I wondered why he hadn't aroused more suspicions at New Life. Anyway, it occurred to me that if he really was her brother, or stepbrother, in a manner of speaking, that could explain his delay."

Moses was frowning. "I don't follow," he said.

"Well, obviously Armbruster didn't recognize David Green as his son," I said. "Of course, the green contact lenses and the facial hair probably contributed, but still. That means that David Green was pretty young the last time Armbruster saw him, if Armbruster had ever seen him in person. Either scenario could lead to anger and resentment on the son's part, and motivate him to go after his father. So, say that was his mission at first—to expose the Right Arm of God as the father of an illegitimate child or a child support defaulter or something like that.

"But once he arrived at New Life, things turned out to be much more complicated than he'd anticipated. Or maybe, since he may have already had some connections to the runaway teen support network, he already knew what some of the complications would be. But maybe what he didn't anticipate was the complexity of his own feelings for his father. I mean, I think the guy's a self-righteous prick, but he has a few good qualities, I guess. For all his posturing, I think he's genuinely fond of Evie, for example. And he seemed to like David Green, and trust him. That kind of approval, however belated, might have been irresistible to a young man who'd missed out on it for a long time."

Moses shook his head. "Deep, Cat. Very deep."

"But pretty accurate," Arpad said. "We found his real name and address on his real driver's license in the safe deposit box. His name was Daniel Verdi. Verdi was his mother's second husband, his stepfather, who had legally adopted him. We also found an emergency contact—a friend of his named Ian McGinniss. McGinniss told us the rest of the story."

I got up and retrieved three more beers from the refrigerator. I wasn't expecting to enjoy the story Arpad had to tell, and I wanted something to do with my hands. I passed out the beers, popped the top on mine, and settled down again with my hands curled around the cold, wet metal.

Daniel Verdi, née Daniel Armbruster, had been thrown out of his father's house at fourteen following an explosive confrontation over some homosexual pornography his father had discovered in his room. Dan's mother, distraught but ineffectual while caught in her husband's force field, had maintained contact with her son and gave him what money she could extract unnoticed from the household accounts. Two years later, though, Vernon Armbruster, not yet the Right Arm of God but rather an insignificant digit at John Hancock Life Insurance, announced that he was leaving her for a file clerk in the accounting department.

By this time, her son's two years on the streets of Chicago had done nothing to improve his health, morals, or prospective longevity. He was sustaining himself on uppers and downers paid for in the usual ways. At seventeen, Dan Armbruster aspired to a criminal career, but his rise to fame and fortune was blocked by an arrest for burglary. He did time on more than one occasion, finally paroled to his mother and her new husband when he was twenty. By this time he was going by his stepfather's name, Verdi. But he was soon back on the streets, and spent his twenty-first birthday hustling, getting drunk, and scoring drugs.

His life would have continued that way and ended soon afterward had he not been approached in a flophouse by a man from a teen rescue organization and handed over to another man, who proved to be a gay minister. These two men changed the course of his life. And the minister had introduced him to the Metropolitan Community Church and the prospect of reconciliation with his heavenly father, if not his earthly one.

A year of G.D.E. classes and two years in a community college while working his way up to manager at a local duplicating service, then two years at the University of Chicago, did not alter the plan Dan Verdi had begun to formulate within days of meeting the Reverend Grant Hammond. At the age of twenty-seven, Dan Verdi entered the Chicago Theological Seminary and was himself ordained as a minister in the Metropolitan Community Church four years later. He was his father's son, after all.

But before he began his ministry, he had, he told his friend Ian, some unfinished business to attend to. Although his father had never attempted to communicate with him, or ever paid a penny of child support to his mother, Dan had not entirely lost track of his old adversary. In recent years, he had followed with interest his father's rise to prominence as an evangelical minister, and he had received with particular contempt information that reached him through the MCC grapevine about his father's reputation for bringing troubled youths to Jesus and curing homosexuality. Dan had decided to put an end to his father's masquerade. Over Ian's strong objections, he had moved to Cincinnati under an assumed name and found employment at New Life. Life on the streets had taken its toll on his features, and a beard, moustache, and green contact lenses, worn over his hazel eyes, had completed his disguise. His father, he said, had harbored no suspicions.

"I'm paid to take care of my baby sister," he'd crowed during one of their frequent long-distance conversations, "who is a chimpanzee. And damned if she isn't the best of the bunch of us—the white sheep of the Armbruster family, so to speak."

But as time went on, according to Ian, Dan had found himself entangled in New Life. He'd found out a few things about some of the men who were working there, and he'd wanted to be sure there wasn't more. He'd grown to like the work, and enjoyed being with the kids, even though it meant working with the Reverend Ted Settles. He adored Evie. And all of the hatred he'd cherished for his father all those years had, when exposed to the light of his father's friendship and approval, dried up and blown away, leaving only a kind of sadness and pity. He'd continued to insist that his father was a dangerous man and had to be stopped, but he took less satisfaction than he'd expected in the necessary destruction of his father's house of cards.

He'd put off the day of that eventuality by undertaking individual rescue missions among the members of the New Covenant. He hadn't, Ian insisted, encouraged kids to run away, just intercepted them when he believed them to be on the verge of doing it, and guided them to a safe haven. He'd understood that this kind of intervention was not a permanent solution, but he'd believed that in the short term it was a workable one—until Tony Frank had committed suicide.

Twilight had deepened to dusk as we'd listened to Arpad's story, and Moses got up now to switch on a light.

Arpad didn't seem to notice. "According to McGinniss," he continued, "Dan understood rationally that he wasn't responsible for that, just like he understood that if parents were determined to have their gay kids 'deprogrammed,' they'd find somebody who'd take their money to do it, even if he put New Life out of the deprogramming business. But emotionally—."

"Yeah," I said. I knew that guilt.

"He might have let things slide longer if the New Lifers hadn't been so hypocritical, publicly praising a kid whose fatal depression they'd contributed to. He'd told Ian that he was planning to wrap things up here within the next week or so, and Ian had understood that whatever he had planned in the way of revelations would coincide with Tony's memorial service."

"So do you know any more about what happened that night between Settles and Green?" Moses asked.

Arpad shook his head. "Just what the kids told us. Settles isn't talking."

"What about Armbruster?" I asked. "What does he say?"

"He says Settles called him and said there'd been an accident," Arpad said.

"Right," I said. "David Green's head accidentally made contact with a—what? A lamp or something?" I found myself rubbing my head in the spot where another heavy object had made accidental contact.

"Yeah, a brass lamp," Arpad said. "But that's not what he told Armbruster, according to Armbruster. He told Armbruster that Green had been compiling material to use against the church, including evidence that Armbruster was a child support defaulter. That was true, by the way. In the safe deposit box was a Wanted poster with Armbruster's picture. You know, 'Wanted for $20,000 in back child support.'"

"But why bring Armbruster in on it at all?" I said. "I can understand that he wanted Clay to help him move David's body and the kids to Evie's, and maybe to set up and start the fire. And he wasn't planning for Clay to live to be questioned by the police. But why bring in Armbruster to help him search David's—or should I say Dan's?—apartment? That seems risky to me. He had plenty of time, after all."

"Well, we're not dealing with a master criminal here," Arpad said. "After all, look at his weapons—a lamp and a frying pan."

"And gasoline," Moses put in.

"Yeah, gasoline from the maintenance shed," Arpad agreed. "You want my opinion, I think he wanted something to hold over Armbruster."

"But he already had the information about Armbruster's past," I objected.

"Yeah, Cat, but the past is the past," Moses said. "You got folks on your side to start with, you can talk 'em into overlooking a whole lot of stuff. So, the man threw a gay teenager out on the streets to fend for himself. You don't think some of the men, and maybe the women, sitting in that congregation wouldn't have done the same thing? And those that wouldn't can probably be made to sympathize. So, the man didn't pay his court-ordered child support. You know how many fathers out there are delinquent on their child support? You've seen the man talk. You think he couldn't talk his way out of it?"

"That's right," Arpad agreed. "But covering up a murder is another thing altogether, especially if it's the murder of your own son."

"Did Settles know that David Green was Armbruster's son?" I asked.

Arpad shrugged. "We'll probably never know. What we do know is that he didn't tell Armbruster if he did."

"Who did tell him?"

Arpad grinned. "Moi." His smile faded. "Okay, I admit I wanted to see the smug bastard sweat. I said to him, 'Reverend Armbruster, I'm terribly sorry to have to tell you this, but your son is dead.'"

"How'd he react?" Moses asked.

"Well, he was slow on the uptake," Arpad said. "He thought I was confused, had it wrong. I'd swear the man had forgotten that he had a son. Then, it sank in, and I might as well have whacked him upside the head with Settles's frying pan. You could see him, replaying the last seven months in his imagination, searching for clues. I got called out of the room then, and it was just as well. I might have said something—."

"Unprofessional," Moses supplied.

"Yeah."

We sat in silence for a few beats, and then Arpad turned to me. "But you were hired to find out who killed Peter Baer, weren't you, Cat? You made any progress on that front?"

I nodded. "Yeah," I said. "I think so."

We exchanged a long look, and he nodded again. "I think so, too."

Chapter Thirty-three

GUSSIE BAER'S LIVING room was as cluttered and furry as before, and smelled of something baking—something fragrant with spices. She let go of her walker to sweep a long-haired tabby from a chair and I was afraid she'd lose her balance and land on top of him. But she righted herself and toddled to the recliner she'd sat in during my last visit, backed into it like she was docking a spaceship, and dropped down in a cloud of fur and dust.

Her eyes were bright. "You've got news," she said.

"In a way," I said. "I've concluded my investigation." It sounded stiff, and I was aware that I wasn't going about this very well.

"And?" She leaned forward and peered at me over her glasses, reminding me once again of a curious bird. But 'curious' wasn't the right word, because there were layers of sadness and anxiety beneath the brightness in her eyes, and some of it was ready to well up and spill over.

I hadn't come up with a good way to say it, so I was direct. "I think you need to ask your son and daughter-in-law what happened to Peter."

Her forehead creased in bewilderment. "George and Vanessa? What do you mean?"

"I think," I said with care, "that they know how Peter died. You need to talk to them about it." I paused to let that sink in, then added, "The police will be talking to them about it, too."

She stared at me for a long time. Then she turned away and I thought she might be weeping into the chair, but she was leaning over to rummage in something next to the chair. She straightened with a crumpled newspaper in her hand. She laid it on her lap and smoothed it. Then she handed it to me. The story she had circled in pencil was not the lead story. It was about the New Covenant club, and its connection to the murder of David Green/Dan Verdi. Tony Frank's name wasn't mentioned; I knew because I'd read the story carefully. And the black-and-white bracelets weren't mentioned, either, though I happened to

know that the press knew about them. But there was a discussion of gay
teen suicides and runaways.

"It's something to do with that, isn't it?" she asked. Her voice
fluttered with emotion. "That's what you're saying."

I nodded.

The tears began to trickle down her cheeks. "There was always
something about him," she said. "Something different. I never knew
what it was until now. I thought he was unhappy, but I couldn't see any
reason why. I thought—well, I thought it was his parents. And he didn't
have to put up with them for very much longer. I—." She faltered. From
her pocket she brought out a crumpled handkerchief and dabbed at her
nose. "I felt very close to him."

I said, "Everybody keeps a few secrets."

"But that was such a big one," she said. "At least, it was to him."

I reached out a hand and took one of hers. "He knew that you loved
him," I said. "That's what matters. He was never afraid of losing that."

I didn't know that to be true, but I felt that it was true. I'd heard her
talk about Peter, and I'd seen her with Monica, and I didn't think either of
them would ever doubt her.

I didn't say any more. I left her to wrestle with her feelings for her
son and daughter-in-law, and with the images I knew her imagination
would generate, as mine had. It's possible that Arpad's crime technicians
would be able to establish where Peter died if he chose to pursue it, but I
suspected that the Baers would confess in the end. In my mind's eye, I
saw Peter hanging—in the garage, in his room, I didn't know where, but
someplace where he could be sure that Monica wouldn't be the one to
find him. Maybe he left a note, maybe not, but they found things in his
room and on his computer that explained what he'd done.

Or maybe it hadn't happened that way at all. Maybe he'd simply
been experimenting with the sexual effects of strangulation, and passed
out before he could save himself. I didn't think that version would have
been much more acceptable to his parents than intentional suicide, but it
could have happened that way. What Gussie had said about Peter's
unhappiness, though, and even Kirstin's hesitance when asked about his
emotional state, made me lean toward the first scenario.

His parents had found him. And then? They'd removed his body,
dressed in what he was wearing, because by then, rigor mortis would have
made it impossible to undress or dress him. That explained the absence of
a jacket on that cold day he disappeared, though they'd reported one
missing and had probably even removed one from his closet. They had
driven to a store that sold polyester marine rope, to insure that the rope

around his neck wouldn't be identified as theirs, and someone—George, I assumed—had replaced that rope with the new rope. Then they had dumped the body in the river, somewhere upstream from where it was found. And gone home to remove all traces of homosexuality from his room, to sanitize it. Maybe they'd even planted the *Playboy* at that time.

They'd done all of these things to save themselves from the disgrace of having a gay son, and a son who had committed suicide. A son who was perfect in every way but one.

Arpad would charge them with something, and an expensive lawyer—somebody who was on their Christmas party list—would plea-bargain it down, and they would end up doing community service. Monica would pay the highest price for their crimes.

These thoughts put me in a poor frame of mind for David Green/Dan Verdi's memorial service. It was held at the local Metropolitan Community Church, which proved to be a small plain building near the university, not five minutes from New Life. I had several offers of company, but I chose to go alone. I had some idea of sitting in solitary misery, but before my eyes had adjusted to the indoor light, I felt a tug on my arm and a familiar perfume enveloped me.

"I was hoping you'd be here," Joy said. "There's not too many people I know, except the kids, of course. And they've all been real sweet, but it's more comforting somehow to sit with an adult when you go to a funeral, you know?"

Joy was towing me in the direction of a row of folding chairs.

"I don't want to sit too close, do you?" She craned her neck to see around a knot of kids I recognized from New Life. "This should be okay." She sat down and pulled me into the chair next to her. "Especially when you're in an unfamiliar church," she added. "My husband says he feels too uncomfortable in an unfamiliar church. I can't get him to go to a Catholic church, not for a wedding or a funeral or anything. He gets so confused!"

She looked around with unabashed curiosity. "I don't know, though. He might feel right at home here—it seems more like a place for a business meeting than a memorial service, doesn't it? Not that the Lord cares. As long as a place is sanctified by the hearts of the worshippers, it's a church, is what I say. Why, New Life took some getting used to when I first started there."

The place was filling up and already the air was becoming close. Joy waved at some members of the New Life congregation, and they waved back. I said something about the crowd.

"Well, David was a fine young man," Joy said. "And if all the people who thought so were here today, why, you couldn't get them all in here!" She dropped her voice. "I think it's just scandalous how many people are afraid to come and pay their respects, Catherine. Why, do you know I've had more than one person say to me that they were afraid of contracting AIDS if they came?" She leaned back and studied the effect of this news on me. I don't think I showed sufficient disbelief or outrage, but I made some kind of noise she took to be appropriate, because she continued, "I mean it! You wouldn't believe the ignorance!"

I wasn't sure what Joy knew or understood about my role in the events that had shaken the foundations of New Life, but she seemed to have chosen me for her confidant.

"Look! There's Betsy with Evie," she said, nodding her head. "Evie's taken this thing so hard! She looks kind of subdued today, but she's been wild, I'm telling you! Well, you can't blame her, poor little thing! She saw him dead, and then she got moved to this new place—it's like a temporary building. And then everybody was so tense, and Betsy moved out, and she won't even give Reverend Armbruster the time of day! Evie, I mean, not Betsy, though Betsy isn't talking to him either, I don't think. They say she didn't know about the son, so I can't say as I blame her. But Evie—I don't know what she knows or how she knows it. Somehow she seems to blame the reverend, though."

Joy shifted in her seat. "Look! Do you think that's David's mother she's talking to? I know he's really Dan, but I just can't think of him that way."

I told her it was. I'd picked up Mrs. Verdi and Ian McGinniss at the airport the day before. Mrs. Verdi had struck me as pretty shell-shocked, and seemed to rely on Ian to think for both of them, which he seemed capable of doing. He stood next to her now, a hand at her elbow. If he felt any rancor toward Betsy Armbruster, he didn't show it.

The service was conducted by a plump woman about my size, who wore her gray hair cut short like mine. It looked good on her, as if it had been cut to emphasize her bone structure and frame her smile, which never wavered. At first, the smile irritated me. I wondered if she'd been informed that this was a fucking memorial service, after all, not a christening. But then it grew on me. I began to see it as the outward sign of an optimism rooted in hard experience—a more complicated optimism than Joy's, I thought, but that assessment was probably unfair to Joy.

That was okay. It was an unfair world. If it weren't, David Green and Tony Frank and Peter Baer would be alive today.

While people talked about David or Dan, and told stories about him, I meditated on justice. I thought about the bald injustice of making someone feel ashamed of themselves for the way they were made—for things about them that they couldn't help. I thought about all the people who shared in the guilt for the three lives lost, and I counted myself among the guilty. I thought about all the other lives destroyed that I didn't even know about. I worked myself up into quite a state.

The only thing that distracted me was Evie's trip to the altar to place a flower in the vase in front of David's photograph. She stared at the photograph for a long time before Betsy managed to wrestle the rose away from her and drop it into the vase. Evie turned away, and then froze. She was staring at something.

Betsy bent over her and started to tug on her arm, then looked up and started. She pressed her lips together and stood up. They held their poses so long that everyone in the audience turned to follow their gaze.

Standing in the doorway was the Reverend Vernon T. Armbruster. He wore a dark suit and a solemn look. He had aged twenty years since the last time I'd seen him. He was oblivious to everything except the two figures at the front of the room.

Then Evie dropped to all fours and made her slow, deliberate way down the aisle to him. She sat down at his feet and slipped her hand in his.

The congregation exhaled a sigh.

Not me. I turned away.

I was in no mood for easy reconciliations, happy endings.

Which only went to show that, compared to Evie, I had a smaller share of that cardinal Christian virtue that comes so naturally to all higher mammals and so unnaturally to humankind: forgiveness.

This book is dedicated to the next generation of activists, including the Lubbock High School Gay-Straight Alliance, and to their indefatigable supporters, The Lambda Legal Defense and Education Fund

Acknowledgments

I'd like to thank John Lukeman and Ralph Grooten of Delaware Marine for their information on marine rope.

For background material on chimpanzees, I've relied on Jane Goodall's work, as well as Roger Fouts's *Next of Kin*. As usual, whenever Delbert appears, I depend upon Eric Raymond's *The New Hacker's Dictionary* for translation.

And last but not least, I'd like to thank Helen Hahn, Hilda Lindner Knepp, and Rosa Ruggles for writing to ask whether there would ever be any more Cat Caliban books, and Sue Clark, my agent,

D. B. Borton lives with two cats in a small Midwestern college town. She teaches writing, film, and literature at a small liberal arts college. As an academic writer, she has published work on film, women's literature, and the supernatural. In addition to her two mystery series, the Cat Caliban series and the Gilda Liberty series, she has written for *Ms.* magazine.

A native Texan, Borton became an ardent admirer of Nancy Drew at a young age. At the age of fourteen, she acquired her own blue roadster, trained on the freeways of Houston and the broad stretches of oil-endowed Texas highway, and began her travels. She also began a lifetime of political activism, working only for political candidates who lost. She left Texas at about the time everyone else arrived.

Borton has lived in the Southwest and Midwest, and on the West Coast, where she has planted roses and collected three degrees in English without relinquishing her affection for and reliance on nonstandard dialects. Borton realizes that her detective's language may shock and offend some readers. She can only say in her own defense that it shocks her as well.

Printed in the United States
20864LVS00003B/230